Barbara Martens
248 W Oakcrest A
Northfield, NJ 08225-1714

C0-AMR-265

The Purple Robe

To Tina,
From
David Dean
May 2015

The Purple Robe

by

David Dean

TUMBLAR HOUSE
'Bona Tempora Volvant'

Arcadia
MMXIV

Printed in the United States of America

ISBN 978-0-9883537-4-9

The Purple Robe
Copyright © 2014 by David Dean.

All rights reserved.

This is a work of fiction. All of the characters, organizations, places, and events portrayed in this novel are either products of the author's imagination or are used fictitiously. Any resemblance to any persons, living or dead, is purely coincidental.

No part of this book may be reproduced in any manner whatsoever without written permission, except in the case of brief quotations embodied in critical reviews or articles.

Visit our website at www.tumblarhouse.com

Acknowledgements

Since I began work on this novel some years ago, the world has experienced three popes, each with very different styles and personalities. It seems particularly appropriate to me that the publication of "The Purple Robe" should coincide with the papacy of Francis I. Not least for the reason that he is our first Latin American pope and my story is likewise located there. But more importantly, Pope Francis brings with him a joy in Christ, and a humbleness of spirit, that my poor protagonist, Father Pablo, could have related to, were he a real man.

Yet, this new and laughing pope also carries with him a distinct whiff of change, and even the possibility of miracles, two things that would have terrified my young curate. Still, I'd like to think that Pope Francis might like this all-too-human, if entirely fictional, priest should they ever meet.

There are many influences that contribute to a work like this. Most remain bound up in the weave of this writer's life and are not easily identified. Others are quite obvious and their positive effect on this book demands at least a word of gratitude, a word I am happy to supply.

This book is dedicated to Christians throughout the world who, despite these violent and darkly seductive times (when has it ever been different?), hold fast to their faith. And to the people of Mexico, whose kindliness and resilience of spirit provided the spark of creation for this book. Most especially I want to thank the Reverend Fathers John A. O'Leary and Antony Savari Muthu, and the late and sorely missed, Monsignor Donald D. Velozo, for their guidance and inspiration over the years.

I also dedicate this effort to my wife, Robin, whose simple trust and faith in God, and less understandably, me, has been both a guiding beacon and a warming fire during every season of my soul.

Finally, I give thanks to Our Lady of Guadalupe, Patroness of the Americas, for the gift of her Son, as well as her prayers and intercessions, without which the writing of this book would have been impossible.

Vivat Jesus!

CHAPTER ONE

Father Pablo Diego Corellas glanced nervously over the chalice at the scant gathering of morning worshippers, his consecration of the wine that would become the living Blood of Christ, halting in mid-sentence. Several ancient faces grimaced in concern.

Since Monsignor Roberto De Jesus had suffered his heart attack and been swept away to Mérida, they had come to expect these precarious moments. In fact, they were the topic of numerous conversations throughout the town, both humorous and vitriolic, depending on the age and piousness of the gossips.

Taking a deep breath to steady himself, Father Pablo focused hard on the golden chalice he held aloft. As the sense of vertigo faded, the monkey-chatter in his head was soon replaced by the familiar words of the liturgy and he cautiously resumed.

"Blessed are you, Lord, God of all creation," he piped, hoping that this was where he had left off. "Through your goodness we have this wine to offer."

Suspecting that wine played a large part in Father Pablo's tribulations at the altar, it was said by some that he was allowed to run a tab at the cafés along the Malecòn.

"Fruit of the vine and work of human hands, it will become our spiritual drink."

A murmured response of "Blessed be God forever" rustled across the church like a dying breath.

Father Pablo, refraining from sighing aloud, thought, *There, I've done it. I'm back on track.* Lifting the goblet on high into a stray beam of sunlight, he then carefully set it back on the altar, stepped back, and bowed.

When he straightened, he found himself staring into the basilisk gaze of Doña Marisa Elena Sáenz, whom he had privately christened "La Viuda Negra", *the Black Widow*, in deference to her severe and unapproachable widowhood. With her crippling dowager's hump, she sat like a black question mark in the front pew and appeared to study him with a dry, inquisitorial air. He would not have been surprised to see her rise in a whisper of dark fabric, level her knobby walking stick at him, and cry, "Heretic!"

It was she that had thrown him off earlier with the raptor-like fixity of her grey eyes. Father Pablo found himself unnerved by those eyes, though he knew himself at least well enough to know that many, many things unmanned him, and with even less reason. She joined a host of fellow priests, parishioners, bishops, functionaries (both civil and clerical), his parents and siblings, women in general, and sometimes even his altar servers, who intimidated him.

Even so, he blamed no one, as he agreed with the image of himself that he saw in others' eyes: He was young, soft and pale, with a pebbled adolescent complexion, unimposing, nervous, barely competent in his duties, and lacking in the spiritual courage he had so admired in the martyrs of his seminary studies. In a word, unfit.

The idea of becoming a priest had not been his, but rather an inspiration of his mother's, or as she would have it, a revelation, the Blessed Virgin appearing to her in a dream as the unborn Pablo rested in her womb. In the holy Mother's arms she carried a babe, but not the infant Christ as might be expected in such visitations, for there was no halo to proclaim his divinity. No, his mother had insisted, this was a mortal child, red-faced and squalling.

Appearing a little out of patience, the Queen of the Universe had thrust the burden into her arms, saying, "Return him to me when he is ready." At these words she was awakened by the breaking of her water.

Later that day, as his exhausted mother had taken him for the first time to her breast and looked into his face, she proclaimed that this was the child of her vision, the selfsame infant delivered into her arms by the Mother of Christ. Thus a dream had decided Father Pablo's fate before he had even had a chance to escape the womb, and being the final child of five boys even his father had been content to give him up.

In any event, he had grown from a fussy baby into a flaccid youth, and the idea of fighting his mother's energetic obsession required more spirit than he could muster. Allowing himself to be carried along by events, he now found himself washed up on the somewhat hostile shores of Progreso.

At this moment, however, Father Pablo congratulated himself; he had progressed to the reception of Communion without further mishap. Holding aloft the Host, he proclaimed as confidently as he could in his high, thin voice, "This is the Lamb of God who takes away the sins of the world. Happy are those who are called to His supper."

The few worshipers responded almost jubilantly, for they were as relieved as he that their uncertain pastor had finally stumbled to the climax of the Mass, "Lord, I am not worthy that you should enter under my roof, but only say the word and my soul shall be healed."

Placing the Host in his mouth, Father Pablo prayed that he would not choke and begin to cough as had happened two weeks before during a packed Sunday Mass. On that occasion, an altar boy had slapped him on the back several times before he was able to proceed. Red-faced and watery eyed, he had served Communion to a line of parishioners who could no longer look him in the eyes. Several had broad smiles on their downcast faces, and shoulders that shook with barely suppressed mirth.

Several days later, the same altar boy who had come to his rescue rather meanly informed him that he had been awarded a nickname by some of his parishioners—"Padre Tomate"— *Father Tomato*, in commemoration of his flaming red face during the unfortunate Mass.

Feeling a familiar dryness in his throat at the memory, he reached hastily for the chalice and set it to spinning with his fingertips. With a second lunge, he rescued the cup before a drop was spilled and then, ever so carefully, brought it up to his lips in both hands. He could feel the tremor in them transfer itself to the goblet and so carefully set it down after his drink. No harm had been done. Perhaps no one had even noticed, he thought.

Refraining from looking out at La Viuda for confirmation, he busied himself with the Hosts that he must now bring down from the altar to his few communicants. It being a weekday Mass he had no altar servers or Eucharistic ministers to assist him.

The first in line was, of course, La Viuda. Standing impatiently at the foot of the altar she watched him disapprovingly, and he hurried to her, hoping to avoid looking into those cold, wintry eyes, yet finding it irresistible to do so.

It had been the same when he had been a child on his father's ranch in Chiapas and discovered a hornet's nest beneath the eaves of the stables—terrified of their painful stings, he would return again and again to stare in dread fascination at their comings and goings, listening to the angry hum that emanated from the grey, papery ball they dwelt in—the same grey as La Viuda's eyes and beehive hairdo, he thought irreverently.

The beginnings of a smile lifted the corners of his mouth, but La Viuda's eyes had their usual effect of dispelling all levity within their bleak scope. He froze with the Host in his hand before her.

She waited for the words that had flown from his head as the line of old women behind her shuffled impatiently. At last, she glanced down meaningfully at the Host in his pudgy fingers and Father Pablo, recovering himself, whispered dry-mouthed, "The Body of Christ."

Answering, "Amen," in such a way as to convey her disapproval, she then stuck out her tongue. He carefully placed the Host there, quickly withdrawing his fingers as if from a trap. With bowed head, she moved on as the next person came forward. The older parishioners insisted on being administered Communion in this manner. Father Pablo, decades younger than most of his flock, found the ritual distasteful as well as archaic, and though he strove not to show it, his inability to control his facial expressions betrayed him with grimaces and pursed lips.

After the blessing and dismissal, and as he was gathering the implements of the altar, a cough interrupted him, and he looked out into the church to find La Viuda awaiting him. "Oh," he cried out like a small boy caught at mischief. "La Viu..." he halted just in time and then continued rapidly, "Doña Marisa! I hadn't heard you there. Have you been waiting long?" Once again, he hurried to join her.

Awaiting his attendance with the same impatience she had shown during Communion, she didn't bother to answer. When he arrived she sat down in the front pew, as it was more comfortable for her to sit than stand, though she was forced to lean forward by the hump on her back. Father Pablo was not invited to join her. Turning her rather long face awkwardly up to his, she spoke, "Señora Alcante is wondering about her boy's whereabouts, and whether you've seen him of late. He uses heroin," she added dryly.

Staring down at the small, black lace kerchief that rested on the improbably large hairdo of La Viuda, Father Pablo tried to appear pensive, though in fact he had no idea of whom she was speaking. "God forgive him. Let's see...Alcante. Wasn't he one of Monsignor Roberto's altar boys before...?"

She cut him off with a look, "He's the cripple that always sits in the back and never comes up for Communion, though I don't wonder at that. As soon as Communion starts, he hobbles out the front and lies in wait for everybody so that he can beg some change; must do pretty well too, to support a drug habit. His Christian name is Juan...got his legs crushed in a car accident several years ago, so I'm told."

Suddenly he did remember—a young man about his own age, thin and dirty, smelling of dried urine and sour wine. He had given him money on several different occasions out in the plaza. Though the young man had been on crutches, his movements had been quick and facile, placing himself directly in Father Pablo's path. Each time, he had demanded money in a lazy, surly manner, while offering no deference whatsoever to the priest's collar, nor had he attempted to elicit any sympathy for his plight.

Father Pablo had found his long, brown rat's teeth and slitted black eyes intimidating and frightful, and he took every pain to avoid him. He recalled, with some guilt, his great relief that the crippled Juan Alcante never brought himself forward to participate in the Eucharist with his dangerous rodent teeth.

"How long has he been missing?" he inquired.

"Several weeks, she tells me. Haven't you noticed his absence yourself?" she asked with a sniff. "Even the incense can't hide his odor when he's here."

"Ah…ah," he stammered, feeling the familiar heat rising to his face. "I thought so…at least two weeks," he lied unconvincingly. Once again La Viuda had exposed his faults as a priest. "I will keep an eye out for him and inform Señora Alcante the moment I have any news. The poor woman must be worried sick."

Arching an eyebrow at him, La Viuda struggled to her feet, "That won't be so easy, as she stopped coming to Mass several weeks ago. I only see her at the market from time to time now. It seems she's had a crisis of faith and fallen in with those Assembly of God people in the east end of town." Swinging her cane suddenly to illustrate the direction, Father Pablo stumbled out of harm's way. "Do you know them?"

Naturally, he was vaguely aware of the competition, but had given them little thought, and nodded.

"You may find a few of your flock have strayed there—it seems the last few weeks have tested many in their faith," she added pointedly.

Father Pablo understood her to mean the untimely departure of Monsignor Roberto De Jesus, and his own inability to fill the beloved pastor's shoes. It wounded his heart to think that his shortcomings as a priest were as obvious as he had feared, but worse, that those failings were weakening the very fabric of the church with which he had been entrusted. So wrapped up in his own struggles to master the administration of the Sacraments, their reality had been lost to him, and it was this, he could see now, that he communicated to the faithful like a venereal disease. How could the wine and bread be transformed into the actual Body and Blood of Christ in the hands of someone like himself?

Turning from Doña Marisa, he was confronted by the now-barren altar and, as if further reproach were needed, the unfinished Chapel of Our Lady of Guadalupe that lay to the north of it. Monsignor De Jesus' beloved project remained neglected and untouched since his departure, as the monies for the craftsmen had become depleted weeks before and Father Pablo had been unable to organize a drive for funds or convince the workers to return without them. From her shadowed alcove of stacked bricks and colorful, dust-covered tiles, the Mystical Rose of Tepeyac peeked out at Father Pablo with an expression of firm and luminous hope—she too, appeared to expect much.

"Well, if that's all then. I've got duties to attend to," he said quietly.

"There is something else, perhaps," La Viuda spoke gently, sensing that she had gone too far, yet never one to be put off by emotion. "Have you heard anything from the Archdiocese about what's happening in the countryside?"

Father Pablo was well aware that there had recently been an exchange of gunfire between the State Police and some insurrectos not far from town. It appeared the police had stumbled onto a checkpoint set up by the rebels, or bandits (depending on who you talked to), and a brief and inaccurate exchange of gunfire had ensued, yet why the archbishop in Mérida would be concerned, Father Pablo was at a loss to understand.

"No," he replied rather hoarsely, regaining his composure and turning to her with wet eyes. "The Church does not normally concern itself with police matters, Doña Marisa."

"Who said anything about the police?" she responded. "I'm talking about the rumors coming out of the country. Shouldn't they be investigated?"

"What rumors?" he asked petulantly, suddenly tired and wishing to be rid of the old woman.

She affected not to notice his tone, but remained squarely planted in front of him. "Country people are coming into the market on Saturdays with nothing else on their lips. They're saying miracles are being performed on some old sisal plantation, that the sick are being healed, the blind made to see. Can you believe it…in this day and age?"

Doña Marisa had grown more animated on this subject than Father Pablo had ever seen her.

"And don't think those *Assembly* people aren't making the most of it, no sir," she continued. "Those holy rollers are preaching that it's Papist superstition and worse—demon worship, and have forbidden their people to attend." She halted abruptly, appearing to await a similar pronouncement from Father Pablo.

The priest could think of nothing to say—the idea of his parishioners wishing to attend some sorcerer's chicken beheadings struck him as comically ignorant—undoubtedly Doña Marisa was overreaching herself on this one.

Smiling, he said, "Now Doña Marisa, surely to even bring this up is to give it a dignity it doesn't deserve. I'm confident that none of our parishioners would give any thought whatsoever to tramping out to some God-forsaken farm for occult rituals. It's just some kind of superstitious fad. In another few weeks it will be forgotten."

She peered at him for a long moment before saying, "You are so young in the world—how, in God's name, did you ever become a priest?"

The flatness of her statement was like a slap, and the smugness of his smile flew off like spittle. He felt like a chastened child standing before this woman who, in this moment, appeared much younger than he had previously thought. She could not be more than sixty, he now realized, though her widow's black, and the deformed spine, gave the impression of long years. In fact, she was rather handsome. "Doña Marisa I didn't mean to give the impression I..."

Turning away, she shuttled down the long central aisle to the entrance doors with surprising rapidity, calling out over the great protuberance that rode her back, "Look to your flock, Little Father. Have you not noticed the empty pews of late?"

With that said she dipped her fingers in the font of holy water, crossed herself, and was burned away like a conscience-stricken dream by the brilliant sunlight that shot through the opening door.

CHAPTER TWO

It took most of the morning for Father Pablo to shake the sense of failure that Doña Marisa had burdened him with, but as he had never taken himself very seriously, he found it easier than most to regain his normally cheerful demeanor. So, after compiling his list of the bed-ridden and hospitalized, and carefully planning the route that would cost him the least amount of shoe leather, he set out with his small kit to administer to the spiritual needs of the sick and the dying in an improving mood. His first stop would be the Centro Medico Americano that sat across the plaza on Calle 33. After seeing to his people in this rather depressing institution, he would then make his way to the various homes of the ill, scattered throughout the city of Progreso.

With a small thrill of anticipated pleasure, he planned his route to include a stroll along the Malecòn where he could enjoy the morning breezes off the Gulf of México. Having been raised hundreds of miles inland, the proximity of the sea and its seemingly boundless horizon produced in him a kind of child-like wonder. This effect had not been diminished by Monsignor Roberto De Jesus' warning that he had yet to experience a great storm, or worse, a hurricane. This, he had assured him in his kindly manner, might make him look to the sea with a more jaundiced eye, "That is nature, my young friend. Do not mistake it for God."

It was true, of course, Father Pablo had only been in the Yucatán for less than a year and so had no memory of the sea that had divided Progreso in half during the hurricane of '91. He was perfectly content with the shallow green waters that lapped the beaches of Progreso and this quiet ocean pleased both his eyes and mind.

In anticipation of this delightful reward for his clerical duties, Father Pablo strode across the city square with increasingly light steps. The November sunshine bathed him in its warmth and his own youthful ebullience rose through the surface of his skin like dew from a melon.

Across the plaza sat the Government House with its Spanish-style façade, busy with the comings and goings of officials, policemen, and citizens, pleased or aggrieved, depending on the answers they had been given within. Loitering on the steps were clusters of young girls, secretaries and clerks, enjoying their coffee in the morning sun before the day became too hot to do so.

Father Pablo could see several of the prettiest were laughing appreciatively at some comment made by a male passer-by, and he briefly wondered what the young man could possibly have said to please them so. As he had only the slightest of experience with young women, and that having been of the most circumspect nature while still in school, he often found himself entranced by such scenes—like a naturalist who chances upon some species cavorting uninhibitedly in its own habitat. When they saw him looking in their direction, the young women raised their hands to their mouths and whispered, and as he angled away towards the hospital, their laughter erupted behind him like a flock of pigeons taking wing. Father Pablo felt his face grow hot with discomfort.

With his downcast eyes on the sidewalk, he would have passed the police captain without acknowledgment and been smashed into the hot pavement, had his arm not been seized.

"Careful, Little Father, the drivers around here will run you down, collar or no." He pointed to the red traffic light at the intersection Father Pablo had been about to enter, and suddenly the noise of the cars and motorbikes returned to his burning ears.

"Oh, oh yes." Father Pablo attempted to assume an expression of somber thought, but only managed to look like a boy caught with a nudie magazine. "My mind was on other things. Thank you, Captain Barrera."

Still holding his arm, the captain smiled easily past him to the girls on the steps, nodding in their direction, "It's all right, Little Father, my mind is on other things too, sometimes. I would think less of you if yours wasn't. We are both men, after all." He released the priest's arm.

Father Pablo's eyes followed the Captain's and he blushed again at having been so caught out. "No, Captain, you've misunderstood. It's the sick, you see. I have so many to visit today. So my mind, naturally, is preoccupied."

The policeman, tall and almost European-looking in his sharply creased uniform, ignored the priest's sputtered explanations and lit a cigarette, all the while coolly appraising the ebb and flow of people and traffic that animated the street. The press of pedestrians parted well to either side of him, their conversations assuming hushed tones or simply dying away altogether, until rejoining their fellow citizens on the other side where normal speech was restored. Even if they were not aware of Captain Antonio Francisco Barrera Huelta's reputation for fearlessness, he nonetheless bore the serene, capable look of a dangerous man.

Father Pablo, for his trouble, found himself jostled several times by passers-by anxious to avoid contact with the captain, and now was beginning to perspire as the day's heat drew on. He thought longingly of the cool green sea but a few blocks away and resented the officer's interference with the schedule that would lead him there, so was surprised when the captain said, "I'm in the mood for a coffee on the Malecòn. How about it, Father? Doesn't that sound delightful…at Le Saint Bonnet perhaps? Please join me; my treat, of course."

Before Father Pablo could raise a half-hearted objection, the officer took his arm once more and steered him towards a police truck parked at the curb with its passenger door standing open. Within, a young Yucatecan officer watched his superior approach with the priest in tow and started the vehicle, his broad, dark face revealing nothing.

Father Pablo knew Captain Barrera from Sunday Masses, where he always sat near the front with his beautiful, exhausted-looking wife and their five children, all girls. They had been introduced on several occasions, but Father Pablo had always had the impression that the captain had not recalled their previous meetings, and so was somewhat astonished and uneasy at the officer's familiar attention now. In fact, he was alarmed.

Though he knew it to be irrational, he could not help but think of all those bloodied martyr priests of the Cristero War, murdered at the hands of the police and army, perhaps kidnapped off the streets—much as he felt he was being at this moment. Father Pablo glanced about to see if anyone was as startled as he, but found the faces of his fellow citizens closed or simply placid. No one was even watching them as he was bundled into the cab of the truck and then sandwiched between the officers.

As Captain Barrera slid effortlessly into his seat and slammed the door, he felt the butt of the senior officer's .45 caliber pistol jut painfully into his ribs. Until that moment he had been unaware that the policeman even wore a gun, so awed had he been by the man's threatening elegance that it had gone unnoticed.

"Really, Captain," he squeaked. "I've no time today, though your offer is much appreciated…some other time, perhaps?" He swiveled his head to the driver, as his narrow shoulders were pinned between the two uniformed men, "Just across the way there…the hospital. The front entrance will do fine."

The truck jerked into traffic, forcing two cars to slam on their brakes, and raced towards the hospital. Father Pablo had just the briefest moment of relief before the vehicle rocketed past the building. Perhaps he *was* being abducted he thought with rising panic.

"Officer, you've driven right past it. But that's all right, anywhere along here will be fine, it's such a beautiful day anyway."

The driver did not slow, and Father Pablo turned to the open window next to Captain Barrera wondering if he should shout for help, or if that would only worsen his uncertain situation.

The captain spoke over him to the driver, "Le Saint Bonnet."

"Thank God," Father Pablo almost said aloud. "We're just going for coffee, after all."

As the truck swung into the next right turn Father Pablo found the captain smiling at him. "You're sweating, Little Father, maybe something cold for you instead?"

It was true; he could feel the beads of nervous sweat standing out on his forehead. The captain offered him a folded handkerchief, as clean and neatly pressed as the man himself, but the young priest refused. Instead, he fished out a wadded, stained one from his own pocket and dabbed at his face. "It has grown quite warm," he said.

They turned right again at the bus station and then left onto Calle 80. A few blocks ahead lay the sea, fringed by the few surviving palm trees after the legendary Hurricane Gilberto. Taking the last right possible, they slammed to a halt in front of the café. Father Pablo could not recall their slowing at a single stop sign along the way.

Holding the door for him, Captain Barrera helped the priest out onto the sidewalk. Standing on solid ground once more he felt his knees shaking.

"Don't worry, Little Father, we will just relax for a few minutes, then I'll take you right back to the hospital. In fact, if you have many house calls to make, I'll have my driver take you door to door. That will more than make up for lost time and, I hope, for any inconvenience I've caused you."

Feeling foolish now for his earlier fears, Father Pablo allowed himself to be steered into the cool, shadowed recesses of the palm-thatched café, while protesting, "That's very kind of you, Captain, but no," as he patted his slight pot-belly almost happily. "You see, I need the exercise."

The captain glanced at his stomach and then away without comment, as if silently agreeing, leading him to a table that looked out over the ocean. As soon as they were seated a waiter appeared at the officer's elbow. "A coffee for me," he commanded. "And you, Little Father?"

Father Pablo hesitated for the briefest of moments, his surroundings triggering a desire to relax and enjoy the breezes off the Gulf. A rum and coke sounded delightful.

As if conjured by this thought, the aroma of sweet caramel rose to Father Pablo's nostrils and for no other reason, he thought of the dance pavilion of his boyhood. It was there that he had enjoyed his first tentative sips of rum, brandy, tequila, and beer. It was also the place in which he discovered his love of God.

Consisting of a large cement slab, the pavilion was mounted over with a great tin roof, a roof stained by years of rust to the color of dried blood. A ring of pillars supported its edges, while an ancient mesquite tree, its great, gnarled limbs stripped away by forgotten storms, rose up to shoulder the peaked center.

The tree had been dead for as long as anyone could remember, gargantuan and petrified by decades, perhaps hundreds of years, of hot winds, and had presented an insurmountable challenge—for where once its overreaching branches had blotted out the sun and created the very place to site the pavilion, its unyielding trunk had refused to surrender to ax or saw.

After several months of contemplating this intractable obstacle to progress, with words like dynamite and fire being angrily bandied about, the solution had appeared like a common dream, its obviousness making everyone laugh and pull faces at their shared foolishness. The roof tree was now part of the village's proud history and presided over every birthday party, baptism celebration, and wedding dance like a kindly, silent grandfather.

On Saturday evenings, it provided the village's gathering place for celebrating the end of the work week. A makeshift bar circled the bleached and seamed trunk, the tree's frozen undulations evoking alien landscapes and the contorted faces of ancient gods or dimly remembered ancestors, while stacks of colorful bottles sparkled beneath bare light bulbs like heathen offerings.

Before this benevolent totem, he and his brothers had sat like a row of owls on the benches that defined the dance floor. Alternately titillated and terrified, he had silently watched the inexplicable antics of his elders—the alcohol they consumed allowing hidden facets of their personalities to dart out onto the dance floor, unexpected and sometimes dangerous, like a jaguar sprung from a cane thicket into their midst. Sometimes there were knives and blood.

Even his mother and father sloughed off the skins they had sported during the long week and danced like young lovers, their bodies joined at the waist, their gleaming faces but inches apart, leaving no room for labor, children, or chores.

The gulf young Pablo felt at such moments was not shared by his older brothers, who snorted, made crude jokes about their parents, and worked up the courage to ask girls to dance. Their zeal to join in the carnal parade of village life was keen and natural and Pablo watched them with envy and even admiration.

The tots of rum they slipped to him from time to time, concealed in plastic cups of sweet lemon and lime sodas, soothed his anxieties and made him feel that he was somehow being included without anything actually being asked of him, and this suited him well.

The reality was that his brothers were embarrassed by his awkwardness and had no wish to be burdened by his tagging along with them onto the dance floor. Pablo understood this without resentment.

The rum and tequila were purchased from older boys in the darkness that lay just beyond the pavilion, and available to any willing teenager with a little money. Pablo's brothers saw to it he got his share and he proved that he could hold his own. In this manner they satisfied themselves that he was not a complete sissy.

As the sweet rum uncoiled within his stomach and sent its soothing fumes upwards into his brain, Pablo's shyness and fears would retreat like unwelcome, but polite, guests to wait in the darkened corners.

Once left to himself, the soft, pimpled teenager was able to open his eyes to the spinning, tumultuous world before him without fear, and found it beautiful in its desperate joys and exalting sorrows—the villagers' poverty becoming a noble imitation of Christ, the silly girls from his school reflections of the Madonna at the various stages of her holy life.

Even the profane and swaggering teenage boys wore the haughty, handsome faces of Roman Legionnaires, their mortality and beauty made evident, and all the more poignant, by the presence of their exhausted, sagging fathers staggering around the dance floor in tight jeans and pregnant-looking bellies.

It seemed the religious studies the Salesian Brothers taught him at school contained all that was needed to know and endure the world, while the rum made him a contemplative—finding Christ's love in every face. The pairing of earthy liquors and the sacred remained confusingly inseparable for him—his hangovers a bleeding, throbbing crown of thorns—the bottle an increasingly heavy cross.

"Your usual, Father?" the waiter asked helpfully.

"What? Heavens, no!" the little priest cried, startled from his reverie. "You know it's far too early for that," he chided the boy. He could not even look across the table at the captain he was so embarrassed. "A coffee for me, as well," he concluded primly. The waiter did not smile, which *was* helpful.

Turning to the beach, he was just in time to see another waiter delivering an iced soft drink to the police driver, who had seated himself beneath a palapa. He had not seen the captain place the order, so he concluded it must be something of a ritual here. It was somehow reassuring to think that the captain took care of his men.

Regaining his composure, Father Pablo turned guiltily to the captain, only to find him watching the shallow waves lapping the shelved sands of the beach. He appeared to have taken no note of the waiter's revealing question, staring into the distance as if alone at the table. For the first time, Father Pablo wondered what this police officer really wanted of him.

"It's entrancing, isn't it?" the priest ventured softly. "God must love us very much to give us such things to enjoy."

The officer turned and scrutinized him a moment. "The beach needs cleaning; it's strewn with bottles and wrappers. The Mayor is dropping the ball on this, you know. How can we ever hope to be the next Cancún if the beaches aren't cleaned regularly?"

As was becoming a habit on this most disconcerting of days, Father Pablo was at a loss to answer. The beaches appeared quite beautiful to him, but of course he had never been to such upscale resorts as Cancún or Cozumel.

Waving away his question, the captain posed another as their coffees were delivered, "Do you find it as difficult being a priest here as I do being a police officer? I ask you this because you are not from Yucatán, and are in position to be objective about it. I think I have lost my own objectivity somewhere along the way."

The priest thought that he did, indeed, find it difficult, but that it had little to do with his current posting and everything to do with his own ineptitude. Looking across the table at the handsome, competent policeman, he doubted their situations were in any way similar. "Well," he ventured, "things are more personal here."

The captain slapped the tabletop with an open hand and barked a dry laugh, "You've hit it right on the head, Little Father...personal, yes."

A startled couple at a nearby table glanced in their direction. Father Pablo guessed that they were Canadians, or Americans, by their appearance. Progreso hosted a small number of them during the winter season, though Father Pablo had met very few as most seemed to be Anglicans. He noticed that some of his coffee had found its way onto the table cloth.

"Close is another way to put it ...or cloying," Captain Barrera continued. "Everyone knows everyone else's business, or soon will. We are what...fifty, sixty thousand people now? Yet, we are still a small town, not much more than a *pueblito*, if you ask me...if you judge by our behavior. Don't you think so, Father? Why, we still have burro men, for God's sake!"

"Well yes," Father Pablo agreed. "I guess that's true, but don't you find that it's rather nice to know your people? That is, to be on a personal basis with those whose care you are charged with?" He felt keenly his own hypocrisy in mouthing such platitudes, as he had made little effort to get to know his own parishioners. When he had first been sent to Progreso he had been content to dwell in the shadow of Monsignor Roberto De Jesus, and had hoped to remain carefully shaded there for many years to come—the Monsignor's heart attack had come as a cruel stroke indeed, leaving him exposed as it did. "I truly believe that one can make a real difference in such a place as this," he heard himself saying.

Captain Barrera regarded him blankly, as if disappointed in such a speech; then offered him a cigarette as he shook another from his pack for himself. Father Pablo accepted it, though he was not normally a smoker when not drinking, but being in an establishment that served alcohol had triggered his desire and he inhaled gratefully as the captain lit his cigarette from a plastic lighter. He noticed that the foreign couple was watching him with thinly veiled contempt. "Perhaps Anglican ministers are not allowed to smoke," he wondered, uncomfortable under their glare.

Catching them at this, Captain Barrera blew a steady stream of smoke in their direction. The man looked as if he wished to say something, while the woman turned away and made a display of fanning the air with her napkin, though in fact they were several tables away from the priest and the policeman. After a moment, the man angrily threw a handful of change onto the table and the couple rose and left, their retreating postures a study in disapproval. They had words with the waiter on their way out.

"Smoking is permitted," the captain announced quietly to the now empty room, before returning his attention to Father Pablo. "The Norte Americanos have it right," he said, leaning forward confidentially and indicating the departing couple with his head. "They live in a large world, go wherever they wish, and are people of power and action. We..." he set his cup down, opening his arms to embrace all of México, "...carry too much luggage. Between our families, our culture, our customs, and yes, Little Father, our religion, we can never finish packing. And so, we never leave, or if we manage that much, we arrive as we began and never learn, or more importantly, change. Do you see what I mean? It's all the same. Too personal, as you put it."

Father Pablo bought time to respond by downing the last of his coffee and taking a long drag on his cigarette. He found himself warming to the tall, elegant officer, but sensed he was being probed, that some deeper question lay beneath the captain's discourse on the Mexican character. He looked beyond the officer to the sea and the miles-long pier that ran like a white ribbon towards the horizon. A cargo ship was being off-loaded by a giant crane; the men involved appearing the size of ants.

"Perhaps the burden of your responsibilities is weighing on you, Captain," Father Pablo began reluctantly, the chafing of his collar reminding him of La Viuda's earlier chastisement, egging him on. "It can't be easy, as you said yourself, to be a senior police officer here. You must find yourself petitioned on every side with people wanting special favors or treatment, in need of your judgment or advice, I should think."

Captain Barrera's features had once again lost their animation, and the priest found himself staring, like Progreso's criminals, he imagined, at the unreadable face of authority. He stumbled on nervously.

"And families, of course—a wife and children. Their care can cause a man great worry. Not that I would have experience with that end of things!" He giggled and lifted his empty cup to his plumy lips, then set it back down hastily in his confusion. "If these are things you wish to discuss, privately, I am always available, you know. You are a devout man, a man of faith. I see you and your lovely family every Sunday. Your girls are quite beautiful!" The captain's face remained unmoved, "Your wife too…striking!"

Silence rushed in to fill the vacuum of Father Pablo's awkward speech and the captain lit another cigarette. This time he did not offer one to the priest but turned away, crossing his long legs.

After several moments of studying the white, puffy clouds stacked in towering columns above the flat sea, he spoke, "Personal, you see. I'm disappointed in you, Little Father. Being an educated man, having spent time in México City, I expected a little more. Yet, you proved my point. I had hoped to have something of a philosophical discussion, but, as usual, it becomes personal. So be it."

Bowing his head, Father Pablo picked nervously at a spot on his cheek, "I'm sorry to disappoint, Captain. Monsignor Roberto would have made you a better companion." He said this without rancor, but as a sad fact.

"No," the Captain responded with a sigh, "no, he wouldn't. He would have spoken exactly as you did."

In spite of the overwhelming sense of loneliness that radiated from the policeman, Father Pablo was buoyed by his words. He was comforted by any comparison to Monsignor Roberto De Jesus, even an unfavorable one.

Captain Barrera spun back around to face Father Pablo, his expression businesslike. "Now then," he began crisply, "as to the matter of the missing Alcante boy." Father Pablo noted a peculiar emphasis on the word *missing*. "You've undoubtedly noticed that he no longer graces us with his presence at church, nor has he harassed anyone in the plaza for several weeks now. Ordinarily, I would see this as a blessing and give it no more thought. He is an adult and free to take himself wherever he wishes to go, and as far as I'm concerned, the farther the better. His mother, naturally, does not agree."

"No, of course not…poor woman," Father Pablo intoned.

"However, her feelings do not make this a police matter."

"No, I can see that, even so, it would be a great comfort to her to know that he is alive and well, I'm sure." Obviously, the captain did not know that Señora Alcante had jumped ship, as it were, and thought she was in close contact with her priest. The irony of representing this lapsed parishioner, whom, until this morning he had been unaware of, struck Father Pablo as singularly absurd, but the sting of Doña Marisa's tongue had done its work.

"Perhaps it would, perhaps it wouldn't," the captain resumed. "I'm not sure in this case. What you can tell her is this: He's been spotted in the countryside at some farm or old plantation. Apparently, if my sources are to be believed, there's some group he's holed up with out there. Some kind of criminal gang or cult, I hear. You can tell her that part, or not, as you see fit."

La Viuda's words came back to Father Pablo, but for reasons he could not articulate, he chose to keep them to himself.

"In any event, *if* it turns out his little gang was involved in that shootout at the crossroads, you can assure Señora Alcante that her son's whereabouts will most definitely become a police matter, and that I will drop everything to find him at that time."

Rising, he placed some money on the table, looking down on Father Pablo all the while. "One other thing she may wish to know. It seems a number of witnesses have seen him moving freely without his crutches—apparently, the country life agrees with him."

Captain Barrera looked out at his driver beneath the palapa who was already rising, as if by an unseen signal. Taking Father Pablo by the arm, he led him towards the entrance, observing dryly, "It appears we live in an age of miracles, Little Father."

CHAPTER THREE

James Arbor left Le Saint Bonnet with the ache in his jaw that had become a familiar source of discomfort since his retirement. He likened the sensation to small steel rods inserted at his jaw hinges and then too tightly screwed down. It made speech painful and difficult, and lent to his rather fleshy face the rictus of a man about to spit or scream.

As he and his wife made their way east along the Malecòn, he couldn't refrain from taking another look over his shoulder at the café. The arrogant police officer and the disheveled little priest could not be seen beneath the cool shadows of the palm-thatched roof. He hoped they were watching and noting the open challenge on his face, even as some quiet rational spot within his brain hoped that they were not. He was, he needed no reminding, in a foreign country where anything could happen, and sometimes did.

"James, stop it," his wife, Brenda, hissed. "My God, he's a policeman. We didn't come here looking for trouble, we came here to relax. Please."

He twisted his head back around and felt a sharp pain run down his neck. "I thought this was the land of *machismo* where men were courteous to women above all things. He blew smoke right at us…at you…a woman! I should have walked over there and knocked that self-satisfied look right off his face, knocked him right out of his chair!"

His jaw ached with each word he squeezed out, but he knew he could have done it. The policeman may have been twenty years his junior, but he knew that he was large enough and in good enough shape to take him...in a short fight anyway, he'd concede that to his sixty-two years.

But he also had kept himself in great shape for his age. Not only had he played fullback in college, but he had jogged and worked out in the gym his entire corporate career, and run younger men into the ground playing "no quarter given" handball. In spite of his widening hips and inexplicably spreading girth, he still possessed illimitable confidence in his prowess and size, these things being the natural outgrowth and physical manifestation of his own inner self.

Even so, since departing the executive playing fields of his adulthood, he felt a creeping sense of having left behind an essential something that, though glaringly apparent to others, eluded him. Looking down on his wife, who had grown suspiciously quiet, he asked, "You think I couldn't have?"

Brenda Arbor only reached his shoulder, and so gave her husband the sidelong, upwards glance that never failed to rouse something in him. It was a teasing, coquettish effect that suited her small face. Though seventeen years her husband's junior, she could easily have passed for five years younger yet, and was well aware of this. Just as she was more painfully conscious that neither would she be mistaken for his "younger" mistress or grown daughter.

When they had married, he had been forty years old and she, his second wife, just twenty-three. James had been in the full vigor of his mature adulthood, both in terms of his clout within the research and development field, as well as his earning ability. The absence of children, and Brenda's inability to conceive, seemed as natural a part of their lifestyle as having them would not have been. James took Brenda's silence on the subject as acceptance if not contentment with their lot. Satisfied with the visits allowed him to his son and daughter by his previous wife, the subject simply never developed into that of an issue.

"I think you could have," she asserted, her small smile still intact. "But I think you need to look up the word *machismo.*" She turned her small, neat head away from him to look out on the sea. "And stop grinding your teeth."

James slowly stretched his mouth wide, like the jaws of a bear trap being cautiously pried apart. "Sorry," he said, after a moment of this exercise. "I don't know when I started this, but it's gotten worse since I retired."

A group of policemen were lounging in the shade of a concrete gazebo built into the wide bricked strip of the Malecòn. They all wore wrinkled-looking fatigues and baseball caps, appearing so young that they might have been American Boy Scouts in their dark blue uniforms. Only the sergeant, identified by his stripes, maturity, and forage hat, wore a gun. The rest were armed only with batons and lay sprawled about the structure in various postures of seeming exhaustion.

Watching their approach with only mild interest, the sergeant was the first to see the American couple. Except for a few vendors, the promenade was largely deserted as the heat of the day built up.

"They look like a bunch of blue lizards," James said, chuckling at the image.

"Shh…" Brenda warned, as the sergeant's small, dark eyes seemed to sharpen and focus at the sound of their voices. "What has gotten into you today? Are you trying to pick a fight?"

The sergeant's expression altered to one of subdued alarm as he watched the approach of the very large American and his woman. Raising their heads with what appeared to be great effort, several of his young officers peered at them in a perplexed, shy manner; then allowed gravity to pull their faces downward once more to contemplate their boots, or the sand-covered floor of the gazebo.

"Buenos días," Brenda smiled at the sergeant as they passed.

"Buenos días," he returned automatically then, like the younger men, looked shyly at his boots. A tired chorus of "Buenos días," rose dispiritedly from the crumpled group.

"Don't bother getting up," James said for Brenda's benefit after they were out of earshot. "What a sorry-looking crew. Can you imagine that in the states? Cops sitting around on the pavement like a bunch of derelicts? Honest to God."

"They were nice, honey. They greeted us just like they would their own citizens. It's a different culture, that's all."

"You had to speak first. Otherwise they wouldn't have said a word. It was reflex. In any case, what's up with all these cops everywhere? Have you noticed? You can't walk two blocks in this town without running into one kind of a cop or another—blue uniforms, green uniforms, brown uniforms. Your friends told us that the State of Yucatán had the lowest crime rate in México, so why all the cops—or is this how they deal with unemployment down here?"

"Maybe that's *why* they have the lowest crime rate," Brenda countered. "Have you thought of that?"

"That Canadian bar owner told me they've had some trouble around here recently. Common wisdom, so he says, is that it's some kind of home-grown militants patterning themselves after the *Zapatístas* over in Chiapas. You know the kind of thing; kids running around in jungle fatigues, wearing bandanas around their faces and waving M-16s, shotguns, machetes, or whatever else they can lay their hands on."

"I haven't read anything in the papers."

"Really...?" James was well aware of his wife's fluency in both written and spoken Spanish. "Well, like you said, there's no *crime* in Progreso...at least in the papers," he added, rather meanly.

It had been his wife's idea for them to spend a month in the Yucatán, exploring the Mayan ruins, the capital city of Mérida, and the "Emerald Coast," as the Mexican Tourist Board had dubbed the rarely visited Gulf shore. She had taken a vacation to the region the year before in the company of two of her more adventurous girlfriends and inexplicably, in James' mind, fallen in love with the place. She was even talking up the idea of buying a vacation home in the area.

It had been his wish to bask in the more sanitized luxury of familiar Cancún. But, in light of her current infatuation with all things authentically Mexican, he had thought it wise to accompany her before he became an inadvertent investor in Mexican real estate.

Angling away from her husband, Brenda stopped, placing her hands on the waist-high wall that separated them from the beach. A group of three couples lay baking on blankets in the littered sand. Judging from their pallor and the skimpy bathing briefs the men wore, she guessed they were recent arrivals, Canadians or Europeans.

As she watched, one of the men suddenly leapt to his feet and rushed into the surf, shouting and waving for the others to join him. A woman, not the one he shared his blanket with, raised her head, shading her eyes with one hand and waving tiredly with the other, as if the swimmer were departing for a long journey.

Overhead, several frigate birds coasted in the breeze like kites, looking down on the fleshy scene with the predator's keen, unhurried interest. No Mexicans shared the beach with the foreigners, as it was not their season. They preferred the summer months of July and August when their children were out of school and it was hotter.

"What do they want...these militants? Did your Canadian barkeeper tell you that?"

"Want?" James repeated, dazzled by the sun and the glinting, gently undulating green waters. "No one seems to know. They just don't want the authorities snooping around the interior, it seems. That's the reason for the roadblocks, checkpoints. Protecting something, I guess...some kind of narcotics operation, probably. It seems that any group that sets themselves up in the drug business down here likes to style themselves as revolutionaries. It gives them an air of respectability.

"The local cops are worried that this gang will start trying to move their goods into Progreso for the fishermen to ferry offshore to freighters. My guess is that they don't want to get cut out of the action, and are just waiting for their chance to take a bite...a *mordida*, isn't that what they call it down here?"

Smiling absently at her husband, Brenda's thoughts went back to the policeman in the café. Suddenly, in spite of his arrogant good looks, her lover of the year before did not appear as dashing as he did vulnerable. Sighing, she said, "I just hope there's no trouble while we're here."

* * *

As promised, after dropping his commander off at police headquarters, the captain's driver took Father Pablo from house to house on his visits. But the presence of the police vehicle, with its priest and silent driver, appeared to worry the occupants of the narrow streets they traveled. It took several stops before Father Pablo grasped the consternation and alarm he was creating and understood the crowds that were drawn to each household he visited—the people assumed that the police had sent the priest to announce the death of some loved one in a car accident or other tragedy. Feeling foolish, he dismissed the driver with his thanks to Captain Barrera and trudged through the rest of his list on foot.

By mid-afternoon, he had completed his rounds and was hot, tired, and thirsty. A *norte*, as the locals called the high, cool winds that blew down from the north during the winter season, had started up, and might have been refreshing but for the fine grit and sand it carried off the beach. Instead, the abrasive peppering only served to add to Father Pablo's discomfort, and he was exasperated and irritable when he finally arrived back at the rectory.

When he found the housekeeper's note on the little side table where she always left messages, he could not refrain himself. "Damn the woman," he muttered, as he kicked off his shoes and sat down heavily in the overstuffed chair. "She overreaches herself."

The note, written in Señora Garza's large, looping script and littered with exclamation marks, informed him that the mayor would be coming to supper at eight o'clock. Undoubtedly, Father Pablo thought disgustedly, the mayor has invited himself and Señora Garza has agreed on my behalf. It had been a regular custom under Monsignor Roberto De Jesus and it appeared the mayor, and Señora Garza, intended to continue it. A postscript noted that she would be back by six-thirty to begin preparations and that she had placed some cold beer in the refrigerator for Father Pablo's refreshment. This last perked him up and he hastened to retrieve a chilled bottle from the kitchen.

After two of these, Father Pablo began to feel much better about the mayor's visit and to see it less as an imposition. "After all," he thought, nodding sagely, "I am the pastor now, so it only stands to reason that the mayor should wish to visit me. It's to be expected under these circumstances."

Sitting in the cool shadows of the high-ceilinged study that his predecessor had occupied, with its heavy, imposing furniture and long windows, Father Pablo indulged in the temporary sense of well-being that the beer afforded him. "It's only fitting after a morning spent with a captain of police, that I should now entertain the mayor. In spite of La Viuda's opinion, I am, perhaps, a personage of some weight, some gravitas."

His head began to sink to his chest, even as fleeting thoughts of the notes he must make for the morrow's homily buzzed uselessly about his ears, unable to gain entrance. Surrendering to oblivion, Father Pablo's concerns drifted out the open windows to join the silent bats flitting to and fro in the comforting twilight that gathered over the plaza, and he slept.

CHAPTER FOUR

Father Pablo managed to nap during the forty-minute bus ride into Mérida, awakening as the lumbering vehicle hissed to a stop at the terminal on Calle 62. The heavy diesel fumes rolled in as the door was thrown open and he groaned quietly, clutching a stomach sloshing with the heavy, acidic residue of last night's drinking.

Standing, he felt the blood run from his face and gripped the seat back in front of him until the spell of dizziness passed, all the while waving on the other passengers who had stopped politely to let him enter the aisle. His supper with the mayor had not gone as he had expected, and it was surely a judgment from God, he thought, that of all mornings for the archbishop to summon him, it would be this one.

Who would have thought that the mayor would be such a jolly, convivial fellow? From the moment of his arrival, a bottle under his arm, he had been a whirlwind of jokes and tales. Commandeering the rectory, he had enlisted Father Pablo as a boon companion even before they had been called to table.

Requiring little in return, the mayor's booming voice carried even into the kitchen, where, on occasion, Father Pablo could hear the cackling laughter of Señora Garza erupt at his scandalous stories. It had been impossible to resist the man's infectious high spirits. Just as it had proven impossible for

Father Pablo to resist his vintage brandy, which he insisted be shared, glass for glass, with the priest.

After the mayor had proclaimed Señora Garza's meal a stupendous success, and she had cleared away the dishes in an unusually cheerful mood, bidding the men goodnight, he had produced a pack of cards, two good cigars, and a beaming smile.

Father Pablo had difficulty remembering the rest of their evening with any clarity, recalling only snatches of ebullient conversation and loud laughter that now seemed tainted with overindulgence and guilt. At some point he had been deemed an excellent fellow, if a little young, and a poor gin rummy player. At another, he had attempted some wit about the mayor's hair and its complex, lacquered arrangement. Unfortunately, he could not recall the mayor's reaction, or even when he had left.

Morning Mass had been a waking nightmare and he had sweated profusely throughout. Miraculously, it had gone without a hitch, even La Viuda appearing satisfied, and Father Pablo had been breathing a sigh of relief as he hastened to his room and bed when Señora Garza intercepted him. "For you," she had informed him tersely, handing him a slip of paper with a telephone message on it.

It had been Señora Garza who had shaken him awake this morning, her nose wrinkling in distaste at his sour smell. It was also she who had discovered the additional, and empty, bottle of brandy Father Pablo had retrieved from Monsignor Roberto De Jesus' now violated wine cabinet. She had delivered the summons from the archbishop with the grim satisfaction of a well-earned pink slip, though the actual message had simply requested his presence at 11:00AM and offered no further details.

These jagged, hazy memories made Father Pablo squirm with shame and he hastened to escape the now-empty bus. Stepping into the fresh air only renewed his light-headedness and nausea, and as he bent at the waist and seized his knees to wait for it to pass, he was treated to his own rank odor. With a small cry of disgust he straightened up and began the short, but seemingly impossible, walk to the archdiocesan offices near the cathedral.

Father Pablo made his appointment with only minutes to spare, and yet was made to wait an additional twenty minutes as a parade of ecclesiastical personages came and went from the archbishop's inner office. A hushed murmur of important business seemed to fill the air of the mahogany paneled room. Few acknowledged the young priest as he sat nervously awaiting his audience.

The world outside intruded from time to time with the faint toot of a car horn, or the grinding, muted roar of a passing bus. Twice, Father Pablo caught the archbishop's secretary, a cool-looking, neat young man of his own age, peering hard at his sweat-stained collar, and he found himself self-consciously touching it, as if that would have some ameliorating effect.

At last, the secretary's phone buzzed and he swiftly lifted the receiver.   After listening to what seemed like extensive instructions, he returned it to its cradle, looked up at Father Pablo, and simply waved him towards the door.   Father Pablo took a deep breath and entered.

His Excellency, Archbishop Guillermo Inigo Valdes Aguera, appeared delighted to see him and held both hands out to greet the young priest from Progreso.   It took a moment for Father Pablo to grasp that the archbishop was not sitting behind his desk but standing, so slight was his stature.   When Father Pablo had first been assigned to this archdiocese and made his obligatory visit to the archbishop, he had found him out of the country on a pilgrimage to Rome, and so they had not met.

He tried not to show his surprise and hurried to take the little man's proffered hands, kissing his ring of office as he did so.

"Pablo Diego Corellas," the little man crowed, all the while shaking Father Pablo's hands up and down.   "It's so wonderful to meet you at last. Wonderful you could come. Please sit, make yourself at home."

Father Pablo waited until the archbishop had once more seated himself before doing the same.   "Thank you, Your Excellency," he managed, baffled at his warm greeting.

The archbishop waved this away, all the while smiling and studying the young priest with a keen, friendly interest.   "You've nothing to thank me for; I've summarily dragged you away from your beautiful seashore and your duties. Heavier duties, no doubt, than you signed on for, what with Monsignor Roberto De Jesus' illness. You do look tired, my young friend. Did they offer you anything to drink? Some water, perhaps? You look thirsty." He made to pour a glass from a carafe on his desk.

Father Pablo was dying of thirst, but he recoiled at the thought of having the archbishop wait on him. "No, please, Your Excellency. That's all right. I'm just fine, really."

"Hush, now," the older man commanded gently, "you're tired and thirsty after that long bus ride and hot walk. You need some water."

Father Pablo wondered if his superior recognized how hungover he was. Surely a man of his long experience could read the roadmap of Father Pablo's weaknesses and see that they led straight to this moment. Probably La Viuda had written this good man and detailed, as only she could, all the failings of Progreso's second-string priest.

Or Señora Garza, perhaps…after last night's performance she had probably wasted no time in calling the archdiocese with her insider information. What an earful she must have given them! It's no wonder that the archbishop's secretary looked at him with such pity and disdain. Possibly it was the mayor himself who had done it, having tested him the night before and found him a weak vessel.

When Archbishop Valdes handed him the glass, Father Pablo's hands were shaking so much that water sloshed over the side, and he brought it to his parched lips in a two-fisted grip.

As he lowered the glass, setting it carefully back on the archbishop's desk, he found the little man smiling at him once more.

"See, you were thirsty…thought so."

"Yes," Father Pablo admitted, "I was. Thank you." He felt near to tears with gratitude.

"There, now," the archbishop soothed. "There, now."

Father Pablo studied the older man in silence, noting his light green eyes and a faint scattering of freckles across his broad cheekbones. Though it was difficult to determine in the muted light of the office, he thought he could discern traces of reddish hair running through the thin grey strands of the archbishop's pate. He could see now that Monsignor Roberto's story of the archbishop's lineage was true; his Irish grandfather peered out from his eyes.

"Let's talk, young man," the archbishop resumed gently. "Tell me about Progreso. How have things been for you in your new parish?"

Father Pablo understood that this was the moment—his opportunity to bare his soul, confess his unworthiness, and tender his resignation. What, after all, was left for him? So he began, "The truth is, Your Excellency, not well. Not well at all, really. You may have heard things."

The prelate nodded in agreement, his smile fading somewhat. "I've been hearing a few things," he agreed. "Go on."

"I'm not the pastor Monsignor Roberto De Jesus was, at least, so it seems. The people of the parish loved him; he was so competent and good. While I…I'm neither good nor competent."

Archbishop Valdes remained quiet, a slight look of puzzlement clouding his pale, merry eyes.

Father Pablo continued; his relief growing as he provided his superior with everything he needed to remove the onerous burden of responsibility from his shoulders. "You see, I never thought of myself as a pastor. I certainly never thought I would find myself in this position when I was sent to Progreso. It never occurred to me that anything might happen to Monsignor Roberto De Jesus and that I would be left in charge.

"It's ridiculous for me to be in charge," he laughed aloud at the absurdity of it. "Of all people…*me*. It was bound to come out. Of course, I didn't realize it would become so obvious so quickly. I've been praying every day to Our Lady for a new pastor…" A sudden thought came into his head and he stopped speaking to look up at the archbishop's face, whose expression had altered yet again, to one of mild amusement.

"Is there a replacement? Is that what you've brought me here to tell me? Thank God, if it is," he cried.

The older man shook his head, his small smile still in place. "No, I'm afraid not, Pablo. There's no relief in sight just yet. After Monsignor Roberto De Jesus' recovery, we will assess the situation. He may yet be able to return."

The archbishop's words struck Father Pablo like a hammer blow. *After Monsignor Roberto De Jesus' recovery we will assess the situation!* Sweet Jesus, that could be months down the road! Hadn't the archbishop been listening?

He resumed, more desperate than ever, "Your Excellency, perhaps I haven't made myself very clear—I am unsuitable for my posting, you can ask anyone in Progreso. Believe me it's no secret...have you not heard this from Doña Marisa Sáenz?"

The archbishop shook his head, asking, "Who is this woman, Father Pablo?"

"She is a humpback with no time for foolishness," the young priest answered meanly, "a black widow who wishes me gone from *her* church."

"Ah, one of *those*," the older man chuckled, then added, "These things take time, Pablo, you are just uncomfortable in the newness of being in charge, that is perfectly natural under the circumstances. Given a little time..."

"No, Your Excellency," Father Pablo dared to interrupt the old cleric, "time is not the issue. A year from now will find me no better. Perhaps I will muddle through the rituals and sacraments a little more proficiently, but that will be all, and the people will know that. They know it now!

"I lack the faith required for a pastor. The truth be told, I lack the faith to be a priest at all. I am awkward and easily flustered in front of the people because I know this. I am silly and cannot help it because I am afraid. And my drinking," he began to weep openly now, the stress of his situation and his brutal hangover combining to illustrate the essence of his words. "Well, it must be rather obvious to you at this moment."

Gripping the edge of the archbishop's desk he looked up into his eyes, as his own threatened to bleed down his quivering cheeks. "Please help me, Your Excellency. I am not fit to be the pastor of Progreso." His own vomitus breath came back to him, foul and desperate. "My faith is the faith of a parishioner, not a clergyman—I belong in the pews, not at the altar."

The archbishop clapped his hands together with a loud pop, startling Father Pablo into sitting back. The man was actually grinning, though his hands remained together in the attitude of prayer.

"That's it, you see," he said, almost happily. "That's just it! You *are* the pastor of Progreso, that's undeniable! Are you worthy? Are you a poor priest? Do you lack enough faith? *Who knows*? Are any of us worthy of these collars and robes? I doubt it. I seriously doubt it."

Pouring another glass of water for Father Pablo, he handed it over his desk to him. "Yet, here we are. And how did we all get here?" He watched contentedly as Father Pablo gulped down the water. "How did I become archbishop, for God's sake, and you, poor boy, the only priest in Progreso?

"I'm sure it can all be explained away quite easily. In your case it appears straightforward enough—Monsignor Roberto De Jesus had a heart attack. Mine is somewhat more complicated, yet I'm sure it could easily be dissected and the component parts revealed as stepping stones leading, however circuitously, to my present situation. Are you with me, my boy?"

Father Pablo nodded miserably while staring at his lap.

"The only part that I find hard to get around is that you *were* there when Monsignor Roberto fell ill. There could be dozens of perfectly explainable reasons of why you were his assistant at that moment, but what we are left with is that it *was* you, and not someone else, not someone more suitable, as you say...but *you*."

Father Pablo tiredly slid the now empty glass back onto the prelate's desk, and allowed his head to flop back until he was staring at the high ceiling. "You won't relieve me?"

Leaning forward, Archbishop Valdes answered, "I don't believe God maneuvers us about like chess pieces, Pablo. But I would not be a Catholic, much less a cleric, if I did not believe His influence is felt within us. If we allow it and open our hearts to Christ, even if it's just a small fissure, we, and the rest of the world, are influenced in ways we cannot fathom. And not once did you tell me you do not believe, only that your belief is not strong enough. I cannot judge what strong *enough* is, and neither can you. You opened your heart some and maybe that will suffice. Now relax and allow Christ to do the work."

Father Pablo began to gather himself and rise from the archbishop's comfortable leather chair. He felt so exhausted that he wondered if he might just fall to the floor and sleep for a while on the cool tiles before his return journey to Progreso.

He had come dreading being exposed as the fraud he truly believed he was, and had ended by being disappointed that he had not been relieved of his duties after all. It was all so anticlimactic and draining. What better show could he have put on to convince the archbishop of the plain truth? He felt like a man who had been given a postponement from the gallows, not a reprieve. It was only a matter of time before he would be hung by the cleric's collar he wore like a yoke around his neck.

"I appreciate your trust in me, Your Excellency," Father Pablo said without conviction. "Thank you. Now I'd better not take up any more of your time." He had begun to shuffle towards the entrance when the senior cleric stopped him.

"Poor boy, did you think that was why I had you come here? What a terrible journey that must have made for you. I would have given your housekeeper more details, but I didn't think it wise just at the moment. I am sorry."

Father Pablo turned back to face his superior, stoop-shouldered and tiredly bewildered, the greasy hair on the back of his head standing up from its contact with the visitor's chair. "Pardon, Your Excellency?"

The older man resumed, "You asked earlier if I had heard news from out your way, and I said I had, it's just that it wasn't about you. It seems that something is afoot in the countryside."

"Afoot," Father Pablo repeated listlessly.

The archbishop chuckled at his own choice of words, "Yes, at least that's the rumor: Healings—the lame made to walk, the blind to see, that sort of thing...*miracles*. The pastor of the church in Barrio de Itzimna discovered some of his flock organizing a pilgrimage to some secret site in the country— that's how I heard about it. He was able to learn very little, as his parishioners were acting on the vaguest of rumors—it seems someone claims to have a holy relic. Have you heard anything yourself?"

Father Pablo shook his head as if to clear his thoughts, "A little, yes—just recently I was told of a cripple from my parish seen walking without his crutches." Thinking of the rat-faced, drug-addicted Juan Alcante, he warned the archbishop, "I wouldn't put too much store in that news, Your Excellency; it's possible that he could walk all along."

"Excellent," the archbishop exclaimed. "A man with some inside knowledge is just what I need."

"What do you mean?" Father Pablo asked.

"Find the people who have this thing and take a look at what's going on, then report back to me. Don't put anything into writing, of course. This is just an informal matter, for now. If word gets out that the archdiocese is involved it could breathe life into an unhealthy situation. It's wise to be cautious in matters of faith, *if* that's what we're dealing with here."

"You want me to go out there? Archbishop, the police tell me these people are *insurrectos*!"

The prelate appeared hugely amused, and it was only belatedly that Father Pablo realized that he was once again standing. "If that's the case, then they will certainly have no use for you and you need have no fear."

"And if they aren't?" Father Pablo asked forlornly, as his superior took him by the elbow and walked him to the door.

"Then they'll be happy to see you, I should think. They'll want you to verify the holy properties of their relic."

"But what if I can't?" This prospect seemed more dangerous than the insurrectos.

"What if you can?" The archbishop countered playfully, laughing. "We'll have our hands full then, I'm afraid!"

Father Pablo tried one last time, "Your Excellency, I am not suitable for a task such as this—I have too little experience."

Ushering the young priest out of his office, the archbishop replied, "Perhaps, poor boy, but it is, after all, your parish, isn't it?"

CHAPTER FIVE

Father Pablo had just nodded off when he felt, rather than heard, the bus slowing and easing its way onto the shoulder of the state highway. As it was probably stopping for some passengers to depart, he did not open his eyes. Allowing the warm, dark vortex of exhaustion to draw him downward into himself, his consciousness folded closed like the petals of a rose at dusk. Even the hiss of the door and the resultant stamp and shuffle of feet failed to rouse him, though somewhere in his mind he registered a murmur of concern ripple across his fellow travelers; still, nothing alarmed him.

Rather it was the repeated question and response that at last wormed its way into his ears and gently but firmly, began to draw him up from his deepening slumber: "*Con su permiso*," then, "*Gracias*," repeated again and again like the proclamation and affirmation of priest and communicant at the moment of receiving the Host.

"The Body of Christ," he mumbled, waiting for the expected response. But La Viuda only glared at what he offered her from his soiled hands. At last, looking down to see what could possibly be the matter, he found that he was holding a playing card instead of the expected Host.

Worse yet, upon closer inspection it appeared that the card was of the type he had often seen his father and his ranch hands play with on Saturday nights in Chiapas. It was graphically adorned with a photograph of a large-breasted young woman wearing little else but some intricately arranged harness to hold up her black stockings. She was bent at the waist, seemingly smoothing those improbable and obviously unnecessary garments, while smiling coyly at the camera, an expression of happy surprise on her face. It appeared she was delighted to be the Queen of Spades.

When the response was finally given, it was incorrect and in the voice of a man. Father Pablo's eyes flew open and he began clambering to his feet in order to escape his shame and flee his church. He had every intention of running to the bus terminal and boarding the next available coach away from Progreso. Instead, he found himself already on a bus and face to face with a startled young man in jungle fatigues wearing a purple sash around his waist. Everyone on the bus was turned towards him and the rebel.

. "Perdoné, Padre," the Indio youth said, taking a hasty step backwards.

"It's not mine," Father Pablo declared to the bus at large, swimming the last few feet up from the dark pool of his dream. Several of the passengers tittered openly at his confusion.

Besides the young man who had awakened him, Father Pablo could see another fatigue-clad youth standing next to the clearly nervous driver; he also favored the wine-colored sash that was at such odds with their camouflage uniforms. The one closest to Father Pablo held a sheaf of colored papers, which he had been in the midst of offering the passengers when he had disturbed the priest.

He now took the opportunity to offer one to Father Pablo, though he appeared reluctant, almost embarrassed to do so. "Con su permiso," he said, holding out the paper like a lump of sugar for a skittish horse. Making no attempt to move on, he waited patiently for the disheveled, sour-smelling priest to accept it or not.

Father Pablo, for his part, stared frantically about, his bloodshot eyes stinging from the harsh daylight that flooded the interior of the bus. At first, he was convinced that the guerilla was trying to give him a pornographic picture, so fresh was the Queen of Spades in his mind. But, as his painful glance took in the additional rebels, armed with some type of rifles and stationed outside at either end of the bus as look-outs, the reality of his situation became clear. In an instant, the unendurable shame of his dream was burned away by the simple mortal fear of death. With a gasp, he turned back to the young man who remained patiently awaiting his decision, his broad Mayan face and obsidian eyes unreadable.

Putting out a hand that he could not stop from shaking, Father Pablo managed to say, "Gracías," thus completing his part of the litany that had disturbed his dreams.

The Indio placed the leaflet in his hand without a word; then gently sidled by him to complete his rounds. After a few moments more, as Father Pablo became aware of the humor he inspired by the expressions of his fellow passengers, it occurred to him to sit back down, and he hastily did so.

Meanwhile, the rebels concluded their business, climbing off the bus with a friendly wave to the driver, who wasted no time in closing the doors and pulling back onto the highway with a great roar and a cloud of dust and diesel exhaust. Chattering excitedly, the other occupants of the bus began to show the leaflets to one another as proof of their shared adventure.

Father Pablo looked back in time to see the insurrectos toss the stolen police checkpoint sign onto the flatbed of their pickup truck and grind their way rapidly down a sandy side road cut into the forest. In a few moments all that could be seen of them was the dust of their progress rising above the stunted trees of the coastal interior.

Only then did Father Pablo turn his attention to the crumpled, sweat-stained paper that lay clutched in his fist. Taking a moment to wipe his palms on the legs of his trousers, he smoothed the paper out on his lap and studied it.

It was a crude drawing, all lines and angles, and appeared to be a depiction of Christ Jesus—his triangular head crowned with enormous thorns, his emaciated body draped with a heavy, purple robe. Blood rained down from his scalp in great droplets, staining the shoulder of the cloak, while his face was an abstract of great agony, or uplifting joy; it was impossible to determine which.

The figures surrounding Jesus were intended to be Roman soldiers, but Father Pablo thought they more resembled ancient Mayan warriors, with their elaborate feathered headdresses. One of them, he noticed, clutched a war club edged with obsidian blades, and this confirmed his suspicions. Two wore identical robes to their captive; the third, the club-wielder, only a tunic.

Father Pablo thought that the drawing revealed the exuberant hand of a tattoo artist. Beneath the passionate, if amateurish, rendition were printed the words, "Ask, and ye shall receive," in bold capitals. There was nothing else.

Suddenly lightheaded with relief at having been loosed by their near silent captors, Father Pablo held the paper out to his nearest neighbor, exclaiming, "They stopped us for this? I don't understand it. What does it mean?"

The old man across the aisle shrugged nervously and shook his head. A number of passengers were once again looking at Father Pablo with interest. Others appeared to be studiously ignoring him. Was this what the Archbishop and La Viuda were worried about, he wondered. It seemed ridiculous, if perplexing. The insurrectos were nothing but zealots, perhaps, playing out some kind of childish mystery, though what it could mean certainly was not illuminated by the paper they had been so keen to distribute. The leaflet was probably nothing more than a means to lure people into the countryside where they could be robbed at leisure, he concluded.

Yet he was forced to admit, if that were the case, why hadn't they robbed the passengers on the bus when they had them at their mercy? No, it just didn't make any sense. *Ask, and ye shall receive.* Yes, he knew it to be a quote from the Gospel, but what the devil did the guerillas mean by it?

"Excuse me," he said rather more loudly than he intended, while waving the drawing above his head. "Does anyone understand this?" All heads turned to him. Even the bus driver appeared to be studying the young priest in his rearview mirror.

Father Pablo shook the paper in his hand like a lure, but one by one his fellow passengers turned their faces from him. A girl of about twenty, with an unfortunate scarlet birthmark covering nearly a third of her face, was the last to turn away.

"I am a priest, you know," he declared rather forlornly to the backs of their heads. "I have a right to know what's going on in my own parish."

The old man across the aisle reached over and patted Father Pablo's arm consolingly, nodding in amiable, but mute, agreement. The rest of their short journey was uneventful and accomplished in unaccustomed silence.

Exiting the bus at the Progreso terminal, Father Pablo began the short walk to the rectory with the faltering gait of a man uncertain of what might happen next. It seemed that La Viuda's confrontation with him (Was it only yesterday morning?) had initiated a chain of events in which his role was that of clown and victim.

"She is a most unpleasant woman," he thought hotly, and deliberately did not upbraid himself for such uncharitable thoughts. "I will deal with that at my next opportunity for confession," he promised. Until such a time, he was content to hold his resentment of her close, like a warming ember, as some small recompense for the suffering she had caused him. "Hateful woman," he muttered under his breath.

Realizing that he was still carrying the leaflet the guerilla had given him, he angrily wadded it up and looked about for a trash receptacle. Seeing none, he threw it forcibly into the gutter. His actions went unnoticed on the busy thoroughfare of Calle 80, as the denizens of Progreso made their way to the mercado in one direction or the plaza in the other. His feet dragging, he made his way slowly back to the rectory.

When he finally arrived he was greeted at the door by Señora Garza, who quite unexpectedly seized him by the shoulders, kissing one of his stubbled cheeks. "I was so worried that I prayed for you all morning," she cried.

"You were…you did?" Father Pablo said in astonishment.

"I didn't know what to think," she continued breathlessly. "Being summoned to see the Archbishop…I was frightened for you. I even thought of calling him to say that you are trying very hard, doing your best, but I hadn't the nerve."

"I see," Father Pablo said, touched in spite of her inadvertent indictment of his tenure so far. He patted her plump shoulder awkwardly. "You needn't have worried so; it seems he is content to let me stumble on."

"All will be well, you'll see," she promised, wiping a tear from a lightly furred cheek. "I pray every day to the holy Virgin for you. Oh," she suddenly exclaimed. "I almost forgot—you have a visitor."

"A visitor?" he stammered, unable to conceal his petulance, "Now?" Visions of a cold beer and his narrow bed drifted apart like an old cobweb.

"Who is it?" he asked, as he had to almost push his way past Señora Garza to gain entry. "What does he want?"

"It's a young woman, and she wouldn't say. She's just arrived ahead of you," Señora Garza replied.

"Confession…?" Father Pablo asked plaintively, not listening. He stripped off his dusty, black coat, revealing the large sweat stains beneath his armpits, and flung it onto a settee. "Why can't she come during the posted hours? What can be so important?"

Señora Garza shook her head while regarding the priest's jacket with distaste. "She said she must speak to you privately. She said nothing about confession, so I had her wait in the parlor. She seemed to know that you would be along momentarily. I, of course, had no idea when you would arrive, or if…" She did not complete the thought.

Who would know when I would arrive, Father Pablo wondered? How odd. The thought brought him up short, piquing his curiosity and momentarily dampening his petulance. He pointed at the closed double doors leading into the parlor. "She's in there?" he asked.

Señora Garza nodded once with raised eyebrows.

"May I have some water? I'm as parched as the Sonoran Desert!"

"I'll bring some in for both of you," his housekeeper assured him, turning for the kitchen as she spoke. "I hope cold cuts are all right for dinner? Since I had no idea when you were returning it made planning a hot meal difficult."

"Yes, fine," he conceded gratefully.

The young woman rose to her feet as he entered the dim room, and a shaft of late afternoon sunlight fell across the side of her face with the scarlet caul. In the brilliant illumination the skin beneath the mark had a pebbly look, much like a sheet of coarse grade sandpaper improbably dyed.

Remembering her from the bus instantly, Father Pablo was no less surprised for that, and it took him a moment longer than it should have to close the door. She could not be more than twenty, he guessed, and other than her disfigurement, was a pleasant looking enough girl—no beauty, perhaps, but buxom and dark, with a patient intelligence in her eyes. Her clothes were very stylish and businesslike, with a short, tight-fitting skirt and white, starched blouse. Her birthmark though was, at best, distracting, and she wore long, silver earrings as if in defiance of it.

She must have had a dreadful time at school, he thought sympathetically, having himself suffered at the hands of his fellow students for his chubby inability at athletics, poor social skills, and in later years for his splotchy complexion. The seminary had provided a blessed haven from the casual cruelty of his childhood companions, but he doubted that this young woman had ever been afforded such a respite.

Realizing that he was gaping, he awkwardly recovered himself and signaled for her to be seated. Crossing the room, he took the chair opposite. "I know who you are," he began, then corrected himself. "That is, I remember you from the bus ride."

She arched an eyebrow at him, as if to say, "Of course you do, it was only a few minutes ago, and after all, I carry the mark of Cain on my face for the world to see." Instead, answering pleasantly and without a trace of nervousness, she said, "Yes, I was going to speak to you then, but thought better of it, you seemed so upset…amongst other things."

"What *other* things?" Father Pablo asked. In the shadows of the parlor her disfigurement was not so pronounced.

Her eyes moved this way and that, coming to rest on his face only at moments. "Other people, I guess. I wasn't sure it was wise to speak with you when there was so many other people close by."

Father Pablo shook his head tiredly. The last few days had been so strange and it seemed this day would end no differently. His head throbbed with his hangover; the nap on the bus provided him only temporary relief from its ravages and now it pounded with renewed energy. "Why should that matter? Unless, of course, this is about reconciliation…do you wish to make confession?" Rubbing his temples, he grimaced unconsciously.

"No," she laughed lightly; it had a charming sound to Father Pablo's ears, like the tinkling of wind chimes. "I'm all right, that way," she assured the priest.

"Good," Father Pablo murmured. "That's good…excellent."

"Are you okay, Father?" Reaching across the short distance that separated them, she touched his sleeve. He nearly leapt from his chair.

"I'm quite all right," he assured her. "I've had a very stressful day, that's all. Now, what exactly is your business, young lady?" The pompous phrase reverberated through his aching skull, and placing a sweaty hand across his forehead, he closed his eyes for a moment. Would this day never end?

When, after a few moments, no answer was forthcoming, he opened them again to find the young woman studying him. Looking back at her in confusion, he wondered if he had misjudged her age, as she now seemed older, more mature, than he had at first thought.

Appearing to reach a decision, she said, "You *did* ask…back there on the bus, after the centurions had left, you did ask, didn't you?"

"Centurions," Father Pablo managed to splutter. "What on earth are you talking about…do you mean those guerillas? And what did I ask? I don't understand you."

There was a light tap at the door and it began to open. The girl raised a finger to her lips in warning as Señora Garza entered with a pitcher of lemonade and two glasses on a tray. Sensing the sudden silence, the housekeeper's back stiffened and she glided noiselessly across the room, setting the tray and its burden on a small side table, and returning the way she had come without a word. She closed the door behind her with only slightly more force than was required.

Grabbing at the pitcher, Father Pablo began to pour himself some of the refreshing liquid, sloshing some over the side in his haste. Just as he brought the glass to his lips, he remembered his manners, and thrust it at the disturbing girl. She waved it away with a small smile, and he quickly began to gulp down its contents.

"Now then," he managed to gasp, setting down the empty glass and wiping his mouth with the back of his hand. "Where were we? Ah, yes, my question. *What* did I ask?"

The girl appeared to give this careful consideration, as if it were important she recall his words with precision. "You asked if anyone understood this."

Retrieving the colored flyer from her purse, she carefully unfolded it, placing it on the side table for him to see. She pointed at the lettering and read it aloud, "Ask and ye shall receive." She glanced up at the priest to see if he had understood. "You *did* ask, you see."

Father Pablo was used to being seen as a fool, but not a moron, and he spoke with barely concealed sarcasm, carefully enunciating each word, "What, exactly, shall I receive...and from whom?"

The girl didn't blink, "*What* depends on you alone, though it must be done with good intentions; from *who* must be obvious to a clergyman."

"Well it's not obvious to me. This all sounds like mumbo-jumbo. Are you referring to what's been going on out in the countryside? I have to tell you that I've heard some disturbing rumors about all that. I should be told what's going on!"

"I *am* telling you, Father. That's why I'm here. I didn't want to say anything on the bus because I wasn't sure who knew anything and who didn't. You're not supposed to tell anyone unless they ask, you see. That's the rule—you have to ask to receive."

"Yes, yes," Father Pablo mumbled impatiently. His thirst was somewhat slaked, but his headache raged. "I get it. But what goes on out there? I hear someone's performing miracles and such. Is it some renegade priest, or one of those so-called sorcerers?"

"It's neither, Father. There are no priests or sorcerers. But there is an old woman...a lady," she corrected herself, "Doña Josefa Maria Lafuente-Lasada, whom you might wish to meet.

She is the last of a prosperous and respected family in these parts and lives on an old sisal plantation outside of town."

"A *bruja?*" he asked derisively in an attempt to cover his alarm at the thought of a clandestine meeting with some witch in the jungle.

"No, no…" the young woman laughed. "…far from it. Doña Josefa is a very pious woman. *Unusual*, yes," she laughed again, as at some private recollection, "but devout, nonetheless. You will come to no harm."

"I am not concerned about that," Father Pablo raised his voice, even as he blushed. The young woman's clear-eyed perception had stung him. "It is blasphemy and the faithful being led astray that concern me." He wondered if the Jesuit Inquisitors of medieval times had sounded as self-righteous and unconvincing as he. "How does she do it—with a laying on of hands, or some such thing?"

The young woman smiled patiently at the priest even as she snapped open her purse and deftly retrieved an elastic band. Without a trace of self-consciousness she began to gather her dark hair into one fist while somehow coaxing the heavy tresses through the band. With a snap, she was done and the luxuriant tangle of her hair had been tamed into a girlish ponytail. Father Pablo could see the sheen of perspiration on her newly exposed neck and thought longingly of removing his own chafing collar.

"She does no such thing," she continued. "She has in her possession a relic, a holy relic that has been handed down through her family for many generations. It is this that she brings out for veneration—after Mass, of course, as she has no wish to interfere with the Church."

"What *relic* is this purported to be?" Father Pablo asked, still feeling the shame of being thought a coward.

For the first time in their interview, the girl appeared to grow uneasy, trying to hide it behind a set expression. Even so, Father Pablo noticed her hesitation. "It is the remnant of a garment worn by Our Savior during His trial."

She had allowed her eyes to wander away from him during this astounding announcement, now, turning back to him, she held his attention. "…a piece of the purple robe stained with the holy Blood of Christ Jesus Himself."

Suddenly, the crude rendering revealed its meaning to Father Pablo—it was meant to depict the robe the centurions forced Christ to wear, along with the crown of thorns, when they mocked him as "King of the Jews."

"You can't be serious," he chuckled nervously. "I mean, how on earth would an old woman living in the Yucatán come to possess such a thing, for God's sake? It's all too incredible. You appear to be an educated woman; surely the likelihood of such a thing must strike you as fantastic, as well. Reason must be applied, yes?"

The young woman stood, clutching her purse, and looked down on Father Pablo. Her expression was pensive, almost unhappy. "*Reason*, Father? We are Catholics, surely the last people to shield ourselves with reason in the face of the miraculous. Do you not, at every Mass, witness the transformation of a simple wafer, and a cup of cheap wine, into the very Body and Blood of Christ?"

For the second time in their meeting, Father Pablo felt himself revealed by the unflinching perception of this strange young woman. Her words flew about him like wasps, stinging him again and again—how obvious a charlatan he must appear to her.

"How would I find this place..." he asked contritely, remembering the archbishop's command "...if I were to want to?"

Halting at the door, the young woman smiled at him encouragingly, "After Mass on Sunday, walk towards Yucalpetén Harbor and a car will pick you up. Please don't tell anyone," she added.

Thinking of the camouflaged and armed Indios, he asked, "Why not...why all the secrecy?"

"The police appear to have taken an interest, and Doña Josefa believes that only those seeking in faith should be allowed to come. Don't be afraid," she added, "I will be in the car."

Father Pablo did not even bother to deny the obvious and just nodded. Almost too late, he thought to ask her name.

"Veronica," she answered.

"Of course," he replied, chuckling once more. "What else?"

As the door shut behind her, he realized that his swollen head had stopped aching at last.

When Señora Garza shook him awake from his slumber in the chair and he stumbled from the parlor to his late supper, he wondered if he had dreamed the entire encounter.

"You've had too long a day," his housekeeper observed.

"Yes," he replied, his eyes unfocused and his voice still hoarse with sleep, "though I didn't understand any of it."

CHAPTER SIX

Father Pablo stood staring down at the dark waters that lapped the bulkhead, watching the tar oils from the sodden timbers leach out as rainbow-colored membranes. Occasionally, fish heads, and other less recognizable viscera, would bob along through the greasy sheen, nibbled at by schools of minnows darting ceaselessly to and from the depths. Shuddering, he turned away, only to find the fishermen arrested in the act of unloading their ungainly, filthy vessels, staring uneasily at the priest that had appeared in their midst. Several of them nodded politely, while the rest returned to their work with unnecessary vigor, as if it were paramount to ignore this inexplicable curate who now wandered amongst them.

Returning their nods uncomfortably, Father Pablo turned his back to them and walked across a large expanse of concrete to stand in the shadow of one of the packing plants. From within reverberated the cries and clatter of men unloading the wooden crates containing the day's catch—it appeared such work was not halted for the Lord's Day.

The unhappy priest glanced about in hope of the promised car's appearance and was again disappointed. He distinctly recalled being told that he would be picked up on the *way* to Yucalpetén Harbor. And here he was, tired and footsore, having been allowed to reach the harbor itself, and *still* no car!

The toot of the car horn made him jump and cry out, its approach having been masked by the din from the warehouse. The small, battered Ford idled several feet behind him. Sitting in the front seat, Veronica smiled at him through the dusty windshield. A good-looking young man about Father Pablo's own age was behind the wheel, scrutinizing the priest with an unwelcoming expression. Behind him, almost concealed in the shadows of the back seat, was another young man, his silhouette alert and attentive, like a dog on point.

Sticking her head out the window, Veronica said laughingly, "We thought you heard us pull up—climb in." The rear door was thrown open and Father Pablo caught a glimpse of a dark Mayan profile as the second young man leaned across the back seat.

Behind him, he heard the laughter of several fishermen who had witnessed his jumpiness. Squeezing himself into the tight confines of the passenger compartment, he cast them, what he hoped, was a severe look.

The car rattled into movement before he had the chance to properly shut the door, and the driver executed a fast U-turn. Within moments the packing plant was lost to view.

"I've had a very long walk and I've been waiting for some time…" Father Pablo began. Veronica turned in her seat, offering him a bottle of water.

"This is my brother, Hernando," she said, cutting short the priest's complaints while patting the driver affectionately on the shoulder. "He's a little worried about bringing you along; he thinks you might cause trouble. But don't mind him, he thinks everyone is about to start trouble. I'm afraid he's learned this from being my big brother." Touching the great mark on her face, she smiled shyly at Father Pablo.

It had been a simple gesture, but Father Pablo understood instantly—it could not have been easy growing up as the protector of such a girl. Even so, today the mark did not seem as bad as before. One gets accustomed to these things, he thought. Behind her, he could see the stern, wary eyes of the driver watching him in the rearview mirror. "Pleased to meet you, Hernando," Father Pablo murmured nervously.

"And you," the brother replied evenly.

"That is Manuel next to you," Veronica continued. "We call him Manny, of course." Father Pablo turned slightly in his seat to confront his companion and found him smiling merrily back and holding out a hand. "He's very sweet, you see. He scares everyone with that warrior face of his, but it's all an act."

As Father Pablo took his hand, Manuel's sparkling black eyes swiveled for the briefest of moments to Veronica's face and then back again. Even to someone as inexperienced as himself, Father Pablo recognized the devotion in that glance. "My pleasure," Manny said happily, though the priest could see that it was not *his* company that pleased him so.

The introductions had distracted Father Pablo. As he took a swig of water, he peered out the window in hopes of gaining his bearings once more. But the sandy road along which they beetled through the jungle offered no clue as to where it might lead. We might be anywhere, he thought forlornly.

The roadblock took them all by surprise. Father Pablo understood this instantly by the terse whispers that flew back and forth between Veronica and her brother in the front seat. The police truck lay parallel to their approach and blocked the intersection, and as Father Pablo watched, two uniformed figures stepped out from the shade of some roadside trees. They appeared to be carrying machine guns and the taller of the two was lazily swatting the humid air in a gesture meant to slow them to a halt. Their car trundled on without slacking its speed.

"They're waving us down," Father Pablo announced needlessly. Glancing over to Manny, whose face was composed and alert but otherwise impassive, he noticed that a tail of dark fabric, like a dog's tongue, hung loosely from the cargo pocket of his khaki trousers. He's one of them…a Sentry…or Centurion, or whatever they're called, Father Pablo thought in a panic. The car sped on. "Aren't you stopping?" he cried. The policemen gripped the weapons that dangled on their slings and brought them around to their chests, their chins rising.

Veronica hissed something at her brother that Father Pablo could not quite make out. He caught only the word "foolish."

When they were a scant hundred feet out, Hernando braked with unnecessary violence, causing a large cloud of dust to drift forward over the approaching policemen. The two men strode to either side of the vehicle with the expressions of sleepy children awakened from a hot, cranky nap. While not directly pointing their weapons at the car's occupants, they nonetheless carried them high, where they could be easily swiveled to do so.

Father Pablo kicked Manny's foot and nodded slightly at the purple cloth that dangled from his pocket. Without acknowledgement, the young man gently worked the material back in, his placid face betraying nothing.

The taller of the officers leaned down to Hernando's window. "Are you blind?" he asked pleasantly.

Working his way to Father Pablo's window, the other officer contemplated him for several moments before shifting his gaze to the Indio. He did not look pleased with the occupants. Manny continued to stare ahead, as if contemplating distant and mysterious horizons.

"I thought you might be bandits," Hernando replied. "What with all this dust, and at a distance, it was hard to be sure. All I could see were two men with guns blocking the road in the middle of nowhere. What would you have thought?"

"I would have thought, 'There's a big vehicle marked *Police* in the middle of the intersection, perhaps I should stop.' But, that's just me, of course.

"Perhaps you could now provide me with your license and identification papers…all of you?" It was only in the form of a request. His eyes swept the remaining passengers and lingered for just a moment on Father Pablo. "You're a long way from any church, Father," he observed.

The officer lifted his head and nodded meaningfully at his partner on the other side of the car. Father Pablo's door was suddenly opened and his arm firmly seized.

"What is the meaning of this?" he squeaked, even as he was drawn out onto the roadway. "I am a priest!"

"He is a priest!" Veronica echoed.

"I can see that," the tall officer assured them both, even as he rounded the vehicle to stand face to face with Father Pablo. "The rest of you remain inside the car!" Whispering something to the first, the other officer then set to collecting the identification papers from the remaining passengers.

"What is the meaning of this?" Father Pablo repeated weakly. Standing beneath the hot sun he began to perspire freely, beads of sweat rolling from his forehead into his eyes.

Raking a hand across his face, he began, "I am the pastor of…"

"There's no need to get into a panic." The policeman cut him off. "I know who you are. My partner there recognized you from church. He is a religious man, you see; me…not so much. He has told me a number of stories about you, in fact. Apparently you have made quite an impression in Progreso." The policeman's smile radiated from beneath the shadow cast by his rakishly angled hat, but he stopped short of chuckling.

"I don't see what this has to do with being stopped in the middle of..."

"Well, that's just it, don't you see?" The officer cut him off once more. "There's been some trouble out this way. Perhaps you've heard? Rebels, or bandits, we're not quite sure. So here we are, in the middle of nowhere, as you rightly observed, and along comes a car that doesn't appear to want to stop for us—the police. Naturally, we become curious, and lo and behold, we find a priest, an Indio, a sadly ugly girl, and a not very friendly driver."

Father Pablo winced at the officer's description of Veronica and felt a tide of resentment roll back a little of his fear. "So?" he managed to say, but even to his own ears his voice sounded more querulous than challenging.

"So," the officer resumed smoothly. "I am wondering when I see these people whether this priest is out for a ride in the country with friends of a Sunday afternoon, or has he been *taken* for a ride by...let us say, less than desirable company? You see, Father, we were just thinking of your own well-being." The policeman waited for a reply.

Father Pablo stared up at the officer for several moments, as large flies, attracted by his profuse perspiration, bumped repeatedly into his bare head. At last he thought to answer, "Why no...*no*, I am not kidnapped—of course not!"

Smiling even more broadly at this, the policeman patted the young priest on the shoulder. "Good, good," he murmured benignly. "That's what I was hoping to hear. So all is well then?"

"Yes, yes," Father Pablo assured him happily, his spirits rising at the thought of their imminent release.

"Excellent." The officer paused and brought a hand up to massage his chin as his expression became thoughtful, almost wistful. "So then, *that* leaves a drive in the country." He glanced at Father Pablo hopefully. "To where, I wonder? Could you say?"

Father Pablo felt his hopes dashed at once. It seemed this wily officer was determined to be satisfied. "My friends," Father Pablo began hesitantly, "are taking me to see Doña Josefa Lafuente Lasada. Perhaps you have heard of her in these parts?" The officer continued to smile encouragingly at the little priest, but remained unhelpfully silent.

Reluctantly, Father Pablo continued, hating to involve himself in lies, yet unable to avoid the conspiratorial role that events had seemingly placed him in. "Her family was of some importance hereabouts, so I am told. She owns a large hacienda where they used to grow henequen…for sisal fibers. You are probably more familiar with such things than I am."

He glanced over at the car where the second officer was questioning the others. What was he asking, and more importantly, would their answers tally with his own? His officer (he now thought of the taller one as *his* officer) remained frustratingly silent, his infuriating smile encouraging him to lie, to play out more rope with which to hang them all. Nodding at his companions, Father Pablo said, "They could tell you as well as me...better really, since they are native Yucatecans. I am new to this area, as you probably already know."

His officer made no reply to this and Father Pablo felt compelled to bumble on, "So, as she is quite old, and not able to get around much, it seemed only right that I should visit and pay my respects, as it were." His officer nodded in happy agreement with this sentiment.

The ebb and flow of questioning emanating from the car had ceased, and Father Pablo twisted around to find that the occupants and the other policeman were now silently watching him. *If only he knew what they had said!* Veronica's face revealed nothing, but Father Pablo thought he could see a line of worry between her eyes that he had not noticed before, her crimson caul appearing to have taken on a darker hue.

He was a priest...he thought suddenly, as if this were a revelation! Obviously, his ministerial duties could take him anywhere, gave him carte blanche!

"Doña Josefa may require spiritual nourishment," he said pompously. "I plan to offer her the opportunity for confession and Communion. These, my friends," he waved airily at Veronica, Hernando, and Manuel, "were good enough to drive me out, as they know the way and have the use of a car."

"Communion," his officer spoke, at last. "Don't you need a few things for that? When I see the priests on their rounds to the sick and housebound, they usually carry a little black bag, like a doctor, with the tools of the trade: a crucifix, wafers, oils, and the like. I didn't notice such a bag in the car."

Father Pablo was dumbfounded. His attempt at confidence evaporated instantly and he felt like an unprepared schoolboy called upon by his teacher. How could he have been so stupid? He had walked into a trap of his own devising.

"A bag?" he repeated, hastening to shovel words into the yawning gap of his credibility. "Well, I couldn't be certain that Doña Josefa would actually desire...you see..."

The policeman's head tilted to one side like a bird eyeing something edible in the grass.

"...the Eucharist must be entered into willingly, something you may not know, not being a religious man as you have said, and as I have yet to meet Doña Josefa, I thought it best to...to just leave everything in the trunk of the car until I understood her wishes on the matter." *There*, he thought, *I've done it. I've answered his question*!

His policeman nodded in agreement once more, as if Father Pablo's explanation was perfectly understandable, the only reasonable course of action for a wise man. "You are a good listener, Father. You heard me quite correctly. I am not a religious man; my father couldn't tolerate religion."

Leaning down to Father Pablo, he whispered conspiratorially, "He was an old socialist—thought the church was the enemy of the people, priests were parasites, all that sort of thing."

The policeman's voice returned to normal. "Me, I'm not like that. I didn't take after the old man. He had his mind made up and didn't need to listen to anyone. But me, I've a curious nature—my mind is open. So, how about a look in that bag to satisfy an old atheist? Who knows, I might experience a conversion—the Holy Spirit might be crouching inside just waiting to leap out on me!" He spread his arms expansively to embrace a world full of wonders, but his face had lost its humor.

"Really, officer," Father Pablo managed to summon up some indignation at last, "this is quite intolerable! I will not stand here and allow you to belittle the Faith of the Church. I *am* a priest, by God!"

He felt some small, unfamiliar kernel of himself swimming up to the warmth of his own anger and was unable to hold it under. The sustained suspense of his predicament had granted him, if not courage, at least the desire to snap at those that bayed at his heels.

"I will not expose the Sacraments to ridicule, even to satisfy your insincere curiosity—of that you can be assured! My *good* friend, Captain Barrera, will be informed by me of this encounter at the earliest opportunity."

Father Pablo was gratified to see just a flicker of uncertainty in the policeman's eyes.

"Gracious, Father, calm yourself," his officer murmured consolingly, even as his expression dissolved into a frozen, dangerous-looking mask. "You will do yourself an injury. If you don't wish me to see the contents of your little bag, so be it. Naturally, I would not force the issue. I was just curious, after all." He took a small step backward towards his truck.

"However, let me save you the trouble of contacting Captain Barrera, as I have a cell phone in my vehicle and he wishes to be instantly informed of anything unusual at the checkpoints." The policeman bowed in mock salute, saying, "With your permission," then turned and walked stiff-legged to his vehicle. Within moments he was in animated, but hushed, conversation on his cellular.

The shorter officer remained with Father Pablo and the car, even as the silence settled over their little group and the flies grew in number and persistence. Father Pablo swatted at them ineffectually, spinning this way and that with his clumsy blows until he stumbled and brought himself up short.

Grinning at him over the roof of the car, the shorter policeman said quietly, "DEET, Father, it's the only thing that works. Until you sweat it off, of course, then they come right back—they are always waiting." He was distracted suddenly by a motion at the police truck. Then turning back to Father Pablo, he said, "Go ahead," and nodded at the open door of the car. The taller policeman had obviously given him a signal that Father Pablo had missed, and he hurried to rejoin the others.

Hernando put the car in gear immediately, but before they could pull away, the taller officer appeared at Father Pablo's window. Bringing his face close to the priest's, he said, "Captain Barrera sends his greetings and says, 'Go with God, Little Father.'"

"Thank the captain for me, officer, and," he added dismissively, "if there's nothing else we would like to be on our way."

"Just this," the taller policeman added pleasantly, "he would like for you to drop by and see him at your earliest possible convenience—he wants to hear all about Doña Josefa and her hacienda. Good day, priest." Father Pablo's officer stood back and swept off his hat in a dramatic gesture to indicate that they were free to continue.

As they resumed their progress down the lumpy, pothole-filled road, Father Pablo squeezed his sweating palms together to stop their tremors. Looking back, he found that the intersection was already lost to the twists and turns of the winding road. The jungle leaned in on either side and scraped the sides of the car with questing tendrils and slashing limbs. When he turned forward again, he found Veronica facing him over the seatback, smiling.

"I wouldn't have thought it of you, Father. You were quite magnificent."

"I was afraid," Father Pablo admitted. "I didn't know what you all were telling him so I wasn't sure what to say. I was just rambling."

Reaching over, she patted his arm.

"After all, we're not doing anything wrong, are we?" he asked the others at large. "There's nothing criminal in all this, is there?"

Hernando spoke for the rest without answering, "It was an unlucky encounter, that's all, but you may want to think about that little tête-à-tête with Captain Barrera, Father...that's not good."

Father Pablo's hands, which had almost ceased their trembling, began anew at Hernando's dire pronouncement. What have they gotten me into, he wondered, and where will it end?

* * *

Captain Barrera snapped his phone shut and set it gently down on the bedside stand of the borrowed beachside condo, while the American woman lying next to him stirred, pulling the sheet up. A wealthy businessman in Mérida had given him the key some years before and insisted he have the run of the place during the off-season—Barrera had allowed some evidence to go missing in a narcotics case concerning the man's eldest son.

"Problems at work…?" Brenda inquired sleepily, in her near perfect Spanish.

Barrera hoisted himself into a sitting position and lit a cigarette before answering. "No…just one of the checkpoints calling in," he replied, exhaling a great cloud of acrid smoke. He watched as it drifted up through the bars of light that fell through the shuttered balcony door. "It seems my name is being bandied about out there, and they just wanted to be sure that I actually knew the fellow."

There was a long pause, and Barrera wondered if his lover had fallen asleep, as her eyes were closed once more.

"Did you?" she asked at last.

"Yes," he murmured. The bank of smoke was being drawn up to the blades of the ceiling fan, the suction pulling tentacles of it ahead of the main body and chopping them to pieces. It made Barrera think of a squid trying to climb into a fisherman's boat and being hacked to bits for its trouble.

"That must happen quite a bit to someone in your position," Brenda observed aloud.

"Yes," Barrera agreed, thinking of the funny little priest, "but only when they are doing something wrong, I think."

Brenda coughed from the smoke; then leaned over to Barrera suddenly with an outstretched arm, two fingers extended. Taking a long drag, he smiled down at her before placing the cigarette between them.

Falling back, she took a long pull from it herself, blowing out the smoke in a satisfied sigh. "You are a bad influence," she announced, handing the cigarette back to him.

"Yes," he agreed, "I am an indulgence for you."

"I meant the cigarette," she replied pettishly.

"I know what you meant," he said, "and you meant both the cigarette and me."

"You flatter yourself," she said, rising and hurrying to the bathroom with her clothes wadded in her fist.

Barrera admired her as she stalked self-consciously across the room. "You have the body of a teenage girl," he observed. It had always impressed Barrera how older American women worked so hard on their figures—dieting, jogging, and doing aerobics. Mexican women, like his wife, seemed to grow handsome, or fat, with age, while these *gringas* strove continually to remain girls in appearance, pretty and athletic-looking. He admired their tenacity—they refused to bow to the natural order of things.

"How would you know?" Brenda called archly through the closed door of the bathroom. "Do you keep a teenage lover as well?"

"I have daughters," he reminded her, stubbing out his smoke. "I live in a house full of women...I see more than I want to, believe me."

"I bet you do," Brenda answered after a long pause, her voice oddly constrained.

Barrera listened to the sound of the tap being run and smiled. That was another thing about this American woman— she gave herself with such abandon between the sheets, but as soon as it was over, she became as chaste and self-conscious as a nun.

He heard the toilet flush and soon after the sound of the running water ceased. After a few moments more, the door opened and she emerged fully dressed in her shorts, sandals, and tank-top blouse. Mexican silver and turquoise glittered around her neck, and her teeth shone like polished pearls against her browned face, even in the darkened room. Barrera thought she could pass for twenty-five in the gloom of the shuttered apartment, with her lithe, slender body. She stood framed in the doorway watching him for a moment before crossing to the bed.

"What about them?" she asked with apparent indifference, as she fastened on her dangling earrings from the bed stand.

"Who do you mean?" he replied, even as he felt the familiar stirrings. It had always been such simple, feminine actions that most aroused him: a woman absent-mindedly putting on her jewelry or makeup, or bending over an oven to inspect the progress of a loaf of bread. Or perhaps his own wife sitting at her dresser mirror in her nightgown, brushing her thick, black tresses with stroke after lazy stroke until it shone like a raven's wing. Those moments, it seemed, when women least had men on their minds but were turned inward to some secret place in the female psyche impenetrable to men, even through the flesh. At such moments, Barrera found women irresistible and entrancing.

"I mean your grand plans to invade the U.S. Do you intend for your family to join you?" Brenda asked.

"Of course, if they wish. If not, they can remain here and I will visit as often as I can. I don't intend to abandon my family any more than you intend to leave your poor husband." He made a grab for her, but she was too nimble and leapt back.

"Oh no," she said, "no more of that…for now, I have to get back soon or Jim will miss me. He's due back from the ruins at Dzibilchaltún within the hour." She picked up her purse; then threw her pillow at him, laughing.

"When will you introduce me to your influential husband?" he asked, just as she reached the door.

Brenda spun about as if to deliver a parting quip, then paused to give his question full consideration. "You didn't make a very good impression on him at the café," she said. "That was foolish and he'll remember you. I can't imagine what you were thinking."

Barrera shrugged, "I got jealous when I saw you with him. I wasn't prepared."

"He won't forget that," she assured him. "You'll have to apologize when you meet him."

Barrera shrugged once more. "Perhaps," he said.

"Even then, it's not likely he'll want to help you back in the States. He's not what I'd call a charitable man. He'll consider his influence a commodity, not a gift, and he'll want something in return. And honestly, though you're a very intelligent, capable, and ridiculously charming man when you want to be, I can't imagine what you'd have to offer him."

Opening the door slightly to the landing, Brenda slid through, so as not to reveal the naked policeman to other tenants who might be passing. She paused to blow him a kiss before shutting it once more.

Barrera listened to her footsteps clattering down the concrete steps to the street and fading away. He slid back down in the bed, lighting another cigarette as he did so, and considered her question—what *did* he have to offer that might open the doors of opportunity for him in the U.S.? He had no intention of leaving his native country to mow lawns or work in some steaming kitchen; these were tasks for men of lesser abilities and education, not for him. He was a leader, an organizer, the kind of man made for great responsibilities—but how could he ensure that his abilities would be recognized and promoted by his lover's husband? It was a conundrum, he thought sleepily, but one he must solve while the opportunity lay within his grasp.

Tossing the cigarette into the ashtray without stubbing it out, he watched the blades of the fan lazily rotate in the growing afternoon heat. Outside, some gulls screeched and chattered over some tidbit of food or garbage, while the surf lapped tiredly at the sand. Thoughts of the sweaty young priest out there in the jungle drifted through his mind like sea mist. What was he up to? Was he really such a fool as he appeared?

A few moments later, Captain Barrera was asleep.

CHAPTER SEVEN

Father Pablo's anxieties were only heightened by his arrival at Doña Josefa's hacienda. Two armed guards, Centurions as Veronica had called them, stood to either side of the vine-covered limestone gateway, one carrying an old shotgun slung from a rope, the other simply armed with a machete at his waist. Like Manny, they appeared to be Indios, and each wore the purple sash of their mysterious allegiance. The wrought-iron gate itself had long ago collapsed to the earth, a victim of neglect and the relentless assault of the climbing vines that sprang up from the jungle floor. Dozens of cars, some that looked as if they had wheezed and crawled to their final destination and would never stir again, and others that appeared to have been driven off the show room floor, were parked at haphazard angles all along the wall.

The Centurions smiled as their small car approached, waving them through and calling out something as they passed, though Father Pablo was unable to make out what was said due to their heavy Yucatecan accents. Manny and Veronica responded merrily in an equally unintelligible dialect, while Hernando simply nodded in his sardonic manner.

As they rattled through and onto the grounds, the years of disuse became even more evident to Father Pablo than the entrance had suggested. What had once been open, park-like grounds dotted with stands of shade and fruit trees now struggled for existence amidst a riot of exultant jungle flora. Hundreds of saplings and young trees, their seeds having been borne over the ramparts like enemy paratroopers by the humid winds, erupted from the rank grasses to challenge their domesticated counterparts. Their sheer numbers ensured the ultimate outcome of the uneven contest.

Here and there, Father Pablo could make out dots or clusters of color within the branches of the once-stately fruit trees— shriveled limes; tiny, brownish oranges; stunted bananas; and soft, mealy mangoes that fell uselessly to the ground to lie rotting amidst a cloud of flies and wasps.

Father Pablo looked on in amazement as they trundled along the rutted, overgrown drive. He could make out dozens of families picnicking beneath the second-growth trees, and the faint, scratchy sounds of music from distant radio stations bloomed suddenly and were as quickly lost with their passing.

It was incredible, he thought, the number of people could not be accounted for by the cars parked outside the walls; they must have been bused in, or made the journey on foot. This scene was not at all what he had expected—it appeared so harmless and…festive. There was nothing more portentous, or threatening, about it than the family picnics that occurred every Sunday in the parks of Mérida, or México City. His anxiety had just begun to wane as they rounded the final curve and the hacienda rose into view.

The mansion still stood, though its builder of some two hundred years before would have been confounded by its current state. The two-story structure appeared to grow out of the earth like a limestone outcropping in the midst of a jungle. The once-friendly shade trees had been allowed to creep up to the walls, their roots mining the foundation, even as their unpruned branches obscured windows and scratched long furrows into the walls themselves. In some instances the limbs reached into the dim interior of the house itself through windowless casements.

The entire structure, its original color long since bleached away by the sun, bore a greenish tint inherited from the surrounding jungle in the form of a pervasive fungus. As they drew nearer, Father Pablo could see that the roof line and the sagging porch over the veranda were home to hundreds of pigeons that strutted, cooed, and fluttered about as they wished, their droppings whitening great swaths of the mossy, ceramic roof tiles.

As Hernando drew the rattling car up to the front of the decaying manse, Father Pablo could see that the steps leading up to the veranda had collapsed on one side, and disturbingly, that the veranda itself had suffered a similar fate. It was as if a fault line had revealed itself in their destruction and might even extend beneath the south side of the house itself. The majority of the steps and veranda remained however, and as Father Pablo and his fellow travelers exited the vehicle, he perceived a triptych of figures watching their approach from the shadowed recesses.

His nervousness returned instantly, and as they carefully climbed the crumbling steps, he began sweating heavily and could feel the stubborn adolescent bumps on his face grow red with the salty, irritating wash.

It was the old woman who riveted his attention, though he was dimly aware that she was flanked by two more of the Centurions. They, like the others, were uniformed in both cast-off fatigues and street clothes, each wearing an old revolver, machete, and the ubiquitous sash wrapped round their waists. Bandanas hung loosely about their necks. They, too, appeared to be Indios, or at the very least, to bear a dominant strain of Mayan blood.

Doña Josefa sat between her guardians like an ancient queen, shrunken and shriveled by her long years—a mummy doll bedecked with silver and jeweled rings, necklaces, and bracelets; dwarfed by the ornately carved high-back chair she occupied. Father Pablo noted that her feet, encased in heavy-looking, clumsy shoes, did not even reach to the floor. Her surprisingly abundant, grey hair was arranged into a tall, complicated coiffure held together with several tortoise-shell combs, and perched atop her large head as if it might topple over with any movement.

Behind her, mounted to the wall, was an exquisitely hand-carved and life-sized crucifix. The flesh-colored paint had flaked off the desiccated and suffering Christ in great patches, exposing the smooth, almost black wood that lay beneath. Surely, he thought, this holy object once resided within a church. At the old woman's feet rested a carved box that appeared to have been crafted from the same wood as the cross.

She called out to them in an unexpectedly strong voice, "Who is there and what do you want?" Father Pablo noticed with a start that she was staring straight at him when she spoke.

Before he could bring himself to address this startling apparition, Hernando answered her cheerfully, "You know who we are, Mother. We have brought the priest Veronica spoke to you about—Father Pablo." He held a hand out indicating the young cleric. "As to why we're here," Hernando continued in the same surprisingly jovial vein, "it is to be in the presence of our Lord and Savior, the same as everyone else and, if we must, to spend a little time with you as well."

The old crone turned her large face to the young man who had spoken, and said, "Oh, it's you...the cocky one. I was hoping you'd stay away from here."

Father Pablo noted a glint of pleasure in the old girl's eye at the sight of Hernando, though she did not betray it with a smile.

"Don't waste your time with me," she added sadly, followed by a rather dramatic sigh and a tired wave of her blue-veined hand.

"No more than is absolutely necessary for courtesy's sake," Hernando assured her.

"Your mother did not cane you often enough," she pronounced. Turning her attention to Father Pablo, her black eyes glittered from within the complex network of wrinkles, furrows, and creases that had replaced the individual characteristics that had once resided there. Only her nose, long and straight, bespoke of her Castilian heritage.

Pursing her lips suddenly, she turned back to Hernando. "He looks like a thief," she stage-whispered. A withered hand, like a chicken's foot, rose protectively to the necklaces around her neck. "A sneak-thief," she added cruelly.

Father Pablo felt his face grow hot with embarrassment and humiliation. "No, Doña Josefa," he managed to croak, "I am your priest. I've come from Progreso."

She looked unconvinced, and Hernando and Veronica laughed. Manny had remained characteristically silent throughout the meeting. "No one is going to take your jewels," Hernando assured her. "I wouldn't let anyone steal them as I expect to inherit them someday soon."

"Hah," Doña Josefa cried out. "Don't you just wish you could lay hands on them, you young scoundrel!"

"You are related?" Father Pablo asked Doña Josefa timidly.

"Don't be a fool!" she fired back. "Anyone can see that he is not good-looking enough to be a member of my family."

Veronica laughed again at this and threw an arm over Hernando's shoulders. "Most girls don't seem to mind his looks," she said to Doña Josefa.

"Then young girls are just as foolish as I remember," the old woman quipped. "Clearly, he is vexatious. Now," she returned her attention to Father Pablo, "what does this priest, if that is what he is, want?"

Father Pablo began to rub his hands together nervously. "I have been told...that is, Veronica has told me of a relic in your possession." The old woman glared at him in silence, saying nothing. "She says...Veronica that is, that it purports to be a piece of cloth from a cloak once worn by our Savior."

Everyone watched in silence, as if his words, or how he arranged them, were of some secret import. He continued awkwardly, "The cloak that He was forced to wear by his persecutors during His trial."

Coughing to cover his discomfort, he hoped that someone else would speak for him. As no one did, he resumed, "Word of this, and the purported miracles arising from it, naturally, has spread...even to the archbishop's office, you see, and, well, he thought I should take a look."

"The archbishop," Veronica gasped. "You said nothing of the archbishop in your office! You let me believe that it was *you* that wished to see the garment. I would never have brought you otherwise. The faith and seeking of *true* pilgrims is what's required here, not..." she spluttered to a stop, searching for the right words "...not secret agents!" The crimson mark on her face had darkened perceptibly with her outrage.

Father Pablo staggered back, looking from face to face, but all were closed against him. "Veronica," he began, "you misunderstand me."

It had simply not occurred to him during their first meeting to reveal the archbishop's assignment. It had not been a willful decision, but one of lassitude, as the whole affair, at that moment, had all seemed too absurd. Besides, he had been terribly hungover and upset, he simply had not been thinking straight. Even so, he could not deny that he had misled her. She had approached him in trust and faith, and he had responded with furtiveness and disdain.

"It was not my intention to deceive you," he offered feebly, though even to his own ears it rang weak and false.

"The archbishop," Doña Josefa crowed. "I haven't seen so much as a country priest around here in decades, and now I have the attention of the archbishop. When shall I expect him for dinner?" she asked Father Pablo; then continued without waiting for an answer.

"In my father's day, before our chapel collapsed, we used to have a priest out here every Sunday afternoon to hold Mass for our family and workers; afterwards, my mother would have the cook prepare a superb dinner. When it was hot, we'd eat right out here," she swept her arm over the crumbling veranda, "candles, silver, and linen," she giggled, "just as if we were in the formal dining room—it was quite jolly!

"He liked our brandy, the priest," she said, then added spitefully. "I bet you would too. You have the look of a drinker."

The old woman folded her bony hands together and her face lost its animation. "Then no one wanted sisal fiber any more—synthetics you know, and we grew as poor as everyone else, then the chapel fell down. After that, no more priests came, except to bury us. There's no one left to bury now, but me. Have you come to bury me, little priest? I don't see a shovel."

Father Pablo, dumbfounded by the old woman's extraordinary speech, took a moment to react. "No, Mother, of course not."

"Don't call me Mother," she commanded him. "I was never married and have borne no children. I only *allow* him to call me that," she nodded brusquely at Hernando, "because he is wicked and cannot be redeemed. I, myself, am a virgin."

Once again, she had struck Father Pablo speechless.

"Take her into the house," she now demanded of Hernando. "Your sister is saddened by this priest and needs a drink. You'll find some sisal tequila in a jug in the kitchen. It's pretty good stuff," she promised them with a wink. "My neighbor runs a still somewhere on my property, and brings me a jug or two, now and then, as rent. At least the surviving henequen plants are good for something."

As Hernando and Veronica, followed by Manny, vanished into the darkened interior of the house, Doña Josefa called out,

"Everything of value is locked up and hidden where you'll never find it, Hernando, so don't bother looking."

"It's no bother," he called back.

"If I had met him sixty years ago, I would *not* be a virgin, I can promise you that," she stated flatly.

Again, he could think of nothing to say to this bizarre old woman. She might be a little mad, he thought, or perhaps, suffering from some form of dementia peculiar to the very old.

"So," she continued, "you wish to know something of the holy relic. Well, sit, sit, I'm not going to keep looking up to talk to you." She indicated the box at her feet. As it was quite low, and the lid somewhat beveled, Father Pablo did not think it would be a comfortable seat, but did as he was bidden.

"Now then," she resumed, "you are supposed to find out if our relic is a fake and report back to the archbishop, is that correct?"

"In essence," he agreed. "He simply wants to know its…its…" he searched for the right word, "…its provenance."

"Provenance," she repeated, "I like that word. What will that tell him?"

Father Pablo thought for a moment. "Well, if we know its origin, then we'll have a better idea as to its authenticity as a true relic. It's not every day someone claims to be in possession of something Jesus Christ Himself wore against His body. And it does seem a little far-fetched, on the face of it, for an old…" he caught himself, but was favored with a smirk from Doña Josefa nonetheless "...for someone living in the middle of the Yucatán jungle to have a two-thousand-year old fragment of cloth from the Holy Land."

"Yes," she agreed, "I can see how that might look." She turned to the Centurions. "Go and find something to eat, boys. Some of those folks will be happy to share with you." She pointed to the dozens of families that had spread their blankets within sight of the veranda.

They hesitated, looking at the priest. "Don't worry about him," she assured them. "He's not going to run off with it. He wouldn't make it fifty feet if he tried," she laughed, indicating the growing crowds. "These lambs would become lions, and he's no Daniel, I think." The guards sauntered off into the grounds.

"Who are they?" Father Pablo nodded at the departing Indios. "Why do they guard the relic?"

"Local farmers, mostly," she replied. "They've lived here even longer than me. Their ancestors built the temples around these parts, you know, and they don't want the government in México City, or the Church, for that matter, to come in and snatch the cloak from them, like they did all their other archeological treasures. Don't be fooled, they're very shrewd, and they know when something's worth fighting for," she assured him.

"I see," the priest murmured.

"Now then," she resumed, "my family has lived in these parts for five hundred years. We were amongst the very first white settlers in the Yucatán to follow after the Conquistadors. In fact, my Great, Great, Etcetera *was* a conquistador. It was he that dragged our family here from Spain, kicking and screaming no doubt, to settle and make our fortunes in the New World.

"He also brought something else from the old country. In fact, you're sitting on it." Father Pablo made to rise, his expression one of horror. "You mean to say I've been sitting…it's in there…my God, woman!"

"Relax, Father, the wood is petrified; you couldn't break it with a hammer."

"That's not the point," he exclaimed. "You've had me sitting on what may be a relic of Christ Jesus, Our Lord!"

"Don't be such a stiff-neck. He is the God that walked amongst us as a man, so I doubt He would want one of His priests standing in this heat when there's a place to rest your bones. It's just a box, after all."

"I'll remain standing," Father Pablo assured her.

"So you believe already," Doña Josefa laughed.

"I didn't say that," Father Pablo answered. "It's just that, well…I don't know, is all."

"Fine, suit yourself. Now, as I was trying to say, the Great, Great, Etcetera brought a family heirloom with him from Spain in that box. It was a reliquary of gold containing a tiny piece of fabric behind the glass. Of course, the story's spoilt for you, as you already know what it is."

"Yes," Father Pablo agreed, "but, with all due respect, Doña Josefa, that hardly explains how your ancestors came into possession of the relic, and five hundred years ago in Spain is still a long way from two thousand years ago in Jerusalem."

Doña Josefa peered narrowly at the priest, as if gauging his intelligence. "Ancestors have ancestors," she pointed out to him. "It seems my Great, Great, Etcetera was descended from a Great, Great, Etcetera that assisted in the trial and crucifixion of our Savior."

Father Pablo looked out on the gathered multitudes. Occasionally, a face would turn to the couple on the veranda, then turn away again to resume eating or chatting. Above his head he could hear the cooing and fluttering of the pigeons in the warm afternoon sun.

"I'm sorry, Doña Josefa, but it's preposterous. Even the Queen of England cannot trace her lineage to the time of Christ Himself."

"I never claimed such a thing," she replied tartly. "I'm simply relating our family history to you as it has been handed down to me. Are you to say that we had no ancestors before the Crucifixion? Now who's being preposterous? Spanish soldiers served in the armies of the Roman Empire; that is historical fact, so why not one of my own people? How else did we come into possession of a piece of the purple robe of Christ? Perhaps it was my ancestor's own cloak that was placed on the Son of God's shoulders."

Father Pablo turned back to the old woman. "Let's say that it is true. We may as well, as I can no more disprove your story than you are able to prove it. So where has it been—this cloak? Why are we just hearing about it now?"

For the first time since his arrival, Father Pablo saw the old woman grow truly still and silent. She remained motionless with her eyes closed for some time and Father Pablo began to become alarmed.

"Doña Josefa," he whispered, hesitantly reaching out to touch her sleeve, "are you unwell?"

She started at his slight touch. "I'm ashamed of this part, but as you're a priest, I guess I should tell it all the same."

He nodded encouragingly.

"We've kept it to ourselves," she whispered. "For hundreds of years, we've kept it hidden within our own chapel, never sharing the miraculous relic with our fellow Christians."

But…why?" Father Pablo asked.

"I can only guess why our ancestors hid it away within the walls of our chapels—we've had many over the course of generations; as soon as one began to crumble, we would build another and place the relic within some secret place. Perhaps it was fear, after all the power of God can be a terrible thing to possess…or maybe it was simple shame at our part in His death.

Certainly, it's not a pretty picture to think of one's Great, Great, Etcetera driving nails through the hands of the Son of Man."

"No," Father Pablo agreed uneasily, "no, it isn't." Her words made him less anxious to see what was within the box.

"When *our* chapel fell down, I was still a young girl, not more than fifteen, I think, and we had already lost everything. One afternoon, late in the day at any rate, because I remember the bats being out, I found my father digging through the rubble. He had managed to drag the crucifix from the debris and it lay propped up against the only remaining wall, looking down on him as he worked.

"As I drew nearer, I could see that he had sweated through the only good jacket he had left, and I knew Mother would be very angry with him. He was grunting with exertion as he dragged chunks of rubble and other debris aside—my father was not accustomed to physical labor, you see. Occasionally, he would curse loudly, unaware that I was watching from nearby. I was very shocked. Times were quite different then, Father, and men of those days were always on their best behavior around women and children. Hardly the case now, I think."

Father Pablo nodded in agreement.

"In any event, he rose suddenly from the dust and dirt clutching a box in his hands...that box," she nodded at the repository for the relic. "And it was then that I saw that he was crying. Wet trails ran through the dust on his face and tears hung suspended in his large moustache. If I had been shocked before,

I was struck dumb at that moment. My whole world seemed to tilt to one side and I felt I might fall off the face of the earth. I had never seen a man cry before, and seeing my father do so made me realize that I knew nothing at all of the world.

"When he saw me standing there, he started toward me at once, the box held above his head, and for a moment I thought he was going to throw it at me. I was frozen to the spot. Yet, when he got to within a few feet of me, he knelt down and placed it at my feet. Remember, I had no idea what it was; until that day I had never heard mention of any relic. I believe I was crying as hard as he at that moment.

"On that day, with the bats darting about over our heads, and the carving of the suffering Christ looking down on us from the cross, he told me the history of our family and the purple robe, and how we had selfishly kept it to ourselves, how we had grown arrogant and forgetful of God in our good fortune. So much so, he confessed, that he, himself, had even forgotten the existence of the cloak until he had been laid low, and that he was now unworthy to be its protector. As his only heir...though I was just a girl...it must now fall to me.

"What do I do with it, I asked? It occurred to me that my father had gone mad and that I'd best humor him, and looking back on it, I think he had...a little. He vanished a few months later on a business trip. In truth, he had gone off on another of his drinking binges and just didn't return. We never did find out what happened to him. Mother died a few years later, bitter and unhappy. She is buried here with the rest of the family.

"He instructed me to pray, Father. That was it. Just pray ceaselessly to the holy Virgin and that she would instruct me—so I have…and so she did."

"She…" Father Pablo whispered, like a man waking from a dream "…the Holy Virgin?"

"None other," Doña Josefa assured him.

"You're joking, of course."

She stared at the young priest with exasperation. "Maybe if *you* prayed a little more, instead of running around calling the faithful liars, you'd receive a visit as well," she huffed.

"You mean to sit there and tell me," Father Pablo continued in amazement, "that besides possessing a piece of Christ's sacred garment, that the holy Mother has appeared to you?"

"Right about where you're standing," the old woman insisted. "I was taking a little nap in this very chair and woke up to find her with the reliquary. At first, I thought she was some peasant girl about to make off with my gold, so I shouted, 'Stop thief,' and threw my stick at her."

Father Pablo gaped open-mouthed at Doña Josefa. She's a heretical lunatic, he thought…like her father. Such conditions could be hereditary, he'd heard.

"The young woman didn't seem bothered by my stick," Doña Josefa continued. "It fell well short of her in any case, as I'm not very strong anymore. She just stood there looking back at me with the reliquary in her hands, so I took a good long look right back. She's not from around here, I thought. I could see that from the unusual color of her shawl—a beautiful sky-blue. No one around *here* weaves such a color, I can tell you.

"Then she started towards me and I grew alarmed, because I could see perfectly well—it was broad daylight—that her feet weren't touching the ground. It's my mother, I thought, it's my mother's ghost come to take me. But as she drew close to my face, I saw how beautiful she was and knew that it wasn't Mama.

"Mama dressed well and had a good figure, but she wasn't very pretty—I took after her, I'm afraid. Then the smell, the aroma, of roses enveloped me and I knew at once who she was, as we've had no roses here for decades. She handed me the reliquary, and I took it without thinking. Then she touched my face.

"I can't describe the sensation, except to say that I no longer felt any of the pains of age or illness, and even the sorrows and regrets that accumulate with a long life vanished—her presence made me no longer fearful of death, but happy about it, though not in a morbid way.

"Then she spoke to me. She said, 'Leave your walking stick where you have thrown it, and take this. Share it with any that seek my Son, as the time is now.'

"With that, she left me—she released her hold on the reliquary and rose up into the sky like a balloon until she was lost from sight. I cried for two days after, I was so sad she had left me behind."

Father Pablo dug a cigarette out of a crumpled pack and lit it. "Doña Josefa," he spoke gently, "how long have you lived out here alone?"

"Too long," she answered. "Why? Here, give me a puff of that."

He handed her the cigarette and she took several drags from it, holding it between her thumb and forefinger.

"Keep it," he said, noticing how wet she had made the end. "Did you receive many visitors...I mean, before this *revelation*?"

Glancing slyly up at him, she said, "Oh, I see...it's like that, is it? Think what you like, Father. Think just what you like."

Tossing the cigarette onto the flagstones, she slid from her chair with surprising agility, taking a moment to grind out the smoldering ember. "No canes for me," she quipped, taking the few steps needed to reach the box, and throwing it open for Father Pablo.

Inside lay the reliquary, fashioned into the form of a cross. It was evidently made of gold and decorated with an array of precious and semi-precious stones that winked like stars against the velvet cloth on which it rested. At the center of the cross-piece was inserted a circle of glass retained by gold filigree at its circumference. The glass itself appeared thick and smoky. Behind it laid a rotted patch of material stained with several dark blotches, so faded with age that its original color was no longer discernible.   Father Pablo thought of the Crown of Thorns raining blood down onto the humiliating garment.

He reached a hand out.

"Don't touch it," Doña Josefa snapped. "It's not for you!"

Lifting it from its container still wrapped in the velvet cloth, she held it aloft for all those gathered to see, and silence spread like evening through the gathered peoples. Even the children went quiet, or were hushed.

After several moments of this, she stumped back to her chair where, much to Father Pablo's surprise, the Centurions had returned unseen and awaited the old lady. Effortlessly, they lifted her onto her seat and resumed their watchfulness. As the faithful formed themselves into line and began to file up to the steps, she said, "Tell the archbishop what you like, priest…that is up to you."

The young priest stood awkwardly to one side as pilgrim after pilgrim approached the relic, knelt, crossed themselves, and placed their lips against the glass protecting the garment. At some point, he became aware of Veronica standing next to him in the shadowed doorway of the hacienda, her expression, as she watched the proceedings, pensive and unreadable.

"Do you know someone named Juan Alcante?" he asked quietly. "A cripple boy from Progreso, rumored to be made whole again by the power of the garment?"

"I don't know about his being crippled, Father. The boy that came here could walk like any other," she answered.

Snorting, Father Pablo shook his head, remembering Doña Marisa's cynical pronouncement—sadly, it appeared she was right yet again.

"As to his being made whole," Veronica continued, "that I can attest to—he no longer craves his drugs and is free of them, though I doubt that will qualify as a miracle in your eyes."

"No," Father Pablo began, "perhaps not, but a great blessing nonetheless, his mother will…"

His words died on his lips as he turned to the girl. In the fading light the blemish on her face appeared as only a faint shadow, shrunken to a circumference of no more than a peso. "Veronica," he gasped, leaning into her and screwing up his eyes. "Your face…"

She took a step back from him, a hand flying up to cover the mark. "I never asked for this," she cried, then fled into the interior of the hacienda once more.

Father Pablo watched, open-mouthed, as she disappeared, while above his head, Doña Josefa's bats began silently crisscrossing the darkening, blood-streaked sky.

* * *

James sat at the edge of the tiny pool set into the concrete patio, the iced drink in his hand sweating and dripping unnoticed, the rum and pineapple juice momentarily forgotten. The plastic chair he occupied gripped him tightly around his hips and thighs and he thought longingly of his "adult-sized" furniture in far-away New Jersey. Even the "spacious" villa they had been promised by the online realty agency, and so deceptively advertised in color photographs, had disappointed—being, in fact, a warren of cramped rooms that he could barely turn around in without dislodging the garish clutter of pottery, paintings, and faux Pre-Colombian figurines the Mexican owners favored. Even the pool was little more than an outdoor tub in which to soak, and he was not tempted to enter it.

Instead, he gazed out across the narrow beach at a sky stained purple at its farthest edges where it rested on a darkening sea. While closer to land, crimson was leached from the heavens in a steady, perceptible retreat, drawing night after it like a shade across a window. Entranced, he watched darkness claim the world in a warm, comforting embrace as he took a long sip of his now-remembered drink.

Within the house, there was the sound of movement in the kitchen behind him, and the sense of well-being that had crept up on him flitted away like an errant thought. He was tired, more exhausted by his trip to the temple ruins than he would care to admit. And his return to his temporary and unsatisfactory home had left him feeling strange and unsettled.

Brenda had been in the shower when he had returned in the heat of the day, greeting him in her bathrobe while busily drying her hair with a towel, and granting him a peck on the cheek before dancing away to her dressing table in the bedroom. From there they had conducted a stiff, almost-shouted conversation, as he had made himself a drink at the tiny bar in the too-small living room. Her questions had seemed perfunctory, disinterested, an odd response from the woman whose idea it had been for him to make the trip in the first place. James had felt a keen sense of dismissal.

Dinner had been a stilted, uncomfortable affair as well, preceded by Brenda's extreme preoccupation with the preparation of their meal. The clatter of utensils, bowls, and silverware necessary to create her authentic Yucatecan dishes had precluded much in the way of interaction.

Her dismal failure at the project and his reluctance to be drawn out on the subject had only added to their mutual discomfort. He had drunk rather heavily as a result, and after several failed attempts to engage her interest in the rather remarkable news he had gleaned on his trip, he had retired to the patio.

A light next to the rear door was switched on, but James kept his bleary gaze on the now hidden sea, where the torches aboard fishing smacks winked and rocked on unseen waves.

He smelled the fresh-washed scent of her skin before she spoke and within it the tangy aromas of her earlier cooking experiment. Turning to look up at her, he thought for a startled moment that she was naked. The flesh-colored leotard she wore shimmered like a child's fresh skin, while around her waist a colorful wrap swung from her slender hips. Her wrists, fingers, and neck winked with glints of light like the boats on the darkened sea.

"You hadn't been in for a while so I thought you might need this." She held out a fresh drink like an offering.

Self-consciously, he set his previous drink unfinished onto the concrete and took the proffered one from her small, ringed fingers. In the pale, cool light of the rising moon, she shed ten years like an old skin, and he contemplated her revealed yet familiar beauty with the same adoration he had felt the very first time they had met—a beauty, an allurement, which had made him cast off his first wife for no very good reason. That woman had loved him as he well knew, and there were the kids too, of course, but these considerations had proved no real impediment to his rapture over Brenda. "Thank you," he said shyly. "You didn't have to do that."

"I know that," she answered, "I wanted to do it."

Seating herself in the flimsy chair next to his, he noticed that, she too, had a large iced cocktail. She didn't often join him when he drank.

They lapsed awkwardly into silence and Jim took a sip, wondering why they were being so tentative with one another. It was as if they had fought and were looking for a way to make up, he thought. Yet, he knew they hadn't and was all the more perplexed for it. He considered that it might be the overpowering strangeness of the place and blamed México at large for their current estrangement.

"You don't much like it here," Brenda stated, as if reading his thoughts.

Jim sat up a little straighter. "No, no," he protested weakly, "it's not that I don't like it here...it's nice enough, I guess; very pretty country...in some ways." He fell silent once more, searching for the words, thinking how tentative he was being tonight, how unlike himself.

Brenda laughed quietly; then took a long draw on her drink before saying, "That's quite the endorsement, darling. I've seldom heard you more enthusiastic on a subject."

Her laughter was as foreign as the moon that rose from the sea, seemingly only miles distant—her voice containing the hint of a stranger...the sarcastic strains of an unfamiliar and dissatisfied dance partner correcting his steps.

"You like it here though," he said quietly, stealing another glance at her from the corner of his eye. "México appears to agree with you very well."

Taking a long sip of her rum, Brenda leaned back in her chair, holding her legs out above the patio and wriggling her feet like a schoolgirl on vacation. An anklet sparkled and spun like a lure on her fragile ankle and Jim felt a sudden jolt of desire like a flare of pain.

After several moments he realized that she was not going to speak and he rushed to fill the widening gap. "The ruins were interesting," he offered. "They were more impressive than I would have imagined—not very well managed, though. I mean, for what should be a major tourist attraction you have to bounce up and down miles of unpaved road to get to it. I thought I'd lose fillings," he added with a forced chuckle.

"That's too bad," Brenda replied vaguely. "I was hoping it might help you to appreciate the culture a little more."

"Then or now?" He asked, feeling challenged and suddenly defensive. "The Mayan Empire crumbled over five hundred years ago, you know; as for *now*...well." He spread his arms to embrace the tiny homes and ramshackle streets of Progreso as Brenda's silence gathered in their shared darkness.

A long quiet followed during which the lights of an airliner winked overhead as it nosed its way east through the night sky, then Brenda asked, "Do you think having children would have made us different people?"

Was that it, Jim wondered? Was it the thought of children that had come between them so unexpectedly? This was a subject they had not discussed in years, and Jim, having children of his own that figured but little into his life, had given the subject almost no thought during their marriage. He had been secretly pleased that the raising of a family would never place obstacles between Brenda and him—he knew that he was not a good father and had no wish to become one again, and could not envision his lovely, sensual Brenda bearing children or rearing them with any joy. He was well pleased to have her to himself.

"Children make everyone different people..." he said "...old and bitter, from what I've seen."

"I wonder," she replied. "When you come to places like this you see so many children flocking around the women, chattering and scampering like monkeys, fighting, playing, crying, laughing, and yet the adults seem so wholly unconcerned...it's like the ocean washing round their feet."

There was a slight pause, and Jim could picture Brenda's concentration, her wistfulness. "No, not unconcerned, that's not what I meant...it's an air of confidence, I think. The children here are so much a part of everyone's lives that there's no doubts, no angst over every little thing concerning child-rearing. The children *know* they are children, and the adults *know* they are as well, and take responsibility for them and expect others to do the same. It's when I see this, when I watch them, that I feel most like a foreigner."

Jim stood abruptly and pointed at the pool. "Have you ever seen such a small pool before?" He swayed from side to side, his face feeling flushed and hot. "What's it for...footbaths? We're fine without kids," he stated. "What would we do with them now, anyway?"

"I don't know," Brenda answered. "What do people ever do with kids?"

Jim stumbled toward the edge of the patio and the beginning of the beach; then stopped, turning back around. "I did hear something interesting while I was out there at the ruins," he tossed into the widening gap.

"Really," Brenda asked, "who from?" Her tone was disinterested and pleasant, her silvered profile serene and unknowable, and it suddenly occurred to Jim for the very first time that it was still possible to lose her.

"The guide, Pedro, I think his name was...maybe Paco, I don't remember, he said something about the local bandits we were talking about the other day, so I asked him what was going on."

Jim could hear himself slurring and concentrated on his enunciation. "He got all cagy about it when I asked, so I shoveled a few dollars on him and he loosened up. He says an old woman on a farm out in the jungle is performing miracles."

"Miracles," Brenda said like someone waking from a dream, "what do you mean?"

"You know," Jim continued, excited that he seemed to have her interest at last, "healings, that sort of thing, if I understood him correctly—he had a pretty heavy accent."

"You're the one with the accent," Brenda reminded him.

"Yeah," he acknowledged, "that's right."

"Go on," she insisted, "I'm intrigued. How does she do it?"

"With some kind of *holy* relic, he said. But he was kind of vague on exactly what it was...either he didn't know or he just wanted more money to tell me."

Jim could see that Brenda was leaning forward in her chair. "But what do the bandits have to do with it?" she asked.

"They protect it," Jim answered, wishing he had not been so cheap with the guide now.

"Protect *what*, exactly?" Brenda countered. "What could it possibly be that they would be willing to shoot someone over?"

Taking a long swig of his rum and pineapple juice, Jim leaned back to look at the starry sky. "God only knows," he said. "He claimed it's something Jesus touched. Can you imagine?"

"Something that Christ touched," Brenda said quietly. "How strange…do they let anyone see it?"

"What…?" Jim asked, surprised and slow. "See it…don't be crazy. Besides, I wouldn't know where to begin; you're the one with all the local savvy. Sounds like a good way to get killed, if you ask me."

He turned to find that Brenda was naked and floating in the pool, her head resting on its edge cushioned by her folded clothes.

"You're not serious, are you?" he managed to ask. "Are you going native on me?"

He watched mesmerized by the moonlight on her skin, the angel's wings of ripples created by her slowly sweeping arms, by her body that lay like an offering beneath the foreign moon and the twinkling dome.

"I'm curious, that's all," she said at last with closed eyes, "you forget I was raised a Catholic…we're *supposed* to believe in miracles."

"That was a long time ago," Jim said; his head spinning. "You told me you were just a kid when you gave all that up."

"Yes," she replied, "I was just a kid."

Suddenly very drunk and sweating profusely, Jim stumbled toward the sound of the incoming tide, leaving the gate ajar as he passed. When his feet found the warm ocean he stopped and bent over, clasping his knees and taking several deep breaths. After several moments of this he felt steadier.

Several miles out, a container ship stood off to wait for the dawn, its superstructure a lighted skyscraper untroubled by the calm Gulf waters of Progreso. When he turned to find his rented house again, he was greeted by an empty pool, its waters smoothing into a mirror for the stars and the moon.

CHAPTER EIGHT

Archbishop Valdes watched in amusement as Father Pablo paced excitedly from one end of his office to the next. It appeared that in his newfound fervor, the young priest had completely mislaid the insecurities and anguish of his last visit, and it was this that the archbishop found both amusing and touching. Perhaps there *were* miracles to be found out there in the jungle, he thought.

"So," the archbishop interjected, even as Father Pablo's narrative wound to a close, "tell me about this young woman, Veronica."

Father Pablo rushed across the tiles to arrive at the archbishop's desk. "Her face, Your Excellency—it is exactly as I've said. The first time I met her nearly the entirety of one side was covered with this awful red caul, but on our second meeting, as she arrived to pick me up, I thought it appeared smaller. However, I didn't give it much thought at the time, as I was very tired and not a little apprehensive, as you might imagine. After all, for all I knew I was being taken to a rebel stronghold. But that evening there could be no doubt; I was as close as you and I are right now. She was one of the first, as I understand it, to believe, to venerate the relic of the robe," he finished breathlessly.

"Yes, so I've gathered," the older prelate agreed, studying the newly-radiant features of the younger. He is alight, he thought with a touch of envy. It would be easy to believe that the Holy Spirit had found a welcome perch on his shoulder. "Yet, she said, 'I never asked for this.' What did she mean, do you think?"

Appearing surprised, Father Pablo admitted, "I've no idea, Your Excellency."

"Well," the archbishop offered, "she ran away, after all. It's doubtful she would have confided in you at just that moment, in any event."

"Yes," Father Pablo agreed quietly, his previous euphoria somewhat dampened by the memory of Veronica's expression. "I should have gone after her," he said, "but I was so excited by what I had witnessed that it was all I could do to restrain myself from joining the rest of the pilgrims in veneration."

"You did the right thing there," the archbishop assured him, "it's early yet for that sort of thing. As to the girl, you'll have a chance to speak with her again, no doubt. She'll be in a better frame of mind then, and when you do, ask if she would be willing to submit to a medical examination—that would be very helpful.

"After all," he continued gently, seeing the alarm growing on the young priest's face, "it's important to eliminate natural causes in these matters, such as a skin fungus that might be cured by one's own antibodies, or a change of climate."

"I gathered from our conversations that this was a condition she has endured since childhood," Father Pablo assured him.

"I've no doubt, but even so, you can understand that we must investigate all possibilities—this is a critical, secular world we live in, Pablo."

It pained the archbishop to witness the joy being drained from his young subordinate, but he knew that he must press on. "Did I understand you rightly that this Veronica girl denied a miracle had occurred in the case of Juan Alcante?"

"Not exactly, Excellency," Father Pablo explained, "rather, she denied that he was ever a cripple to begin with, but that the miracle lay in his withdrawal from drug addiction." He could see that the archbishop looked disappointed, and felt that he had, somehow, let Veronica down in the telling.

"That's a tough nut," Archbishop Valdes murmured. "Is there any chance that Doña Josefa would relinquish the relic, for a short while of course, to be carried up to México City for examination?"

"No," Father Pablo exclaimed. "The Centurions would never permit it; it was exactly this that she warned me against!"

The archbishop raised a hand. "All right, Father, all right," he laughed. "Calm yourself."

Father Pablo took a step back, aghast at his own temerity.

"Would she...they, that is, accept an expert in their midst, if he examined the relic *in situ*, do you think?" the archbishop persisted with a hopeful smile. "That could be arranged, I believe."

"I don't know," Father Pablo answered. "I doubt it, somehow."

"Oh, well—the devil! These folks are not going to make this easy, are they?" The older man asked sadly.

Father Pablo shook his head in answer.

After a few moments of silence the archbishop suddenly clapped his hands together, as he had done during their last meeting, startling Father Pablo, "We'll pray on it, young Father, you and I, and I'm sure an answer will be given us." His pale eyes appeared to twinkle with delight at the thought. "In the meantime, return to the hacienda when you can and learn what you may, your impressions are invaluable.

"I feel like one of those superintendents in a Scotland Yard novel," he laughed, "and you my trusted and dogged inspector…it's a *mystery*, you see!"

Father Pablo did see, but rather than a dashing investigator, he felt like a sleazy informant. Kissing the archbishop's ring, he turned heavily for the door. The archbishop's voice stopped him.

"Be careful, Pablo," he said, his green eyes clouded with concern. "And I mean in every possible way. Passions run high in such matters as these and priests are notorious for getting themselves killed—don't you be one of them, or I will be very angry with you.

"As to the other matter, be cautious, as well. Miracles may indeed be happening on Doña Josefa's plantation, but bear in mind the words of Our Lord to Saint Thomas, 'Blessed is he who has *not* seen, yet believes.' Go with God, Father Pablo Diego Corellas."

* * *

When Brenda awoke it was with the fully-formed intention to seek out the relic. This had not been her intention when she had gone to bed the night before, and she had not dreamed about it that she could remember. Even so, she had no wish to analyze her emotions and thoughts, conscious or subconscious, or hesitate over her actions, but rose from her bed to find her husband and set the task before him.

She found him fully clothed and sprawled across the downstairs guest bed, his snores rumbling like the surf beyond the bedroom wall. She looked down on him for several moments; her arms folded within the silken sleeves of her Japanese-styled bathrobe, then, without warning, ran the lacquered nails of her right hand across the instep of his left foot. With a great snort he sat directly up, his curly hair a ragged nest, his eyes blurred and veined with drink. He gaped sightlessly across the room. "I don't know you," he accused someone in the darkened corner.

Brenda thought, not for the first time, that Jim resembled the illustrations of fairy tale giants from her childhood books—huge and comical, potentially dangerous. She pinched his ear and said, "Jim! Wake up!"

He turned to look up at her and answered while rubbing his sore ear, "I am awake…I've been awake. What time is it?" he asked, looking around the room in bewilderment.

"I'm going to make coffee and pour you some juice while you get a shower. I'll meet you in the kitchen."

Jim shook his head and blew through his pursed lips like a horse. "Okay," he agreed meekly, clambering off the tossed and tousled bed with difficulty.

Without waiting to see that he succeeded, Brenda walked rapidly into the kitchen and set about her stated tasks. When she heard the shower running on the second floor, she dialed Barrera's number on her cell phone.

He answered on the third ring and Brenda began without preamble, "Antonio, it's me. What do you know about a holy relic being venerated out in the countryside somewhere?"

"Good morning," he answered, "I am very well, thank you…and you?"

She ignored his tease and went on, "I'm serious. Jim is in the shower and may be down any moment…have you heard of such a thing?"

Barrera answered briskly after a small pause. "I am aware of some kind of goings-on, a cult if you will, though I lack many details at the moment. Doña Josefa would be your woman, I think. She owns an old henequen plantation out in the jungle; it's been years since it was properly farmed, so I am informed.

"I wouldn't recommend you going out there, Brenda. I'm not at all sure what you might walk into and I have no way to protect you if you get into any trouble. Do you understand me?"

"Yes," she answered, glancing up at the ceiling as the shower fell silent.

"A holy relic," he repeated, "how interesting. Who told you this?"

Brenda cupped the mouthpiece with her hands while listening to Jim's heavy footsteps cross into the upstairs bedroom; then whispered, "Jim heard it from his guide at the ruins yesterday. Do you think it could be true?"

"You're asking me?" Barrera laughed. "It would appear your sources are as good as mine."

"I'm serious, Antonio. What do you think?"

He paused before answering, "I think you should be careful, this country creates a lot of dreamers and satisfies very few of them. Why should you be so interested, I wonder?"

"I don't know…it sounds like an adventure, like a story my grandmother might have told me when I was a little girl. When I went to bed last night I wasn't even thinking about it, but when I woke up this morning I couldn't think of anything else. The idea…the possibility of something…I don't know."

"Hmmm, I see," Barrera answered untruthfully. "I still think you're being foolish, but I'll put in a call to someone I know out there. He'll keep an eye out for you and let me know if you run into any trouble. I'll put a patrol in the area, as well."

"You have a man out there?" Brenda asked.

"If you can call him that," Barrera said. "He's not a policeman, he's an informant. I sent him out because I thought they were setting up a narcotics operation, now it seems I'm the last to know differently. Perhaps we can talk when you get back and you can fill in the details?"

Brenda glanced up once more counting Jim's footsteps crossing the landing to the stairs. "I have to go now," she whispered, "right now," and snapped her cell phone shut and slid it into the pocket of her housecoat, turning as she did to pour a large mug of coffee. As Jim stepped into the kitchen she handed it to him.

Jim automatically took the steaming mug and cradled it beneath his nose saying "I don't know what got into me last night. It's not like me to drink like that...hell; I didn't know I *was* drinking like that. I can't even remember what we're doing this morning. What did I miss?" He stopped, looking at his wife in confusion. "I'm sorry," he said.

Brenda stood on her toes and pecked his freshly shaved cheek and came away with a hint of lime and unidentified chemicals. "Drink your coffee, sweetheart," she said, "then get in touch with that guide of yours and see if he'll take us out to see the old woman and her relic. I'll get dressed myself while you make the arrangements. I won't be long," she promised with a smile.

As she hurried up the stairs he had just descended, Jim called after her, "You're kidding, right? You've *got* to be kidding me." He sloshed coffee onto the tiled floor and muttered something indistinct.

As incentive for good behavior Brenda allowed her kimono to slide to the floor just before she stepped through the doorway into their bedroom. The silence that followed told her that Jim had indeed been witness, and several minutes later she heard the muted conversation that told her he was on the phone to their guide.

* * *

The bus ride back to Progreso was unaccountably crowded, the packed travelers within chattering excitedly during the dull trip. Occasionally, one would recognize another over the heads of his, or her, fellow passengers and call out to them in greeting, followed by whole conversations shouted back and forth over the length of the entire bus. In this manner, the Méridanos arranged assignations for the coming evening, debated the merits of Progreso's few restaurants, and revealed at which hotels or residences they could be found.

Father Pablo found the festive, carnival-like atmosphere baffling and not a little uncomfortable; even the aisle was standing-room only. He had given up his seat to an elderly woman who, squeezing his arm croaked merrily, "It's a wonderful thing, isn't it, Father?"

Assuring her that it was, he had no idea as to what she was talking about and spent the entire fifty minute ride clutching the seat backs to either side for support. Occasionally, he would glance down to find the old woman deep in prayer, her head bowed over clasped hands from which a rosary dangled, the crucifix dancing and swaying with the rocking of the bus.

When she would catch him at this, she would raise the rosary toward him and smile toothlessly, even as her whispered recitations of the decades flowed without interruption. The third time this occurred, it finally dawned on Father Pablo to make the Sign of the Cross in blessing. This so delighted the old woman that she raised her clasped hands even higher and shook them like a wrestler declaring victory over a vanquished opponent.

Their arrival was delayed by an additional twenty minutes due to a traffic backup just outside Progreso, and Father Pablo assumed that it was the result of yet another of the terrifying, and generally fatal, car crashes for which Highway 261 was infamous. Yet, as they inched their way forward, no carnage was observed, only police traffic details attempting to keep open the intersection with Highway 27 that ran east to west along the coast. Though their attempts were met with only fitful successes, it nonetheless had the overall effect of allowing the phalanx of motor vehicles that had just entered into Progreso to be absorbed and dispersed before the next wave was allowed to wash into the city limits from the south.

Inching their way through the intersection, Father Pablo was able to observe the tired, harassed-looking officers, their uniforms and faces chalky with dust. Suddenly, the crisp, handsome image of Captain Barrera rose up in his mind in unbidden contrast. He had avoided his summons for a week now and was filled with dread at the prospect of their next, inevitable meeting. Even so, he was unable to contain his curiosity and exasperation with the snail's pace to which he and his fellow passengers had been reduced. Shouting out the window to the nearest officer, he asked, "What's happened? What's going on?"

The policeman spun about, equally exasperated, no doubt, at having been questioned and harangued by this sea of motorists, his sweat-streaked, whitened face set to snarl and snap. Upon seeing Father Pablo's collar, his expression underwent a series of transformations: the snarl dissolved into one of embarrassment that, in turn, gave rise to consternation and indignation.

"*You* ought to know," he shouted back accusingly. "Are you playing with me?" The policeman called out something to his fellow officers, whose heads began to turn in the direction of the bus.

Shocked at the man's vehemence, Father Pablo fell back from the window, the passengers he had leaned over regarding him with renewed interest. "Me?" he answered aloud in puzzlement, as the bus lurched ahead to enter the town.

"I have no idea what he's talking about," he offered apologetically to those watching. He now wished desperately to get off the bus and his legs shook with fatigue.

His bewilderment only grew when he was at last disgorged from the packed vehicle. Instead of the quiet, early evening streets of his beloved seaside town, he was greeted with boisterous, noisy crowds worthy of Mérida on a feast day.

As he stumbled out of the terminal making his way toward the plaza, he felt himself suddenly seized in a fierce grip. A booming voice cried out, "Father Pablo! Well met, well met! It's wonderful, isn't it?"

The mayor released one of Father Pablo's arms to sweep his own jubilantly and benevolently over the crowded streets, unknowingly repeating the old woman's declaration on the bus. His tall, pomaded hair quivered with excitement as his tri-colored sash of office fluttered proudly over his ample girth in the freshening breeze. The sash was something the mayor ordinarily wore for official ceremonies and holidays, and Father Pablo was only further perplexed by its display.

"Are they here for Advent?" Father Pablo managed to ask. He had been told by Monsignor Roberto De Jesus to expect a rise in visitors to Mass during the Christmas season, but he had not prepared him for anything like this.

Laughing loudly, as if at a good joke, the mayor spun him about while gripping one arm and guiding Father Pablo away from the rectory. "Let's celebrate," he declared.

As they progressed to the Malecòn the mayor greeted citizen and visitor alike with the bonhomie that was expected of him and was, in fact, part of his very nature. The people reacted with delight at this double blessing of both church and state, waving back excitedly, sometimes bursting into applause at the sight of priest and civic leader arm in arm.

Their arrival at Eladios was of one piece with their journey and they were quickly ushered past the line of waiting customers to be seated at a choice seaside table—it appeared that on this evening, nothing was too good for Progreso's leading citizens. The murmur within the popular restaurant rose to the hum of a busy hive with their arrival and even Father Pablo found himself surrendering to the excitement that seemed to animate the air.

Within moments drinks were brought to them and the mayor saluted the room with his glass held high, proclaiming, "Salud!"

A sea of glasses rose in response as a chorus of, "Salud," was returned. Before Father Pablo could down his first sip of the margarita Eladios was famous for, someone called out, "A blessing, Father, please!" This plea was followed by a chorus of requests. The mayor beamed at him across the table, nodding.

Buoyed by the fervency of belief that he saw around him, Father Pablo set his glass down, and rising to his feet, etched the

Sign of the Cross in the air, saying, "In the name of the Father, the Son, and the Holy Spirit."

The entire room followed suit, crossing themselves in union with the young priest and falling into sudden silence. Even the clatter coming from the busy kitchen subsided as if in expectation.

He continued, "Bless us, O Lord, and these Thy gifts which we are about to receive from Your bounty, through Christ, our Lord." That was good, he thought, he hadn't stumbled on, or missed a single word.

Glancing out at his ad hoc parishioners, he found a number looking up at him expectantly from beneath their eyebrows. Encouraged, he dared to improvise, "Look down on these, Thy pilgrims, and bless them and their families as they so joyously await the Advent of Christ's birth as celebrated in the coming holy season, and shower them with the blessings that come only through the Gifts of the Holy Spirit. Bless their time with us here in Progreso and when they depart to return on their homeward journeys, keep them safe in both body and soul." He took a shaky breath, astounded at his newfound eloquence, but reluctant to press his luck by continuing. "Amen," he sighed gratefully and made to sit down.

Even as the wonderful elixir of salt and tequila washed the dust of his travels from his mouth, Father Pablo became aware of the continued silence that followed his words. Looking out over his fellow diners, he found their heads still bowed; the hush of the room more expectant than respectful. Several of them were sneaking impatient glances of him. He felt the mayor nudge his arm.

"What?" he heard himself stage-whisper. The familiar and unwelcome embarrassment of past Masses climbed from beneath his collar. What in the world had he got wrong, he wondered?

"The pilgrimage," the mayor whispered back, smiling encouragingly. "They're waiting for a blessing on the pilgrimage, Father."

"The...what are you talking about?" Their pilgrimage was at an end, Father Pablo thought—they had arrived for the Advent season.

As the clash of silverware and the clatter of plates resumed from the kitchen, the pilgrims reluctantly returned to their fast-cooling meals. A sullen, inquisitive murmur arose from their tables.

"Oh well," the mayor chuckled, "this is a hungry crowd; they couldn't wait. Don't worry about it." He signaled for their waiter.

"I don't understand. Did I say something wrong?" Father Pablo asked.

"Wrong?" the mayor replied as he dipped into the *botanas* the waiter had hastened to deliver. "No, no, of course not...you can take care of it in the morning. In fact, that would be even better, more appropriate." He appeared to be giving the matter some serious thought.

"Yes," he resumed, speaking around the food in his mouth, "after morning Mass you can give them the Church's blessing from the steps of the church and send them off."

Warming to his subject, he continued, "They will fill the plaza, no doubt, so I had better alert Captain Barrera. He can be very testy about such things, you know. But a good man, I think, even so. He gets things done; no doubt about that.

"Perhaps I should make a few calls to the local news offices as well, just in case they've been asleep through all this." Arching an eyebrow, he leaned forward conspiratorially. "A little publicity would be good for Progreso, don't you think, Father? It will be good for the Church, too," he hastened to add.

"Oh God," Father Pablo breathed, "you are talking about the Purple Robe, aren't you?"

"Of course," the mayor assured him happily, "what else? Your little secret is out, Father. Everyone knows everyone here, and your visits to Doña Josefa's hacienda and with the archbishop are the talk of the whole region. Will his Excellency bless us with his presence soon?" he asked hopefully.

Shaking his head and sighing, Father Pablo set his empty, and now bitter, glass down and looked out to the sea. The sky had turned as yellow as a parrot's breast, while the long, wispy clouds grew dark bellies, and glowed wine red at their edges. The sun had long since sunk below the distant horizon. It was such a sky as this, Father Pablo mused, that Our Lord must have gazed out on from the Garden of Gethsemane as he contemplated his imminent betrayal and death.

"No," he spoke, at last.

"Why not?" the mayor cried, even as their drinks were refreshed and he threw his back with gusto. "It would encourage the faithful," he assured Father Pablo, then added portentously, "and perhaps return the wavering to the ranks of the Church. Think of the converts!"

Father Pablo thought this last somewhat self-serving, as Catholics accounted for some eighty percent of the population of the Yucatán, while the rest were fallen away from the Church, leaving a mere handful for the Protestant faith.

"He's not convinced of the authenticity of the relic...and neither am I." Father Pablo added this last so as to demonstrate solidarity with the archbishop, though his own feelings were far from certain. "I am investigating...so to speak."

"Investigating," the mayor repeated around a mouthful of the last of the appetizers. "You've heard about that crippled beggar boy dancing at weddings and how that awful mark was wiped clean from the face of that Veronica girl, haven't you? A tubercular woman from the shacks down in the lagoons was cured only days ago. She was mere days from death—I know, I go down to visit those poor folks from time to time! I'm their mayor too, you know!"

Taking a breath, the mayor downed the last of his tequila. "Ah well...go on and investigate, if you must. In the meantime, what do you intend to say to all these visitors when they show up at Mass tomorrow morning?"

Father Pablo shook his head once more even as another round of drinks was delivered. "I don't know. I really don't know what to say."

The mayor regarded his young priest for several moments before speaking. "It's not as bad as all that," he assured Father Pablo. "Take it from an old politician—it's all in the words and how they're said. You don't have to endorse the pilgrimage, or the relic, for that matter. After all, they're going whether you do so or not. Just bless their faith. Yes," he cried, his slightly bulging eyes shining with moisture, "that's really it, you see. That will make them happy enough. They deserve that much, at least, for their strivings. The archbishop wouldn't begrudge it, I'm sure; he's a kindly, pious man. We've shared a few drinks together over the years, and I think I know him well enough to say this much."

Taking hope from the older man's words, Father Pablo allowed his third drink to soften his earlier alarm and anxieties. "Yes, he is a good man. I've seen that during my visits. He would not wish to discourage an honest exploration of faith." The mayor nodded in contented agreement.

"Yet," he paused, as he wended his way through the theological labyrinth, and an increasing haze of alcohol, "what if I am encouraging heresy? What if the relic...the cloak of Our Lord is a fake—a knowing, willful forgery? Would I not be seen as condoning heresy? Wouldn't I be a willing participant in blasphemy?"

Folding his hands across his big belly, the mayor pursed his lips in thought for a moment before answering, "If you knew that to be true...yes. But you know nothing of the kind.

"We know of the miraculous works attributed to it, of course, but we may never know its true origin. Does that make it a fake? Do we ignore the rest awaiting an answer we may never have? That's for you to decide, Father.

"I've never been to the seminary, so I am ignorant in these matters. But if faith is strengthened by this bit of cloth, if hearts are opened to God's mercy and will, then that seems good enough for me. It makes me happy."

Smiling now, he shoved a menu at Father Pablo. "You need to eat something, Father; then you'll feel better. That's what I always do when the press of business gets me down." He laughed aloud, patting his large stomach affectionately.

"When you get back to the church, you can pray on the matter. I'm sure Our Lady will act on your prayers and you'll have your answers in the morning. I'm sure of this...in the meantime enjoy a bowl of the *ceviche*, it's wonderful, and I highly recommend it."

A growl of distant thunder rumbled from north to south.

* * *

The Centurions regarded them darkly, it seemed to Jim. But each time he would glance their way, they would look politely down at their feet or resume some whispered and suddenly remembered conversation with one of their compatriots. Even so, the guns made him nervous and his perspiration, already thick and sour from the hangover, seemed to worsen and grow foul with stanched fear. Brenda did not appear to notice or be much bothered by this ragged militia, but studied the outlandish procession of the lame, the sick, and the possessed as they stumbled, staggered, hopped, and sometimes crawled like slugs toward the upraised reliquary.

Their guide had been replaced shortly after their arrival by a sleazy-looking young man that Jim would have recognized as a con man or criminal in any culture or country. Appearing at their side shortly after their arrival, he offered to assist them with any needs they might have, be it food, drink, or if they wished, to lead them to the head of the line of the faithful. But before they could answer, he drew their driver aside and engaged him in a heated and hushed exchange, his hands flying up into the air from time to time as if he might slap him. Pedro, or Paco, Jim could not keep it straight, at first seemed equal to the task of defending his position, but after being shoved violently against a tree trunk, at last lowered his face to these threats and grew silent.

"Hey, we're fine," Jim said in English to the young man's back, "we've got a guide."

Ignoring the giant American, the interloper raised an open hand once more to Pedro. This time Pedro flinched away from the blow like a scolded dog. His dominance clearly established, the stranger turned to Jim smiling, and answered in passable English, "*Now* you do. This man was unsuitable and knows nothing of Doña Josefa's ways. He would have gotten you into real trouble, I think."

He began walking rapidly toward the crumbling hacienda with the mincing gait of a man walking on coals or broken glass. Even concealed by his stained jeans, Jim thought his legs did not seem straight or properly formed.

"I am Juan Alcante," he informed them as an afterthought. Without thinking, Jim and Brenda followed him as their previous guide slunk back to his jeep. "I have told him to wait," their new guide informed them confidently, hitching a thumb at their former protector. "He will wait."

Glancing back at Pedro's retreating, defeated posture, Jim concluded that he had not tried very hard to succeed.

He was startled by the touch of a hand and looked down to see that Brenda had seized his in her own, "Hurry up, slowpoke," she said, giving him a tug.

"*Sigamé,*" Juan called back to them. "Follow me, please."

With feet leaden with uncertainty, Jim pushed forward, smiling in reassurance at Brenda, while feeling nothing of the kind in his heart. The great house lay before them, its line of petitioners snaking back through the low forest until lost from sight.

"Step up, if you wish," Juan said, pointing toward the spilling veranda. He pranced toward a small family group that would be next to climb the low stairs and approach the cross held aloft by the mistress of the plantation.

Both Jim and Brenda were transfixed by the tiny apparition of Doña Josefa and her gold-encased prize, and only at the last moment realized that Juan had begun tugging and pulling at the awaiting family while waving for them to step up. It was then that Jim noticed the Centurions.

The commotion appeared to wake them from their trance-like immobility, their eyes quickening into life even as they glided forth from the sides of their mistress. It was unclear to Jim whether they were about to intervene against Juan's depredations on the hapless family, or assist him in their removal.

An older woman, whom Jim thought might be the mother of the brood, shoved someone forth from their midst and began to hurry and push him up the stairs leaving the rest of her family to carry on the fight. Balking at being culled from the herd, her charge stiffened his body against her efforts.

Jim could see now that it was a boy of indeterminate age, his features soft and downturned with heavy-lidded eyes that sloped dramatically at their outer extremities, his hair fine and wispy, barely a covering for his round head. "Uhnnn…" he bellowed in fear "…uhnnn!"

Doña Josefa's guards appeared on either side of the struggling mother and her stubborn charge, while more arrived from every direction as if by unseen signal. The penitents within sight of the ruckus grew vocal in their support of the woman and her terrified child, even as the armed men stepped between the rest of the procession and the family, allowing their weapons to slide round to their waists for easier access and obvious display.

"Doña Josefa," the tired woman cried above the boy's grunting, "Doña Josefa!"

All of these things had seemed to happen within seconds and only now did Jim understand that this had something to do with Brenda and him. "No…" he muttered at last "…Juan? No! We don't want that!"

As if she were awakened by Jim's voice, Brenda started and cried out in rapid Spanish that they would await their turn and not to molest these people any further.

Jim saw the wrinkled doll-woman holding the relic turn her scrutiny upon them, her expression one of distaste and impatience. The cross, seemingly forgotten, hung from her hand nearly touching the mossy stones.

Spinning round and glaring at them, Juan extricated himself from the cursing and crying pilgrims. Limping back over to them, he was clearly ruffled and aggrieved.

"It is a service that I offer," he said in a tight, lisping voice. "What could it have hurt for these people to have waited five more minutes? It is only for a small fee, I assure you, the money is spread round for the Centurions and the upkeep of the grounds here."

Surveying the torn, churned earth around them, as well as a few, obviously new chemical toilets placed along the pilgrims' line of march, he continued huffily, "The Indios that guard the cloak have to eat as well, you know; it costs them to be here and takes them away from their farms."

Brenda glanced at Jim meaningfully, and he reluctantly fished out his wallet and offered Juan five hundred pesos. With a sniff, he snatched it away and made it disappear like a magic trick.

Looking back up, Jim saw that Doña Josefa no longer regarded them, and the procession had resumed quietly, the contested family already returning from their veneration. The mother's face shone with triumph, though over what Jim could not determine, as the boy's features appeared unchanged, still mired in the permanent, questing befuddlement of severe retardation.

Nonetheless, he smiled in happy imitation of his mother, content to reflect her mood now that the crisis was over. The woman's misplaced optimism and the man-child's drooling mimicry, combined with the heat, humidity, and his incipient hangover, made Jim feel slightly sick. Glancing over to Brenda to see if she might be ready to leave, he found her absorbed in the passion play they had come to witness, rapt with attention as every new family, or set of supplicants, provided each following scene.

He tapped Juan's shoulder roughly, "What is it then..." he nodded at the lofted cross "...the crucifix?"

Throwing him a glance over his narrow shoulder, Juan replied, "No, Señor, it is what's *in* the cross." He turned around to study his charges more closely. "You came all the way without knowing?" He chuckled throatily.

"Within, it contains a piece of the purple robe of Christ Jesus—the selfsame cloak that was placed on His shoulders by the Roman soldiers, along with the Crown of Thorns—to humiliate Him," he added as if speaking to children.

"I'll be damned," Jim snorted. "Is that *right*...a robe...or cape...or something, worn by Jesus—Jesus in the Bible?"

"Jim, don't..." Brenda warned.

"Don't what," he fired back. "You're not taking this seriously, are you? We're out in the middle of the Yucatán jungle for God's sake! They've no more got a piece of Christ's clothing than I've got the Holy Grail in my trophy case, Brenda! This is a sham, a shakedown for money, a country sideshow." His thick arm swept over the crowd, "A *freak* show, if you ask me!"

"I'm not asking you," Brenda spat back. "No one is asking you!"

It was then that Jim noticed the Centurions' attention had come to rest on them exclusively. He lowered his voice. "All right, all right, let's take some pictures and get out of here, okay? Have you noticed all the men with guns?" he asked sarcastically with a quick nod at the nearest one. "I don't think these *Centurions* are going to want too much intelligent scrutiny of their precious relic."

As if to add to their misery, a shower burst from a sky obscured by the closely grown trees and began to soak them in warm moisture. In spite of this no one surrendered their place in line. One of the Centurions standing over Doña Josefa smoothly unfolded a plastic garbage bag from within the cargo pocket of his camouflaged pants, handed one edge over to his companion, and together they provided the tiny woman a canopy for the rain. They appeared untroubled as to their own conditions.

Deftly producing two squares of torn plastic as well, their guide offered them to the Americans. Jim quickly handed one to Brenda while taking one himself. Again he gave Juan money. Juan had reserved a third square for his own use, joining them in their huddle of makeshift rain gear.

Above the heads of the undaunted pilgrims, Jim made out what appeared to be a wooden box being carried aloft. He wiped the water from his eyes in order to better see as it drew closer to the stairs and the relic of the garment. His attention quickened as the object rolled along on the undulating back of the snaking procession, drawing closer and defining itself through the lashing rain. Glancing down at Brenda, he saw that she too had become riveted as realization began to dawn on them both.

"Oh God..." he heard her whisper "...oh, God."

The young man carrying the small box stepped now into full view. He wore a soggy suit so elegantly archaic that it could have been his grandfather's. The woman next to him, also dressed in her finest, was swathed in the damp and sagging lace of her wedding gown, her mantilla dripping and askew. Arranged behind them came several generations of both sides of the family, shuffling and gripping one another in their grief and shared misery, some with umbrellas, most without.

Setting his burden down, the young father carefully removed the lid of the little casket. Jim felt his stomach lurch and his knees go weak as he saw what was within. Instinctively, he reached for Brenda, but she had moved several steps closer to the family.

Dressed in much the same fashion as her mother, the tiny girl within the coffin was smothered within the white confection of her baptismal gown. Her head, with its dark curls, was crowned with white roses grown wilted by the heat and humidity of her wooden box. Even from where he stood, Jim could see that she was grey with death, having assumed the stiff, unmoving rictus of lifeless clay.

As if she might yet be waking, her eyes were slightly open, but the sunken orbs, yellowish as egg yolks, belied this in their fixed regard of nothing at all.

Lifting the box like a cradle, the young father and his family regarded the little corpse that had brought them to this place in their shared sorrow. Several of the older men raised clenched fists to the heavens and shook them, even as they bowed their heads to death's implacable reign. Joined by the other females of her clan, the young wife's quiet weeping grew into a communal lamentation, as her husband ascended the slick steps with his burden.

Following closely, the young mother staggered and crawled after him and the little coffin like a drunk, the driving rain providing the only accompaniment to their stilted ballet of grief.

Doña Josefa awaited them at the top of the steps as she did all before them, but even Jim could see that she, too, was affected. The golden cross vibrated in her veined hands ever so slightly at the approach of death.

Kneeling at the foot of the reliquary, the young man set the casket down, and without rising, reached for the cross, even as Doña Josefa lowered it to his lips. Joining him, his wife knelt by his side as if to reenact their vows as bride and groom. Nearly pale as her dress, she leaned forward to place her lips against the obscuring glass of the reliquary in her turn. Then, without a word, her husband reached into the coffin, lifting their lost, slack child to the cross as the rain pattered down onto her unfeeling face.

This time it was Jim's turn. "Oh God," he said.

Looking once more to Brenda, he saw with a thrill of horror that she had dropped to her knees like everyone around them. Only Juan and he remained standing. "Brenda," he whispered urgently.

Hesitating only for a moment, almost too briefly to be noticed, the old woman brought the glass to the child's dead lips, gently touching them.

The silence that had bewitched the encampment held for several long moments as the parents remained kneeling, refusing to rise and surrender their hope. Amongst the pilgrims, heads began to be lifted for glimpses of what might be occurring, for any sign of one of the robe's miracles. Murmurs of inquiry grew in volume and hope.

But the child remained lifeless, water pooling in her eye sockets, her head rocking awkwardly with her father's despairing sobs.

Taking command with a nod of her large head, Doña Josefa indicated that the couple should rise and take up their burden once more. And without protest, the young man offered his daughter to his wife for a final leave-taking kiss; then did the same himself while leaning over to return her to her coffin.

The wail that met his own lips made him nearly drop the child. Leaping to his feet and holding the baby at arm's length, he danced about as if he wished to flee but was chained to her, his face a study in terror.

With a scream that rent the astounded silence in half, the wife tried to rise from her knees but failed, throwing her arms out for her restored child; then slumping to the wet stones where she lay forgotten and unconscious. Doña Josefa scuttled back like a crab as her guardians crossed themselves and hastened to join her.

Across the grounds of the hacienda, hundreds of people began to rise to their feet in stupefied recognition of what had occurred before their very eyes, and the word swept quickly through the ranks to those who could not see.

The father, now holding the girl over his head with his mouth open to the rain, his gaze intent upon his daughter's face, cried aloud, "Jesus be praised! Christ be praised!"

Even from where he stood, Jim could see the color had returned to the girl's once-dead flesh, her wide-open eyes grown so white with vitality as to have a bluish tinge.

Rushing to seize the child, the family members passed her amongst themselves, laughing and crying, the little girl's own laughter reaching Jim's ears like the striking of crystal in a crowded dining hall.

Across the grounds of the hacienda, a thousand voices swelled and broke in a triumphant shout that drove the pigeons and bats into the sky, even as it silenced the howling monkeys in their treetops.

Jim looked to see that Brenda was crossing herself over and over, her bare knees mired in the mud. Before his very eyes she had become almost indistinguishable from everyone else in the encampment. He stumbled toward her in shock. Up on the veranda, the little girl's entire family was taking their turns to kiss the purple robe in gratitude for its saving power.

Remembered at last, the young mother had been revived and helped to her feet but not yet to her senses, as she would approach and touch her living daughter only to scream once more, fall to her knees calling upon God, then rise yet again to do the same. From the comfort of whichever relative now had her in their possession, the child laughed at these antics and clapped for more.

Jim placed a shaking hand on Brenda's shoulder as she turned her wet, reddened eyes up to his, her face beatific and strange. "Oh Jim," she breathed, placing a hand on his own, "what have we seen?"

A great tremor ran through his body and he shook like a dog throwing off the damp. "A trick," he replied hoarsely. "It's some kind of con...you know that. No one comes back from the dead."

Brenda raised herself to her feet using Jim's arm. The rain having let up, she pulled the makeshift shawl from her head and looked into her husband's face. "I'm not sure of what I know right now," she answered. "Are you...*really*?"

"*Yes*, yes I am. That family...that little girl, they're just *ringers*, Brenda. It was an act...a good one I grant you, but just a show for the gullible, the superstitious." He felt his resolve returning as he warmed to his subject. "They throw in a show like this every now and then to keep people coming, to keep them believing, and most importantly, to keep them *giving*—it's a scam. Come on, we're educated people, Brenda, we know better than this."

She considered his words for several long moments, then said, "Do we, Jim…do we really know better?"

"At best she was comatose, or in an epileptic state of some kind…catatonic, maybe. The rain probably woke her up," he finished, his own confidence largely restored. Now he just wanted to leave.

"We should be getting out of here." He looked around but Juan was nowhere to be seen. "I guess he thinks he got all the pesos from us that he can," he said, turning back to Brenda. "Let's find our way back to the…"

He stopped speaking, arrested by the image of his wife walking away from him to join the procession of believers, her blonde hair and fair skin making her stand out in the line of adherents. Yet even as he watched, she began to converse easily with the strangers around her, their camaraderie facilitated by their common experience, their shared, yet private, hopes and fears.

In that moment, Jim understood what he must do, what he had, in fact, been prepared for by his life, experience, and work, to do—expose the Christ cloak for the fraud it most surely was. And if in doing so, he were to have Brenda return to him as she truly was, as he knew her to be, then all other considerations were minor and unimportant.

The rain began once more as a steady miserable drizzle and Jim stumped away to find their unhappy driver. Glancing back, he saw that Brenda had placed the plastic over her head once more, and but for a glimpse of her blonde, highlighted tresses, she became indistinguishable from all the rest.

CHAPTER NINE

Father Pablo did, indeed, pray for guidance when he returned to the rectory after his dinner with the mayor, but if the Mother of God answered, he was unable to remember her words in the morning.

The effects of the tequila he had shared with the mayor rendered his actions of the previous evening into a hazy pantomime. Brief scenes returned to his struggling memory and throbbing head, but offered little illumination as to his role or intentions. He recalled that at some point he had raised his glass in a communal toast to the holy robe and had been roundly applauded, but now shook his swollen head painfully, ashamed at his lack of restraint and self-control.

What was even worse was his memory of having prayed before the unfinished altar of Our Lady of Guadalupe in a drunken state. Mercifully, he had no memory of his slurred and jumbled entreaties, only the sickening mortification that his blasphemous slobbering had been heard and duly registered in the ear of an omniscient God.

He had only just rinsed the vomit from his mouth when Señora Garza tapped at his door to awaken him for morning Mass. "Yes, yes," he called out, too ashamed to go to the door, "I'm awake—I'm up! Just leave the coffee by the door."

He hastily washed his armpits in a vain attempt to cleanse himself of the sins of gluttony and pride, but the stench clung to him like a hair shirt. "I am unworthy, Lord," he muttered over and over, even as he threw on his clothes and hastened to the sacristy to change into his vestments.

From without he dimly registered a rising murmur, even as he slurped and spilled his coffee down his shirt front. He could think only of his duties now—concentration and perfect adoration of the Host was his only chance of even beginning to atone for his sins of the night before, as he had no confessor. The absence of Monsignor Roberto De Jesus had deprived him of that simple consolation. But these thoughts were arrested as he burst through the door to the sacristy and was himself brought to a halt by the activity within.

The scene was all bustle and motion, as not one, but four altar servers struggled and twisted into their robes, while chattering excitedly as if it were Christmas Day. The oldest and most efficient of the four, the boy who had saved Father Pablo from choking on that painfully embarrassing Sunday, muttered impatiently, "You'd better hurry, Father, you're running late," then added with a smirk, "and you don't want to keep this mob waiting."

Even as Father Pablo took in this extraordinary turnout of assistants, so unusual for a school day, the murmur he had dimly noted from the rectory rose to a subdued roar within the confines of the small room. Cracking the door an inch, he peeked out, but could see nothing for the press of bodies that crowded the entry and extended into the nave and beyond. He fell back with a small cry, "My God, there must be a thousand people in there."

"That's not counting the ones on the plaza that can't get in," his eldest altar server assured him with perverse delight.

Father Pablo was suddenly assailed by vestments being thrust into his hands and thrown over his head. It appeared his young assistants would not brook dither or delay, but were determined that Father Pablo would be properly vested and delivered to the altar in a timely manner. Even as he protested at their rough handling, the bell began to ring the hour and with its cessation, voices within the church rose up in song—even the choir had convened! It *was* like a holiday, Father Pablo thought in astonishment.

Suddenly they were ready. As if in a dream, he found himself at the rear of the procession, following the upheld cross that parted the dense sea of humanity into a narrow channel. Arriving at the altar as the last notes of the hymn drifted up to the vaulted ceiling, they bowed in almost perfect unison then climbed the few steps to the altar. The silence that accompanied these simple acts was as complete as that following the clap of a great bell.

Turning and facing his people, Father Pablo intoned in a loud, confident voice, "In the Name of the Father, the Son, and the Holy Spirit."

Making the sacramental gesture of blessing, he saw its corresponding response repeated a thousand times over, rippling from the altar to the entryway and out into the plaza, where a thousand more imitated in faith what they could not hear nor see. Father Pablo's heart swelled with an unexpected joy, and the throbbing of his head diminished to a distant tapping, the dark smog within his brain swept away by a cleansing breeze.

For the first time in the short history of his ministry, he found himself smiling in pleasure at the people entrusted to his care. In that moment, and in contradiction of the great numbers of people that stood before him, he no longer saw his parishioners as a demanding, querulous, and faceless entity, but as something altogether finer and more kindred. No longer were they a threatening, incomprehensible presence but fellow travelers, vulnerable, confused, and yearning, just as he was. Their hunger for grace was a palpable clamor in the silence following his benediction and he felt like laughing aloud at this tardy revelation to his calling.

No wonder he had been so miserable for all these years, he thought, for in failing to see his relationship to his fellow man, he had condemned himself to a life of loneliness and solitary adversity. He needn't be alone! He was not alone! All were candidates for forgiveness—even he.

"The grace of our Lord Jesus Christ and the love of God and the fellowship of the Holy Spirit be with you all," Father Pablo said with pleasure.

"And with your spirit," the response washed over him like a new baptism.

The Mass proceeded without flaw or error on his part and his newfound confidence wavered but once, when he registered with a slight start that Doña Marisa was not at her accustomed place in the foremost pew. It pained him to think that she had been deprived of her seating by the throng of pilgrims that had arrived at their doorstep. With her deformed spine, she would never be able to stand throughout. Someone had undoubtedly offered her a seat, he assured himself, though he was unable to locate her as he let his eyes rove across the packed believers.

He did not deviate from the homily he had written the week before, in spite of the groundswell of fervency he felt rise from the anxious pilgrims, but found within the words that had seemed so prosaic when written a new and glowing meaning that had been hidden from his own eyes until now. His translation into the spoken word grew wings and soared, a tongue of flame that danced and illuminated.

When time came for the liturgy of the Eucharist, his drunken bleating at the feet of Our Lady returned to him once more, and the stain of that unconfessed sin rose up like bile in his throat. "I am unworthy," he thought once again, but added, "yet, I am all there is to answer, and Your people are hungry, O Lord, so I must feed them. Forgive me and do not punish them for my sins." He continued the preparation of the gifts without faltering.

After the dismissal, and as he stood in the entry to bid farewell to the faithful, Doña Marisa was suddenly revealed as the man he was shaking hands with strode away, unmasking the bowed figure he had concealed with his broad frame. Dressed in her perennial widow's black and leaning on her cane, she shuffled up to him like a dark reproach. The old dread came upon him and Father Pablo hesitated for just a moment before seizing her dry, thin hand. "God bless you, Doña Marisa," he whispered. "I was worried when I didn't see you in your usual place."

Her grey, bleak eyes met his and softened at his touch. "It was kind of you to notice, Father," she answered quietly, then added with her customary severity, "At least *one* of these fools had the decency to offer me his seat since they've taken over our church."

She freed her hand from Father Pablo. "You preached well today, Father." This was the first time he could remember her addressing him as anything but "Little Father."

"A big audience seems to bring out the best in you," she added after a pause, "I wouldn't have thought it."

"Thank you," he murmured in reply, "that's very kind of you."

"You're not going to spoil it all by encouraging these people, are you?" she asked flatly.

Father Pablo felt his old uneasiness return. "What do you mean, Doña Marisa?"

"You know full well what I mean—the talk is that you're about to step out there and bless this mob and their quest for the Holy Grail, or whatever it is. Is it true?"

Father Pablo caught himself stooping in unconscious servility to the older woman. Straightening with an effort and clearing his throat, he replied, "I intend to bless them for their faith. There's nothing wrong in that, I'm sure."

"You intend to bless their unsanctioned search for the superstitious, you mean." She took a deep breath and blew it out. "I had hopes for you during Mass today. I thought, 'Ah ha, at last he has seized his vocation.' You continue to disappoint— how can you be such a fool?" She turned from him and shuttled away through the crowd, her cane flicking dangerously.

Watching her depart, Father Pablo noted that even this great crowd of strangers gave her passage a wide berth. "Why does she haunt me so?" he wondered sadly, then asked himself, "Perhaps God has appointed her my conscience, made her my Socratic inquisitor—what must it feel like to finally please her?"

Shaking these thoughts from his mind, he made his way to the doors, his newfound confidence returning with each step. "The holy water…hurry…and don't forget the wand," he hissed at his sardonic altar server.

The boy gave him a surprised glance, the sneer vanishing at Father Pablo's unaccustomed vehemence, then turned and ran back to the altar for the items.

The scene in the plaza brought the priest up short. Thunderstruck, he wavered in the doorway as he took in the undulating mass of humanity that awaited him. "Holy Mother of God," he murmured.

The entire plaza was teeming with people—men, women, children, whole families of several generations, holding aloft their rosaries, or simply with upraised palms, awaiting his blessing. A number of homemade banners emblazoned with the names of faraway parishes waved in the breeze above the heads of the faithful. Some depicted the Virgin of Guadalupe, while others replicated the humiliation illustrated on the Centurions' leaflets.

Moving through the packed masses, the vendors were making the most of the occasion, selling hand-carved crucifixes of dubious quality, and glow-in-the-dark plastic rosaries in vibrant pinks and greens. Others, having hustled their grills from the Malecòn, charcoaled pork and chicken for those wishing to break their fast, their mouth-watering labors marked by aromatic columns of dark smoke that rose above the crowd in grey streamers. Teams of television crews focused their cameras on Father Pablo from several vantage points.

The streets that bordered the plaza were packed with every manner of vehicle panting and grinding to be away. Several tour buses were parked on the opposite side of the plaza, where they too added to the noise, smog, and confusion—their sides adorned with banners that read, "Ask and ye shall receive!"

"Well," Father Pablo thought a little worriedly, "the secret is certainly out." It was then he noticed Captain Barrera, with a rank of policemen, cordoning off the few steps that led down to the plaza from the church. He was clearly preventing the press of bodies from surging over Father Pablo.

As always, the captain appeared cool and remote, his dashing, uniformed figure half a head taller than the crowd he seemingly ignored. As his officers shoved and sweated in the morning sun, the captain calmly lit a cigarette, crossed his arms, and surveyed the scene. Apparently satisfied, he turned to look up at Father Pablo, a small, tight smile on his face, and twirled two fingers in the air to signal his approval to begin. As if cued by the policeman, both the altar boy and the mayor arrived at his elbows simultaneously.

The altar boy was seized with such nervous violence that some of the holy water sloshed over the side of the aspersorium. Father Pablo had never seen the boy so overwhelmed, and realized with guilty satisfaction that, at last, it was he that was in control. He patted the boy consolingly on the shoulder, causing him to start from his open-mouthed reverie of the seething plaza.

The mayor, on the other hand, his sash of office somewhat soiled but still proudly displayed, faced the great crowd with confidence, even joy. He waved several times to the pilgrims' loud ovation at his appearance, but refrained from addressing them. He indicated this by placing a hand to his mouth, then taking it away to point to Father Pablo, smiling humbly all the while. "Clearly…" he seemed to be saying, "…this is not my show, but Father Pablo's." The fruity odor of percolated alcohol exuded from his pores, reaching the priest's nostrils even above the stench of his own skin.

Nodding to Captain Barrera that he was ready to begin, Father Pablo smiled. The senior officer nodded in acknowledgement, then turned to speak to an American, or European, couple that had appeared at his side. They seemed to be listening intently to the captain, though the man occasionally waved the officer's cigarette smoke impatiently away from his face and grimaced for effect. It was this that reminded Father Pablo of his previous near-encounter with the foreign couple in Le Saint Bonnet café.

The man was large, taller even than Captain Barrera, and heavily built, powerful-looking and red-faced. His wife, or girlfriend, was also taller than any other woman present, with strikingly blonde hair that she wore loose and shoulder length, her long, slender legs exposed by the hiker's shorts she wore. The men nearest the couple allowed their eyes to travel her length appreciatively in spite of their surroundings, and appeared to be discussing her attributes in animated fashion. It seemed Captain Barrera was acting as their host and interpreter, and Father Pablo wondered briefly how they had met, his only memory of them being their extreme annoyance with the police captain at the café.

Feeling a slight nudge to his ribs, he found the mayor smiling at him inquisitively. Father Pablo cleared his throat, raising his right hand. The mob grew silent by degrees, and when at last they were hushed, he sketched the Sign of the Cross and began.

"My dear people, today we shared the Eucharistic Meal of Our Lord and Savior, and in doing so, we became brothers, even as we were strangers to one another only yesterday. So let me speak to you as family this morning."

Someone across the plaza shouted in the pause of his speech, and was answered by the diesel engines of the waiting buses chugging and coughing into silence. The people looked up at him in happy expectation. Gathering his courage, Father Pablo formed his next words carefully.

"The journey you are about to embark on to venerate the relic at Doña Josefa's is one of faith, and I cannot say what you will find there."

A murmur of concern rippled through the crowd at this lukewarm endorsement of their pilgrimage. The Americans' expressions grew perplexed, while Captain Barrera appeared slightly annoyed at Father Pablo's unexpected orthodoxy.

"Many amongst you are ill and others afflicted by injury and disease. Some, I am sure, suffer from sickness of the spirit and mind, while others, like me, are stained with sin which, like a cancer, poisons our relationship with our Creator and Savior. I cannot say with certainty what the properties are of this relic that is purported to be a piece of the purple cloak of Christ, as it is known. But I can say this much—God loves you, no matter your weakness or frailty, so do not fear loss or disappointment.

"Just this morning you partook of the miracle of bread and wine becoming the actual Body and Blood of Jesus Christ, and were made ready for salvation. Do not forget this as you go forth, but let it become your own holy garment and badge of true faith."

A puzzled silence ensued as Father Pablo paused to take the container of holy water from his young assistant. He withdrew the aspergillum, raising it aloft. "There," he thought, "I have not betrayed the archbishop's instructions." And with a downward sweep of his arm scattered droplets of the water across the front line of policemen and spectators, then swinging it sideways, completed the Sign of the Cross, spattering the faces of Captain Barrera and the American man.

Casually crossing his self, the captain withdrew his handkerchief and carefully patted his face dry, afterwards offering it to the shocked and incensed-looking older man. It appeared the woman had avoided the sprinkling altogether.

With that, Father Pablo descended the steps into the crowd, advancing through its middle and scattering the water every few feet. By the time he had circled the entire plaza and returned to the doorway of the church, the water was nearly gone and he felt as depleted as the silvered bowl.

Returning the items to his frozen altar boy, he faced the crowd once more. "Bow your heads for God's blessing," he called out, and a sea of dark heads bent in obedience. "Father, look down on these, Your people, and bless them and their pilgrimage of faith in the Name of the Father, the Son, and the Holy Spirit. Amen. Go in peace, my children."

It was clear to Father Pablo by the sullen mutterings of the pilgrims as they turned away that his meaning had not been lost on them. His hopes of treading the middle ground in the matter of the relic had not succeeded, and the people felt short-changed by the absence of his acclamation—they were much more intelligent than he had hoped and were not so easily fooled.

By honoring the strictures placed on him by the archbishop he had done his duty to the Church, but in his heart he felt that he had failed the faithful. After all, he thought, he had seen the face of Veronica made clean by her veneration of the cloak. Why deny what he had seen with his own eyes and felt within his own heart? Didn't the miracles themselves validate the authenticity of the relic? Yet, he had done his duty to the Church in spite of all this, though his vow of obedience offered scant consolation for what he feared was, in truth, moral cowardice.

Sighing, he turned to reenter his church when a voice rang out across the heads of the retreating masses. "Father, do you not believe in the holiness of the purple cloak of Christ?"

Father Pablo felt as if a bolt of conscience had been shot through his back, and thought longingly of how very close was the sanctuary of his church—just a few steps more and he would have escaped altogether.

As he turned once again, he found the mayor smiling in discomfort, his forehead perspiring freely. The crowd had slowed its steps and hundreds of heads were turning. Scanning the upturned faces for his interrogator, Father Pablo was unable to discern him and the question was not repeated. Captain Barrera and his American friends appeared keenly interested in his answer, as well.

Struggling for the words that would not betray his vows, he answered, "My belief is of no consequence—the relic is what it is, whether I profess belief in its authenticity and power or not. If someone fails to see, or believe, in the miracles wrought by Our Lady of Guadalupe, Fatima, or Lourdes, does that render them false and unworthy?"

The inquisitor wasted no time in responding, "What exactly then is the Church's position on this so-called Holy Garment?"

Father Pablo was able to see his antagonist clearly now, as the crowd had distanced themselves from his impertinence—he was a small, wizened man wearing a straw snap brim hat, a cigarette dangling loosely from the corner of his downturned mouth. He was making notes on a small digital device. Other reporters and television crews slowed their packing and several camera lenses swiveled towards Father Pablo.

"I cannot speak for Mother Church, as this is a local matter at this point," he replied primly.

"How about the archdiocese then, I can't imagine that Archbishop Valdes is ignoring this whole thing?" The man waited, fingers poised over his little keyboard.

"The archdiocese has no official position on the matter as of yet. It is being studied." Out of the corner of his eye, Father Pablo saw Captain Barrera nod his head toward the reporter. Instantly, several policemen began to make their way through the crowd toward the man.

"And you, personally, Father...what is *your* position, if I may ask?" The fingers hovered.

The crowd's silence became charged as they awaited Father Pablo's answer. He hesitated for several moments before answering, "I...*I, personally*...I believe—but, it is not without reservations that..."

The crowd did not require further clarification. The announcement swept through the pilgrims with cheers and alleluias, their previous festive mood instantly restored, even as the reporter was being hustled away by the officers. Many of their number applauded Father Pablo, while others hooted and whistled in excitement. A group of college students began to chant his name while waving their banners in enthusiasm, and the chant was taken up by the plaza as a whole. "Father Pablo, Father Pablo..." rang across the square to echo back from the government building across the street.

The priest felt his arm suddenly seized and uplifted in apparent triumph by the mayor, who beamed at the crowd, pumping his fist in the air. The altar boy fled into the church. "My God," Father Pablo gasped, "what have I done?"

Snatching his arm from the jubilant mayor, he rushed forward several steps to address the crowd, but the din drowned his words—they had heard what they had come for and had no need of further explanation—they knew his heart. In a haze of misery, he noticed Captain Barrera, still untouched by the uproar, shaking his handsome head in bewildered amusement, even as the American couple looked about them in shocked disbelief at the crowd's reaction, appearing on the verge of fleeing. With two simple words...*I believe...* he had laid waste all that had gone before.

Within minutes, it seemed, the plaza was deserted, as the last of the faithful formed up into processions and marched triumphantly into the exhaust of the departing buses and cars. Even before the last of them had vanished into the haze and dust, gulls that had circled the plaza previously unnoticed began to screech and fight over the scraps of meat and tortillas that had fallen onto the ground, fishing morsels of refuse from the overflowing trash cans.

Feral dogs, drawn to the scene by the aroma of the cooking meat, crept out from between buildings to aid the ravenous birds by overturning what receptacles they could and rooting out the most fetid garbage from their bottoms. When anything worthwhile was discovered, the dogs suffered swooping, aerial attacks by their feathered competitors, who often drew blood with their large, cruel beaks. Some of these, however, paid dearly for their boldness when they were snatched from the air to be instantly torn to pieces and devoured by the half-starved canines. Father Pablo watched this scene in a kind of stupefied, waking horror.

Turning for the church, he saw that the mayor, like his altar boy, had fled—no doubt having rushed off to head the procession to Doña Josefa's hacienda; now only the police captain and his new friends awaited him. Captain Barrera, unexpectedly, touched the bill of his hat to Father Pablo. "In deference to my newfound notoriety," Father Pablo thought disconsolately.

"I wouldn't want to be you when the archbishop reads the papers tomorrow," the captain said in greeting.

"No," was all Father Pablo could think to say.

He drew the priest a little apart from the Americans. "You never came to see me like I asked," the policeman stated evenly. "It's too bad, because if I had known then what you and your friends were up to out there at the hacienda, I might have saved you a lot of grief in the days ahead. Perhaps it's not too late."

Confused and disinterested, Father Pablo replied, "I don't know what you mean."

Smiling, Captain Barrera steered him over to the American couple. "Let me introduce you to Señor and Señora Arbor—they are from the U.S.A. This, my friends, is Father Pablo Diego

Corellas." He draped an arm possessively over the priest's shoulders.

The woman smiled sweetly at the dejected priest, offering her hand, "Please call me Brenda, Father." She almost curtsied, but caught herself. Father Pablo noted that her Spanish was quite good.

Giving her a quick glance of disapproval, her husband thrust his large, meaty hand into Father Pablo's own. The priest winced at the power of his grip. "James," the American stated flatly, releasing him.

"The pleasure is mine," Father Pablo assured them in a faint voice.

"Father," Captain Barrera resumed, even as the young priest noted that the captain, like Doña Marisa, was no longer using the diminutive he had so favored in the past, "Señor Arbor…James," he corrected himself with a smile, "has a special interest in the relic that may be of some use to you, especially after today's events.

"You see, he has only recently retired from a very prestigious research facility in America, and still maintains a controlling interest of company shares. He believes that this may allow him to be of some assistance to the Church in this matter."

Father Pablo gawked at the big American for a moment, unable to follow this strange turn of events. "What do you mean?" he asked, addressing Captain Barrera. "Assist in what manner?"

The captain said something in English to James, who replied gruffly and at some length in the same language. When he had finished speaking, Captain Barrera, for the first time in Father Pablo's experience of him, appeared uncertain. It seemed his command of English was not up to the task, and a flush of embarrassment entered his cheeks.

Brenda reluctantly intervened, "My husband, Father, has at his disposal the resources with which to determine the age of the cloth in Doña Josefa's possession; in fact, it may even be possible to determine in what part of the world it originated. He believes that this may go a long way in assisting the Church in its position on the garment."

"I see," Father Pablo said, turning this information around in his mind like a stone that might, unbelievably, contain a precious gem. "Yes, perhaps." This was what the archbishop had wanted after all, he thought.

"In light of today's events, this offer would be of service to you, personally, as well," Captain Barrera added lightly. "The sooner the matter is resolved, the better."

Barrera's observation was not lost on Father Pablo, who understood that in wrong-headedly endorsing the relic, however inadvertently, that he had brought the matter to a crisis. It was now in his best interest, as well as that of the Church, to authenticate the history of it, or disprove and disavow it and prevent the faithful from falling into superstition and heresy. Since he had provoked the issue, it now remained for him to resolve it.

"You would do tests?" he ventured cautiously.

"A number of them," the woman answered with some reluctance, it seemed to Father Pablo. "We would need a small portion of the cloth, an inch square, perhaps, nothing more."

"You have the equipment here to do this?" he asked hopelessly, already guessing the answer.

Chuckling sympathetically, Captain Barrera patted him on the shoulder. "Don't you wish it was that easy? No, Father, they'll need to take the sample back to the lab in the States. This is a great service and courtesy they are offering, and at no expense to the Church! In a few weeks, or months, at most, you'll have your answers. The archbishop will be delighted!"

Father Pablo had never heard the captain speak in such a cheerful, almost careless, manner, and was both puzzled and grateful. It was a wonderful offer he had arranged, but Father Pablo had little hope of its success—Doña Josefa and her Centurions would never agree to part with even the smallest piece of the relic, he felt sure. "I don't know," he mumbled uncertainly.

"Naturally," Captain Barrera continued, "they will need your assistance in negotiating with Doña Josefa. I hear she's a feisty old hen, but she'll listen to you, I'm sure."

"To be honest, Captain, it's very unlikely, but I did promise the archbishop that I would return to the hacienda to observe and interview some of the people who claim to have been cured. I'll try."

"That's all that you can do, but you'll succeed, Little Father, I have faith in you."

Father Pablo noted with discomfort Barrera's return to the usage of "Little," and glanced at him suspiciously. Could it be that the policeman was playing some angle that Father Pablo was not privy to? All the events of this day threatened to make his head spin, and his headache from the previous night signaled its return with a painful thumb in his left eye.

The captain added courteously, "Whenever you wish to visit the hacienda, please allow me to arrange your transportation, and don't worry, we are no longer concerned with the Guardians, or Centurions, or whatever they call themselves—now that we know what they are about—so long as they don't shoot at us anymore, that is." He winked quickly at the woman, and Father Pablo saw her look hastily at her sandaled feet.

The husband, his fleshy face screwed up in scowling concentration, was so engrossed in trying to piece together some sense of what was being said, that he missed this surreptitious exchange altogether.

"You can take Brenda and James with you, as well," the captain continued smoothly. "They have been out to the plantation once before but had no one to formally introduce them to Doña Josefa, so this would give them a chance to meet the old girl and take a closer look at the relic. It couldn't hurt, and might help. I find Mrs. Arbor quite persuasive, myself."

Father Pablo could see the flush climbing up from beneath Brenda's sleeveless, low-cut blouse, and that her husband was now regarding both she and the captain with bewildered suspicion.

"I will see what can be done," Father Pablo spluttered, then bid his fellow conspirators good day, hastening into the dubious comfort of the church.

CHAPTER TEN

In the days following Father Pablo's inadvertent blessing of the pilgrimages, he saw Progreso swell and transform beneath the relentless onslaught of believers. It seemed that no aspect of normal life was to be exempt. Traffic remained in gridlock almost continuously, despite the exhausted efforts of Captain Barrera's beleaguered officers, and only the kindly *Northers* of the season prevented the town from lying beneath a blanket of smog that might have rivaled México City's own. The din and grind of automobiles, along with the impatient sounding of their horns, quickly became a sad fact of life in the town.

No café or restaurant was without its line of hungry pilgrims from dawn to long after dusk had fallen on the tired port. Within the first days of the excitement, the open air market and its more sanitized competitor, the super Mercado, had been stripped of their goods by the famished hordes. Responding to the mayor's pleas, the governor himself prevented a serious food shortage by exerting his influence with the warehouses of Mérida.

However inconvenienced by these conditions, the natives nonetheless recognized and seized the opportunities they offered. Parking became a cottage industry—courtyards transformed into valet parking lots, while young children seized any curbside parking spots that became miraculously available, blockading them with trash cans or whatever obstacles that could be devised.

Inevitably, a frustrated driver willing to pay the day's going rate would be located amongst the hundreds of automobiles crawling by, a deal would be struck and the beckoning curb once again revealed like a shimmering oasis. It was exhausting but lucrative work.

Hundreds of home kitchens sprang into action as well, becoming *cocinas economicas*, and creating bag lunches by the overpriced dozens to be hawked from verandas. Mothers, grandmothers, and daughters, worked side by side, or in shifts, as the demand might dictate and their larders allow.

As Progreso's few hotels were quickly overwhelmed, households rushed in to fill the gap by renting hammock space in any spare rooms, sheds, or garages they possessed. Even roofs and verandas were surrendered, at agreed upon prices, to the shelterless faithful, and the sound of hooks being hammered into walls could be heard in every neighborhood.

As to those wanderers who sought a night's free respite on the beach, they found no solace there. Captain Barrera chose this time to enforce a dusty, seldom-used ordinance forbidding sleeping on the beach, and his men made twice-nightly sweeps to corral the miscreants and send them into the arms of Progreso's new class of entrepreneurs. Like the mayor's actions, his own were seen as beneficial to the common good and roundly applauded.

Father Pablo's bewilderment at Progreso's transformation was only compounded by his own—it appeared that in a single instant he had been elevated from clerical clown to ecclesiastical celebrity. Wherever he went in the streets of the town, he was greeted by native and stranger alike with warm familiarity, and if he tarried, he was soon jostled and swarmed by enthusiastic well-wishers. No one, it seemed, with the glaring exception of Doña Marisa, was immune to the exciting events that had overtaken the town and rippled outwards into the Yucatán from its new epicenter; neither would anyone listen, much less believe, that Father Pablo might entertain doubts or reservations concerning the purple robe and its miraculous power.

Whenever he attempted to explain the Church's unofficial position on the relic, he was met with winks and commiserative pats on the shoulder—they understood, they seem to say with these gestures, that he was caught between the proverbial devil and the deep blue, and were therefore free to intuit his unspoken approval. In spite of his earnest efforts, everyone went away well pleased with him; after all, they too had bosses, and knew what it was like to toe the company line.

As to the *company's* regional manager, Archbishop Valdes wasted no time in contacting Father Pablo after the events on the church steps, calling him by phone that very evening after watching the night's news on television.

"Father Pablo," he called cheerily down the line from Mérida, "the cameras like you! They always make me appear heavier than I think I should look, even under my cassock. But you...you looked quite dashing, I must say!"

"Yes...thank you, Your Excellency," Father Pablo spluttered. "I've been meaning to call you all day. It's just that I was trying to collect my thoughts, you see. I don't think I was fairly represented, exactly. This reporter put me on the spot, and I was taken by surprise and spoke before I had a chance to properly think through the correct answer. Events here, you see, have taken on..."

"Yes, dear boy," the archbishop murmured reassuringly, "I can well understand. You were pushed into the pool!"

"What? I was...I'm sorry, Your Excellency, I'm afraid I don't follow," Father Pablo replied.

"Didn't you ever go to the municipal pool when you were a boy?" The older man continued airily. "Inevitably, as one stands at the edge, pondering the warmth and depth of the water, some boy comes along and shoves you in! Usually, in my case, it was one of my older brothers. They never tired of such sport. And there I would be, shocked by the cold—I always remember the water being frigid—with water up my nose and desperately struggling to regain the surface. This never happened to you?"

Father Pablo hesitated, as his mind was a blank at the unexpected analogy, and he could conjure no such memories.

"Well, no matter, it has now. That reporter gave you quite a shove," Archbishop Valdes laughed. "Your expression, when you realized what you had said, reminded me of what mine must have been so long ago at the pool."

"Archbishop, you cannot imagine the response to what has happened here! People are flooding in from all over the Yucatán, perhaps from all over México," Father Pablo cried, the relief at his superior's kind understanding releasing the panic that had been building in him all day. "It's all beyond my ability, as you've seen now with your own eyes. You saw the crowds on television! Perhaps now you'll take a hand in this and relieve me…"

"Oh no, no, that wouldn't do, my boy," the older prelate interjected. "The cat's well out of the bag. And perhaps, now that your feelings are known, Doña Josefa might be amenable to allowing access to the relic. What do you think?"

He didn't wait for an answer before continuing. "Yes, it may be that your little admission may actually work in our favor. Who better to investigate now than you?"

Again he needed no reply. "So that's it then. Use your influence as God directs and all will be well, you'll see." He paused in thought, resuming confidentially, "Should Doña Josefa and her Centurions be moved to agree to an examination of the relic, you let me know and I'll quietly make some arrangements."

"Oh, yes, that reminds me," Father Pablo replied, "as luck would have it, there's an American here who claims to have the expertise and resources to assist us in the matter."

"An American," The archbishop muttered. "Is he Catholic?"

"I didn't think to ask." Father Pablo recalled the angry red face at the plaza. "I don't think so. Does it matter? He's some sort of scientific researcher. Captain Barrera vouches for him," he added.

"Well," the archbishop replied uneasily, "a healthy skepticism is certainly needed here, but...I'm a little fearful of inquiry without faith."

"I don't understand," Father Pablo answered. In his brief acquaintance with Archbishop Valdes he was not familiar with hesitancy on his part.

"Did you ever dissect a frog when you were in school?" the older man asked.

Father Pablo nodded in perplexed agreement, forgetting to speak into the mouthpiece.

The archbishop continued anyway, "It was disgusting, wasn't it? The profusion of guts and other unidentifiable bits spilling out from that thin skein of flesh...and the smell, good God! Yet, when you see a frog perched on a lily pad in a pond, taking in the sun and croaking contentedly away, it's really quite remarkable, don't you see? It's just one of God's creatures, and a small one at that, but nonetheless miraculous in its completeness." The older man paused as if taking in the whole scene he was describing, resuming sadly, "Under the scalpel it appeared anything but that, just a bundle of organs bound up in a pitiably vulnerable tissue."

"Ah, yes," Father Pablo agreed, while quietly wondering if the archbishop's mind was not becoming unhinged.

"In any event," the old man resumed briskly, "speak to Doña Josefa as soon as possible. As to the American, well...perhaps we should get to know him better before involving him too much. There, I guess that shows me for a skeptic, too. Keep in touch, Father Pablo, don't make me worry."

"I will," Father Pablo promised.

"Good—that's my boy!" The archbishop responded. "And Father, in the midst of all this, don't forget that flock of yours. I'm sure they love you very much and they'll need your guidance and strength in the days ahead...no matter how things turn out; especially if they don't turn out as they hope."

"Thank you, Your Excellency," Father Pablo said. "I'll do my best."

"And with God's help, that will be more than enough," the archbishop chuckled, suddenly happy again. "God bless you, Father Pablo." He hung up.

After a few moments of listening to the dial tone, Father Pablo did the same.

* * *

Captain Barrera sat across the desk from James Arbor and wondered if he had ever dealt with a person he disliked more. It seemed everything about the man was designed to elicit the policeman's poor opinion. His manners were abrupt and challenging, and were it not for the captain's secret designs depending so much on the good will of this contemptible man, he might have slapped his face for him long before.

Even his great size irritated Captain Barrera, casting his own stature (an asset that had served him well as an officer) into shadow. He found that it bothered him no end to have to look up to this man, and when they were on the street together he was certain that he had seen others also making such unfavorable comparisons, grinning behind their hands at him. It was almost too much.

To make matters worse, since Brenda had managed the introductions, a clever, if somewhat humiliating affair (an impromptu tour of the government building during which they had been recognized by a deeply apologetic Captain Barrera), Arbor had begun to drop in on the captain whenever it suited him. And being retired with nothing but time on his hands, these opportunities arose almost daily.

It was fine for him, Barrera fumed, but since the advent of the Holy Garment, he was daily confronted with new challenges to the order of the city.

Making little attempt at conversation, other than dry observations on how Barrera's department might be improved to American standards, the infuriating man would camp out for hours on end. To these observations, Barrera would smile and murmur, "Yes, that does sound interesting. Perhaps we'll look into that."

When the smoke from the policeman's cigarettes annoyed Arbor, he would simply rise and open windows for ventilation without so much as a by your leave, even throwing open his office door for all the clerks and secretaries to gawk at them from their desks and, no doubt, gossip about later.

On two different occasions, once when Captain Barrera had been requested to the scene of a brawl in one of the overcrowded cantinas, and another time when a man had gotten himself cut over a parking spot, the insufferable gringo had invited himself along. Unbidden, he had climbed into Captain Barrera's truck, sandwiching the senior officer between his driver and the American. His humiliation could hardly have been more complete. Though it had occurred to him to stop the vehicle and simply order the man out, he had refrained, and perhaps that was the most aggravating part of all—in order to further his plans and ambitions, he could not afford to alienate the powerful and connected foreigner. During these drives, he ruefully considered the price to be paid for deals with the devil.

"Well, Tony, what about this priest of yours," Arbor barked at him as Barrera hung up the phone—one of his sergeants was booking a Progreso pilgrim who was wanted in Vera Cruz for murdering his wife.

Riff raff were arriving from all over the country, Barrera mused.

The captain contemplated Arbor blankly for a moment longer; he so hated that *Americanization* of his name, not to mention the lack of respect implied by the dropping of his title of rank, something no well-bred Mexican would have done.

"What about him....*Jim*?" he asked in return.

Arbor hesitated for just a moment as well, evaluating this sudden familiarity on Barrera's part, and not liking it. "Goddamn, pay attention! What have we been talking about?"

"The relic, of course," Barrera answered, blowing out a stream of grey smoke, "what else?"

"Well...what do you think?" Arbor persisted. "Will he be able to get me a sample of this so-called purple robe of Jesus? Can we trust him?"

The captain took his time in answering his impatient guest— this was one way, he had discovered, he was certain to drive him to distraction. "Trust him," he repeated, appearing to give the question great thought. He carefully stubbed out his cigarette. "He is a priest," he pronounced at last.

Arbor snorted and shook his large head. "Meaning what, exactly?"

Barrera ran a manicured hand along his jaw, feeling the stubble of a long day. "He answers to God and the Church, though not necessarily in that order. On the plaza, he answered to God; I suspect since then he has answered to the Church." The captain chuckled quietly at the thought of the harried little priest.

Arbor rose suddenly, causing his chair to slide backwards over the marble floor. "For God's sake," he muttered, "you cannot get a straight answer in this country!" He took the few steps required to reach the open window and leaned against the sill with both hands. Barrera watched him from the corner of his eye.

After a few moments of studying the activity in the plaza, the American swiveled his head to regard his collaborator. "Look, Barrera, I came to you with a proposition—you help me obtain a piece of this *miracle* cloth, and I see to it you become one of our V.P.'s of Latin American operations with my corporation…have I got that right?"

Barrera's phone began to ring, but he ignored it, knowing his secretary would answer for him. "Yes, Jim, that is exactly right," he replied.

"Well then," Arbor resumed, turning around to face the policeman, his expression one of slight amusement, "should you fail to produce, or jerk me around on this thing, then Brenda and I will be out of here in one week's time, as planned—but not before I've had a little sit-down with the mayor. Follow me?"

Nodding stiffly, Barrera understood that his dislike for James Arbor was richly reciprocated.

"You're a big deal in this little burg," Arbor went on, "but that's where it ends. Back in the real world—the States, you'd be nothin' without me…just don't forget that…*comprende?*"

Barrera felt the blood draining from his face, but replied smoothly, hating himself, "Yes, Jim, I understand completely."

Clearing his throat, he began fishing the packet of cigarettes from his tunic pocket, but anger made his hands shake so much that he quit mid-gesture. "You needn't worry, Jim, a sample will be obtained and your company will gain great—what is the English word for it?—celebrity, I think."

This was not the word he had been searching for, but his emotions were choking his brain and it was all he could think of. "The newspapers, television networks, everybody will be interested. Publicity equals money in the U.S.A., no? And you, Jim, you will be a big shot again—*El Toro Grande*."

Arbor continued to look out the window for several more moments, then said, "I don't give a damn about all that," and ambled back over to Barrera's desk. Appearing suddenly distracted, he seized a framed photo of the captain's family and began studying it intently.

It showed a younger Barrera in dress uniform, his lovely wife at his side looking proudly up at his face. His five girls, all arrayed in white dresses, surrounded them like a bouquet of gardenias. It appeared they were standing in front of the church on the plaza. The late afternoon sun was making them squint slightly, but their teeth shone like the ivory keys of a piano against the soft brown of their skin.

Shaking his head slightly, Arbor asked, "What was the occasion?"

Barrera had no need to see the photograph to recall the day. "It was the day of my promotion to captain."

"They look very proud of you," Arbor said quietly, still studying the family in the picture. "Is that the church behind you?"

"Yes," Barrera assented, growing a little uneasy at Arbor's absorption with his family.

"Why the church…why not the steps of this building, it is where you work, after all?" Arbor set the picture back on the desk with an unaccustomed reverence.

"We had gone there to receive a blessing from Monsignor Roberto for the occasion." Barrera carefully realigned the framed photograph to the angle he was accustomed to. "You've not met him, he was our pastor. He's now recuperating in Mérida from a heart attack. The young priest I introduced you to in the plaza is only filling in for him. He's not very good," he concluded.

"He looks like an idiot," Arbor agreed without enthusiasm. He seemed to have wilted in the last few moments. "If you ask me, you've pinned your hopes on a slender reed."

Barrera was not familiar with the saying, but nonetheless took its meaning. "I rely on no one," he assured Arbor. "If Father Pablo cannot, or will not, assist us, I have other avenues that can be explored."

"I just bet you do," Arbor said, turning wearily for the door, his sudden deflation alarming Barrera more than his previous threats. Pausing at the door, the American pointed at the photograph he had been examining so closely just moments before. "Your wife reminds me of my own a few days ago in the plaza—only Brenda wasn't looking at *me*, was she?"

Barrera kept his expression blank to hide the shock he felt crawling across his scalp like ants.

"You have a beautiful family, Tony, but Brenda is *all* I have." Barrera watched the huge man appear to shrink and grow old before his eyes. "Don't bite off more than you can chew, *amigo*; don't try to screw me over."

He stepped out, then leaning back in, added, "We can't keep waiting for that priest. I want to go out there tomorrow and see if the old woman will bargain. See what you can do and give me a call at the hotel."

"Yes," Barrera agreed through teeth clamped in tension, "I'll make some arrangements."

Arbor didn't bother to close the door behind him.

CHAPTER ELEVEN

Pulling the battered Ford to the edge of the road some two miles from their destination, Manny climbed out proclaiming, "Sorry, Father, but this is as far as we can go. We have to hoof it the rest of the way."

Astounded, Father Pablo surveyed the gridlock of abandoned cars that sat three abreast and extended up the sandy road until lost from sight. It appeared to the young priest as a scene from the end of the world—what any given road might look like on that day the mighty Archangel Gabriel blows his trumpet, snatching up the living in the very moment of their next breath. Standing there in the eerie silence, he pondered the inert river of metal.

As Manny finished locking the doors and joined him, a parrot began to screech and cry like the last soul left behind on the newly desolate earth. Father Pablo shivered.

"It's a mess, isn't it?" Manny observed with good humor; then began to trudge ahead, leading the way through the labyrinth of baking vehicles. When Father Pablo had sent word to Veronica that he would like to return, once again avoiding Captain Barrera's silken hospitality, Manny had arrived alone to drive him out to the hacienda.

The priest, hampered by the satchel containing the sacramentals, hurried to catch up to Manny as he glided effortlessly ahead through the maze. "What's happened?" Father Pablo gasped, already wilting in the close humidity of the overhanging trees and the heat radiating from the near molten cars. "Where are they?"

Laughing, Manny called back, "It's like this every day now, Father—by dawn they start arriving and by noon it's like this. I don't know why they stop then, but they always seem to...thank God." He strode on as Father Pablo struggled to keep up. "If you think this is bad, you should see what happens after the veneration of the robe, when they try to leave. You don't want to be here then," he assured the already tired priest.

"No," Father Pablo gasped, stumbling against a car, then snatching his hand away and blowing on it.

After some twenty minutes of struggling to keep up with the young Indio's pace, Father Pablo called out, "Manny, did you think to bring any water?"

Slowing to a stop, Manny unslung a small sack from his shoulder. He produced a bottle from within it, offering it to the panting priest. "It's too bad priests have to wear black all the time," he observed solemnly, as Father Pablo greedily gulped down the liquid.

"Yes," Father Pablo replied between swallows, "I think I agree."

A half an hour later they arrived at the gateway of Doña Josefa's hacienda where the sea of cars lapped up to the crumbling walls. Only a small area at the gateway itself had been kept clear by the Centurions. There, Father Pablo could see that the guard had been tripled since his previous visit of only a few days before.

He arrived panting and gulping for air, clinging to Manny's shoulder like an old man, but managed to gasp, "Let's rest...for a few moments...here." His legs were shaking and he stumbled over to a car shaded by a large mango tree. "Here...a few minutes," he pleaded. Manny nodded as Father Pablo settled himself onto the hood of the vehicle, his perspiration spattering down onto the sandy, churned-up soil.

Arriving noiselessly at his side, the Indio offered him the remainder of the water, which he shamelessly gulped down without so much as a thought for his companion. After a few moments, the young priest began to feel himself once more. "Thank you," he murmured contritely.

"No problem," Manny assured him.

Wiping the sweat from his stinging eyes, Father Pablo surveyed the scene before him. The guards, he noted, had not just increased in number, but appeared to have altered somewhat in both character and appearance. Before, they had been alert, but relaxed, and even with their old armaments had not evinced a very menacing façade. These, however, sported automatic rifles that Father Pablo recognized as AK-47s, and their demeanor was both sullen and tense; even with Manny at his side, he felt fearful of approaching these ferocious-looking guardians. Though they had nodded in recognition to his escort, they continued to cast suspicion-laden glances at the priest, and Father Pablo felt his mouth dry up and his bowels gurgle alarmingly.

"Doña Josefa is expecting us?" he managed to gasp at his companion.

"Yeah," Manny replied, as placid as always. "You ready now?"

Nodding reluctantly, Father Pablo heaved himself to his feet once more, and summoning his less than adequate supply of courage, followed Manny through the milling Centurions, who parted without comment to let them pass.

As they entered the estate, Father Pablo asked, "Has something happened?"

Manny took a few moments to reply, "There've been a few incidents."

"Incidents…?" Father Pablo parroted.

"Yeah," Manny agreed. "There're a lot of people coming here," he added unhelpfully.

Turning back from a last look over his shoulder at the Centurions, Father Pablo was confronted at once with evidence of Manny's understatement: The second-growth forest that had sprung up from the untended grounds and sheltered the earlier pilgrims had itself been subsumed by the voracious onslaught of the new. Every tree and sapling had been felled to provide the cooking fires of the hordes of faithful that stretched out before Father Pablo's eyes. Columns of dark smoke arose here and there like the markers of barbarian encampments, their siege having stalled at the very steps of Doña Josefa's tottering mansion, newly-naked in the distance. The aroma of greasy meat blended unpleasantly with the pervasive stench of open sewage and, once again, Father Pablo felt his innards twist uncomfortably.

"Holy Mother," he breathed.

"Yeah," Manny agreed once more.

Undeterred, however, he plowed on through the closely packed peoples with Father Pablo stumbling along in his wake. Even in the docile Manny, Father Pablo perceived an impatient contempt for these new arrivals as he shouldered his way through them. The chorus of curses and challenges their passage evoked, however, fell suddenly silent as the outraged parties recognized the purple sash around the Indio's waist. Their hot looks of anger followed him even so, and Father Pablo hastened to keep up with his guardian, lest he be left behind to answer for this Centurion's arrogance.

Drawing nearer the residence, Father Pablo observed several portable toilets, their doors sprung and gaping, their putrid contents overflowing into the surrounding earth—failed attempts, he surmised, at providing for the pilgrims' more earthly requirements. One lay on its side, looking both absurd and threatening.

He noticed that the press of humanity only allowed those near these now-useless receptacles to edge but a few feet from their spewing filth. How they endured the nauseating odor and the clouds of flies they drew he was at a loss to understand, and observed with disgust the naked footprints of children in the chemically-tinged sludge. His own footsteps became cautious and mincing.

The din and babble of the restive mob rendered conversation with Manny impossible, and they passed from the blaring sphere of broadcasted salsa music into the concussive orbit of rap songs in enforced silence. Occasionally, a chorus of "Salve Regina" or "Te Deum" might be heard drifting above the crowd like the phantom voices of more distant and mysterious times. At last, they reached the casa.

Here, they found the veranda abandoned but for the Centurions, who, like their compatriots at the gates, had proliferated in number, sporting the new military rifles which they wore on slings and cradled ominously against their chests. The crucified Christ remained also, staring sadly down on his militant protectors and the noisy press of humanity that seethed beyond. Doña Josefa's chair was empty, and the carved box that contained the reliquary was nowhere to be seen. Even the pigeons appeared to have fled.

"Everyone's inside," Manny answered Father Pablo's unspoken question, ascending the low steps. The priest hurried after him.

Manny exchanged a few words with his fellows and they were allowed passage, the barrels of the rifles swinging slowly over the crowd as the Centurions parted for them; then reformed ranks like a closing curtain.

After the bright, unfiltered light outside, the darkness inside the entry hall fell like an eyeless hood over Father Pablo's face, and he halted involuntarily. Manny's footsteps continued down the cool passageway until the priest called out, "Manny, wait! I can't see!"

The soft padding of the Indio's feet reversed and drew near again, then Father Pablo felt his arm gently seized. "Just a moment," he pleaded, "my eyes need to adjust. How can you see your way?"

"Memory," Manny replied in his laconic, amused manner, tugging Father Pablo along.

As they made their way toward the rear of the great house, Father Pablo's eyes began to adjust to the new conditions and, like ghosts, furniture and other objects began to materialize and emerge from the greater darkness. A row of ornately carved, stiff-backed chairs lined one wall of the hallway like sentries long-forgotten at their posts. On the opposite wall were hung two portraits done in oils, one of a stern, balding, mustachioed man in a black suit; the other depicting a homely, sallow-faced woman in a white gown and mantilla that might have been her wedding dress but for the young girl clinging possessively to her skirts.

The child appeared tiny, almost dwarf-like, in what, even in the dim light, seemed to Father Pablo a crude rendering. In contrast to her parents' studied formality, revealing little but their class and the outward appearance they wished to present to the world, the child's pinched face was apprehensive, perhaps fearful. The artist's heavy, stolid brushwork had recreated the tiny Josefa as an ugly, ill-proportioned doll. Clearly, the patron's mandate had precluded the artist from softening the impact of the image, and it saddened Father Pablo to think that Doña Josefa's own father had chosen this portrait for her posterity.

The formidable Doña Josefa, Father Pablo now realized, was barely a foot taller than she had been at nine, perhaps ten years old—she had not shrunk with great age, but had failed to outgrow her child's body.

The only beauty the artist had managed to capture in his unhappy task was the matron's shimmering white dress, which floated out from the dark background with a life of its own. It seemed to Father Pablo that the frightened dwarf-child clung to this lace confection, not her discomfited mother, as to a lifeline that might draw her forth from an uncertain world. He continued past this grim triptych with a heart grown heavy in his chest.

Manny and he progressed past murky, unused rooms containing little but broken, dusty chairs and lopsided settees, their burst cushions alive with mice. Leaves and other, less recognizable debris filled the corners of some rooms. It appeared to Father Pablo that the mansion was shrinking to better fit the proportions of its mistress.

As they approached the very rear of the house, a high-pitched voice called out, "Who's there? Is that you, Manny? Did you bring that silly priest?"

"Yes, Doña Josefa, I have him with me," Manny answered pleasantly without raising his voice.

From out of the grey at the corridor's end, two Centurions arose from their rickety kitchen chairs and slid them aside to allow Father Pablo and Manny to pass. One of them politely opened the door to the kitchen for them; even so the little priest had to turn sideways to sidle past them in the suddenly crowded hallway, frightened he would bump their rifles.

The old lady awaited them within, in a room her parents and she would have been unfamiliar with during the heyday of the hacienda. She sat at the head of the small table with Veronica and her brother to either side. An unfamiliar person leaned back against the wall in a chair to Veronica's left, his long, thin legs dangling from the tipped piece of furniture to jerk and bounce with an unheard rhythm, his face in shadow.

"Good afternoon," Father Pablo announced uncomfortably. "God bless all here." Drawing the Sign of the Cross in the air, he smiled particularly at Veronica. She dropped her eyes, but even in the kitchen's early twilight, he could see that no blemish remained upon her face, and that her skin glowed as if lit from within. Fumbling for a chair, he found it difficult not to stare at the transformed, and now lovely, young woman.

As he settled himself, he became aware of the strong odor of tequila that pervaded the room, and that a jug sat in the middle of the table. Cups of old and chipped china rested before each of the table's occupants but Veronica. Father Pablo found Hernando regarding him slyly through heavy-lidded, half-closed eyes, a loose, dangerous grin on his face.

Wagging a finger at the priest, he slurred, "Shame on you, Father. That's my sister, you bad monkey."

Before Father Pablo could protest, Doña Josefa challenged him, "What will you do now, little priest? You've seen them out there! Will you take them back with you when you leave?"

"Take them back?" Father Pablo repeated stupidly. "Doña Josefa, I didn't send these people here. Surely you know that?"

"I know what Hernando told me, and he was there at the plaza. You were preening like a little turkey cock in front of the cameras! How proud your mother must be of her famous little priest! Did you see what you've done? How could you not, wading through that mob and their filth? They're nothing but a bunch of gawkers at a sideshow. They shit where they eat, those animals!" She halted for breath.

Father Pablo remained still, shocked into silence by the old woman's vehemence. He saw Veronica watching his reaction and thought he could detect a trace of sympathy in her large eyes, but she too remained quiet. He understood now the air of defeat and fear he had felt upon entering the grounds of the hacienda—he had stumbled into a council of the besieged.

Hernando leaned over to seize the jug, pouring a little of its contents into Doña Josefa's cup. He spilled some onto the tabletop. "Drink this, Auntie, and calm yourself," he murmured.

"I'm no one's aunt," she replied automatically. "And if *you* get any calmer you'll fall off your chair."

Laughing quietly as he refilled his own cup, Hernando answered, "It's not far to the floor." He slid a cup to Father Pablo and made to pour, but the priest waved it off.

"You see, good Father," he resumed smoothly, after taking a sip of his own, "it would appear that our little show has outgrown its venue. I'm sure you noticed that on your way in— all those believers you had to walk over? It seems that they won't take *no* for an answer. They're not at all interested that Doña Josefa cannot stand out there in the sun and rain from sunup to sundown each and every day. I doubt even you could do that, Father. No, they came for the purple robe of Christ, and the purple robe they must have.

"We've tried denying them, but that didn't work, either. They waited us out, you see. In fact, things got a little ugly. Some of Manny's boys had to crack a few devout heads before it was over.

"Even so, they stayed put, and eventually, we had to give in. They wouldn't leave otherwise. Yet, even when they do, they are replaced by still more. You can see our dilemma I'm sure...after all it was you that threw the door wide open, in a manner of speaking, of course."

"I want them all to leave us alone. I want them to go away," Doña Josefa pouted. "They're like a plague—a biblical plague of locusts! They've eaten my beautiful land right down to the ground! Please, Father," she pleaded a little drunkenly, "Speak to them—send them back!"

If Father Pablo had been shocked earlier at the old woman's vitriol, he was now shamed by her pleas. His own words floated back to him on a wave of self-disgust—*I believe…*

How easy it had been to abandon responsibility and utter that phrase for the enthusiastic crowd, and how pleasant it had been to bask in the warmth and camaraderie of their response. Even as he recalled that moment, he could not deny the pleasure its memory brought him—that sensation of belonging, of no longer being apart and alone. He had been wanted.

Was that why he had said those words, he wondered? Did he truly believe in the authenticity and efficacy of the Holy Garment? Or had it simply been a moment of weakness?

Looking around at its retinue of keepers and the state they had been brought to, as well as the waste and devastation that had washed up to their door like a toxic sea, it no longer appeared very clear. Even Veronica's burnished face seemed flimsy evidence of the supernatural here in this dark room, surrounded by the needy, relentless humanity that feasted, swilled, and shat at their very doorstep. Had Christ Himself faced such peoples on the Mount, he wondered? Was this why he had performed the miracle of the loaves and fishes—to satiate a heaving, demanding mob?

Clearing his throat, Father Pablo spoke at last, "I can see now what I have done. It was foolish of me, but in my defense, they were coming all the same. Though, I acknowledge, by counting myself amongst the believers, and saying so publicly, my words were construed as an endorsement by the Church itself and, so I am told, were broadcast all over México…I can see the result. I was very weak and foolish, and anyone who knows me would not have been surprised."

"I wasn't," Doña Josefa agreed, "and I had just met you."

Veronica finally spoke, "Father Pablo, the endorsement of the Church, or even of yourself, as a priest, was never asked for; I told you as much. The purple cloak stands on its own, supported by the very power of Christ Jesus Himself. We, here at this table, know this. The Church's opinion cannot change that one way or the other. That was never the point.

"When I approached you at the rectory, it was never for that. Mistakenly, I thought you sought what we all did…" she swept her arm over the table "…to be close to our Savior. 'Ask and ye shall receive,'… remember?"

Father Pablo nodded weakly, saying nothing.

Veronica continued, "These people you've sent never ask—they demand. A pilgrimage must begin in the soul, Father, you know that, but these folks arrive with empty sacks to be filled, that is all. Most just want good fortune…we could more easily hand out rabbits' feet."

"Yet," Father Pablo ventured, "the miracles…the cures, they continue to occur, yes?"

Veronica appeared to give this thought before answering, "In many cases, yes, but not always. Some go away very disappointed."

"So long as they go away," Doña Josefa mumbled sleepily from her chair. Her chin barely reached the table's edge, and Father Pablo thought she resembled an ancient doll, out of fashion and long-discarded.

"One fellow with a speech impediment tried to seize the reliquary from Doña Josefa when his speech went uncured," Hernando chimed in. "It was quite a scene, but I must say, Doña Josefa held her own and never let go, though he was shaking her like a maraca."

"It's a family heirloom…its mine," Doña Joseph complained to no one in particular.

"Of course," Hernando continued, "after the Centurions threw him down the steps and the crowd started in on him, I doubt very much whether his impediment continued to concern him. Before it was all over, Manny's boys had to rescue him from the mob."

Hernando's attention swiveled to his Indio friend leaning silently against the wall. "What did you all do with that nasty fellow, Manny? I never saw him again after he was hustled away."

Manny returned Hernando's sardonic scrutiny without speaking until Father Pablo broke the uncomfortable silence.

"Do you perceive a difference in those favored with those denied?" he asked Veronica.

"No, Father," Veronica answered frankly. "The difference must be in their hearts, because it certainly has nothing to do with their appearance or status—the poor are sometimes cured where a rich man is denied, the ugly favored over the beautiful. Often, strangely, the opposite is true."

"Not so strange," the priest said. "Perhaps those that did not receive a cure have more to learn from their sufferings. Does not Christ teach us that suffering is a part of life, and do we not benefit from offering up that suffering and pain for the salvation of our souls? Perhaps we are better off enduring the hurts of this world to ensure a place in God's Kingdom in the next."

Father Pablo's speech was met with silence and Veronica's downcast face.

"Oh," he cried, as the insensitivity of his statement struck home. "No, I didn't mean it was better, as such, just that for *some* it may be required for the sake of…"

"Good one, Father," Hernando exclaimed cheerfully. "Give her hell for being cured; she can't possibly have suffered enough!"

"You're an idiot," Doña Josefa added. "Get out of here and take those people along with you," she hooked a horny thumb at the outer wall, "and don't come back."

Father Pablo instinctively reached for Veronica's hand, stopping short when he saw the tears on her newly smoothed cheeks. He *was* an idiot, he thought.

He turned to face the old woman, saying, "Doña Josefa, even if I leave, those people will not follow me, no matter what I say. You must understand that. They are here for the relic; whether they are worthy or not, I cannot judge, but I cannot make them go now."

"There's not much you *can* do, is there, priest?" Doña Josefa hissed.

"One thing, maybe," a hoarse, raspy voice came from the darkened corner of the room where the young man drummed his feet in the tipped-back chair, "you could let him take the relic to Mérida, or México City, and get it out of here."

Surprised, Father Pablo peered at the young man he had forgotten during the heated discussion. When the speaker struck a wooden match to light his cigarette, the cunning, ratty face of Juan Alcante glowed in its nimbus.

"Yes…yes," Father Pablo stammered in surprise, "if you would allow me to place it in the keeping of the archbishop, just temporarily, of course, then there would be no reason for people to keep coming here, you would be left in peace."

After all, he thought, this is what he had been instructed to do in the beginning, and now it would not only serve the cause of the Church and the faithful, but would certainly improve the situation at the hacienda. Even so, the support of Juan Alcante made him uneasy.

"No," Doña Josefa asserted, "I told you before, it's a family heirloom, and I don't want a pack of strangers, priests or no, pawing over it."

She crossed her arms imperiously over her flat, brocaded chest, but the fear of the mob revealed itself in the quivering of her chin and in the white strain of her leathery features.

"Then you'll just have to make peace with your new tenants," Juan stated flatly, dropping the snuffed match onto the tiled floor.

"The relic will still belong to you," Father Pablo assured the frightened old woman. "I promise you. It would simply be in the safekeeping of the archdiocese while studies were being made. Afterwards, if you still wished, it would be returned."

"Tests, you mean," Doña Josefa quipped. "Your boss wants to run some kind of tests, with chemicals and such. What kind of church needs scientific proof? What happened to faith, and allowing the Holy Spirit to proclaim the inner truth of a thing? Or don't you churchmen care about such things any longer?

"Oh yes," she cried, warming up to her subject, "I know a few things myself, even if I am an old woman, and maybe I know a few things more than a snot-nosed, young priest who wasn't even born here!" Tears stood in her filmy eyes.

"Maybe he's right," Hernando said quietly, sounding sober for the first time since Father Pablo had arrived. "What's the harm, after all? We all know the truth of the purple cloak, so there is nothing to fear in their tests. And you, Little Mother," he turned to Doña Josefa and stroked her hand, "you need to get out from under this thing—the strain is turning you old before your time! Look at you! If you keep this up, I will have no choice but to chase other women."

"You're ridiculous," she assured Hernando, "and more than a little tipsy. You're as bad as all men—worse." The tiny woman gawped grimly at the stained tabletop, even as the corners of her lips curled up in amusement. "And don't drink any more of my tequila, you're cut off," she proclaimed, removing her hand from beneath his, even as a blush faintly colored her reptilian cheeks.

Juan Alcante spoke once more in his odd, sibilant voice, "If the Church doesn't suit you, Doña Josefa, you might want to consider other alternatives: There's an American here from a big research firm in the States that's interested, so I've been told. You might want to consider something along those lines. You wouldn't have to worry about any monkey business from the Church; he's just interested in determining the robe's age and origin, and he would give it back when he's done. He would only need a small piece of the cloth for testing and would probably pay a lot of money for the privilege, as well." Glancing around the ancient kitchen, he added, "You could use it."

Father Pablo started at the mention of the Americans—*how would Juan Alcante know anything of them*? Veronica spoke before he could inquire.

"Juan, I can't believe you! Listen to yourself, you of all people! To suggest that the purple robe be placed in the keeping of some research company in another country! Darling, think about it."

Father Pablo's head snapped around at this last—had she actually called the insidious Juan Alcante, *darling*? Of all the strange events of this day, the hidden world behind this revelation made his head swim.

"Think about what?" Juan asked, eyeing the jug of tequila hungrily, but making no move toward it. "I'm not suggesting she give it away, am I? It's just a loan…for money. Like your brother said, what is there to be afraid of, no matter who has it?" He ground out his cigarette on the tiles.

Veronica glanced at her brother who arched an eyebrow at her teasingly. "My brother is an idiot, sometimes," she assured Juan, "but that doesn't mean you have to be one, too. Think of what it has done for us, the robe—my face, your…addiction," she cast a nervous look at Father Pablo. "It doesn't seem right to place a relic of Our Lord and Savior in the hands of a bunch of secular scientists, don't you see? They have no faith—it feels…sacrilegious."

Leaning back in his chair once more, Juan fished for another cigarette. "Perhaps," he conceded. "Your face, yes, that's really something, I guess. But...my drug habit...," he threw a look of defiance at Father Pablo, "...well, let's be realistic—I had already come out to the country to try and kick it before you...before *I* venerated the Garment. It's kind of hard to see where one begins and the other leaves off."

Glancing once more at his girlfriend, he found her poised to protest. "I get your point though, I'm not stupid, girl." He got his cigarette lit and blew a steady stream of smoke toward the ceiling while his heels resumed their impatient tattoo on the grimy floor.

Outside, the murmur of the crowd seemed to swell with impatience, and Doña Josefa looked fearfully at the nearest wall as if they might come crashing through. With a hop, she dropped onto the floor, only her face visible above the tabletop and said, "You all seem to forget that the relic is mine and I'll do with it whatever I think is best."

Trundling over to the only closet in the room, she pulled it open as Manny detached himself from the wall, joining her. "But one thing you can be sure of, Juan Alcante," she continued, "I will not be turning it over to Barrera's *Americanos* for thirty pieces of silver. That policeman had the audacity to approach me on their behalf this morning and seemed surprised that Father Pablo had not already paved their way, but I refused to meet with them."

Her fierce little eyes searched Father Pablo's face for a moment before fixing on Juan and continuing, "Did he now send you to wheedle and bargain on their behalf? The only mystery to me is that you would speak for them...or is it for the captain? It seems everyone is intent on having what is mine."

Juan answered in a voice clotted as sour milk, "I know Barrera, if that's what you mean...he's arrested me a few times along the way, so we're on speaking terms. As to the relic, I was just trying to be helpful." Looking to Veronica, he shrugged his thin grasshopper shoulders. Her expression was wary and unreadable.

Reaching up to a shelf, Manny brought down the carved box that held the reliquary, and in the lengthening silence said, "I'll carry it for you, Little Mother."

"Very well, then," Doña Josefa answered tiredly. "Let's get started before they start throwing stones through the windows." Turning to Father Pablo, she studied him once more, as if making a decision; then asked in a resigned tone, "Why don't you join us, Father? Perhaps if they see a man of the cloth they'll behave themselves."

He nodded his agreement and they went out to the believers.

CHAPTER TWELVE

Father Pablo stood next to Doña Josefa, but some several yards distant, as if to declare that he had no official position on the relic. Even so, as Doña Josefa had hoped, the pilgrims were well-behaved, and Manny's fellow Centurions were not called upon to quell any disorders as the thousands of seekers crept forward to venerate the purple cloak.

At the near edge of the crowd, Father Pablo noticed the American couple and Captain Barrera. It seemed to him that the men looked at him disapprovingly, and the young priest blushed at having, yet again, avoided the captain and his suggestions of companionship, as well as having done nothing to help them in obtaining a sample of the Passion relic.

The woman, Brenda, stood apart from her escorts, her arms folded across her chest, watching the seemingly endless procession of anguish and desire.

For hours on end they undulated forth, six and seven abreast, until halted at the foot of the steps by the armed Indios and separated into family groups or solitary believers, before being sent on to Doña Josefa. Some were pushed along in wheelchairs, while others hobbled awkwardly on crutches.

The most fervent amongst them insisted upon ascending the rough limestone steps on their knees, fingering their rosaries and praying the decades as they scraped along. When at last they stood before the reliquary, their eyes glistening with hope and devotion, Father Pablo winced at the sight of their bloodied kneecaps. Being a physically timid man, he could not envision himself doing the same. Wasn't the human condition suffering enough, he wondered, without the need to inflict the added pain of self-mortification?

Oftentimes, mothers and fathers would repeat this ritual with the added burden of a child clutched in their arms, the face of their offspring frightfully cloven at the mouth and drooling, or the limbs flailing as the afflicted grunted and made sounds like an animal of the forest or barnyard. In such cases, Father Pablo found it difficult to witness their painful progress and wished to turn away. Yet, the power of the spectacle, and the suspense of the outcome, would not allow it.

Too often, after kneeling and kissing the protected cloth of the robe, the desperate seekers would arise seemingly unchanged, the one leg still shorter than the other, the vision still dark or obscured; the tumor like a malignant vegetable still erupting from the skull.

Worse still were the children whose fowl-like cackling did not suddenly resolve itself into human speech, the corpse left unanimated within his coma, the misshaped head that remained elongated and melon-like on the thin stalk of a neck.

At such moments, Father Pablo could see Doña Josefa's fervency transfer itself into the quivering of her claw-like hands, as if this added effort might be what was required to wrest the requested miracle from the reliquary. She visibly sagged when none was forthcoming and her efforts appeared to have no bearing on the outcome of any request.

Yet, as Veronica had foretold, some were indeed visited with the power of the Holy Spirit and made whole before the eyes of all present, even as the logic and reasoning of the selections remained impenetrable to the human mind.

One such was an old man in the grip of a palsy so severe that it shook his body like a rat in the jaws of a terrier. It seemed to Father Pablo that the tormented man would be unable to complete the short journey up the steps before being thrown down again by the violence of his affliction.

Still, he came on, throwing himself first one way, then another, to offset the seismic tremors that threatened his balance and beset his progress, deigning any assistance all the while. Both Father Pablo and the throng below observed his attempts in awed and expectant silence, fearing each moment he would be flung back down the steps that he had so painfully negotiated.

At last, stumbling up to the reliquary, he fell to his knees with a crack that made Father Pablo feel faint. Seizing the relic in his trembling hands, he hauled it to his lips, his spasms nearly wrenching the cross from Doña Josefa and tumbling her over in the bargain.

Veronica rushed forth from the shadows of the veranda to assist the old woman, standing by her side as an audible sigh arose from the crowd at the completion of the old man's arduous journey, followed by a hushed expectancy as to the outcome. Father Pablo found himself leaning forward in anticipation.

Mumbling his devotions, the ancient attempted to sketch the Sign of the Cross on himself before beginning the daunting task of rising from his knees. His hand and forearm vibrated alarmingly. Unable to find his forehead, his hand darted this way and that, making asymmetrical patterns in the air about his face and chest. At last managing to seize his right wrist with his left hand, he brought his fist to his lips. Then, suddenly, he was still.

As if waking from a dream, he slowly released his wrist and brought his hand before his face, contemplating the newly-stilled appendage. The wonder and relief at his release from a life of constant and erratic movement was, for a moment, concentrated in this simple contemplation of the obedient fingers held up before his fellow pilgrims like a benediction. These same people stared with him in awed silence, as if they, too, had just experienced the self-same miracle.

Slowly raising the left hand as well, he compared it to its brother and gawped in open-mouthed astonishment and joy at the twin gifts bestowed upon him. Tears coursed down the dry rivulets of his seamed face.

"Viva Jesus!" he cried, clamoring to his feet on legs made sturdy pillars of the temple, holding both hands aloft.

The crowd screamed back, "Viva Jesus!" in a roar that swept across Father Pablo, Doña Josefa, Veronica, and the Centurions like the hot, moist wind of a summer storm, electric and terrifying with possibilities.

Before Father Pablo could regain his senses, the wind reversed and the chant swept back across the throng in an ever-widening wave that carried the news to the farthest outskirts of the hacienda, the cry diminishing in the distance.

As the old man danced away, turning his pockets inside out to throw whatever money and valuables he could find at the feet of Doña Josefa and the relic, Father Pablo shivered at the enormity of what he had witnessed. Yet, even as he did so, he could not refrain from questioning the restoration of an old man who had but a few years left to his life, when so many families and their children had been left to twist in the wind.

Yet, even this was not consistent. On his previous visit, he had seen a young boy who had lain insensible for two years after falling out of a second floor window, roused by the touch of the holy cloth to his dead lips.

The child had walked away clutching the hands of his weeping parents and chattering like a cockatoo while distractedly rubbing the concavity on his head that marked the spot of his long-healed injury.

Even this day, a young girl, white as her first communion dress, was cured of the internal bleeding that threatened to outpace her small heart. The only external evidence to this that

Father Pablo could discern was the undeniable bloom that rose up through her blanched flesh like the sun's radiance behind a summer cloud.

Within moments of the touch of the Garment her near transparent skin became suffused with color and health, her deadly languor replaced with the animation reserved only for the very young and healthy.

If these, more subtle, occurrences failed to impress the gathered masses, their effect on Father Pablo was incalculable. Now that he was confronted by God's undeniable power, it seemed his devious human nature must devise other snares of faithlessness, and he questioned the seemingly capricious nature of God's will and was ashamed.

Much later that night, after the last of the pilgrims had placed their lips against the reliquary and returned to their world beyond the walls of the hacienda, Father Pablo stood on the abandoned veranda, contemplating the day's events. Two torches guttered nearby and were all that remained of the row that had illuminated the procession that had continued long after darkness had fallen.

Even so, several hundred pilgrims had been turned away to wait until morning as Doña Josefa's strength had finally failed her, as did Veronica's in her turn. Now they huddled in dispirited makeshift encampments of torn plastic sheeting and palm fronds.

Adding to their misery, a heavy shower had drenched the penitents shortly after nightfall, turning the churned earth of Doña Josefa's devastated plantation into mire. Now mosquitoes filled the thick air with an insistent hum.

Other than the insects, the silence that remained lay like a thick blanket, and Father Pablo felt as if it must presage yet an even greater storm.

Interrupting his reverie was the unmistakable sound of a hand slapping against unprotected flesh. It seemed to originate from the greater darkness at the far end of the veranda. Without understanding his own motivation, Father Pablo stepped back beneath the eaves of the casa, stilling his breath.

By degrees, barely audible murmurs grew in pitch and depth, pulsating with suppressed emotion. Even so, the cadence and rhythm of the speech eluded his understanding until it occurred to him that it was not his own language being spoken, but that of English.

Edging along the wall to be closer to the source of the voices, he was halted by the sudden flare of a match. He flattened against the pebbled surface of the casa as the faces of two men appeared to float in the air before him but a few yards distant. One lit the cigarette of the other, then his own; then the faces vanished with a puff of breath.

In that instant, Father Pablo recognized the features of Juan Alcante and Captain Barrera.

Yet these men were not the source of the voices, which lay several yards beyond them. Squinting hard in that direction, his eyes becoming accustomed to the stygian darkness of the Yucatán night, the American couple began to take form in shades of blurred, gray motion. Clearly, they were in disagreement over something.

The slapping sound had originated from the woman, who had unwisely worn only shorts and a sleeveless blouse for her visit to the hacienda, and now provided a feast for the voracious mosquitoes. It appeared to Father Pablo that her ire was not directed at the annoying swarm of insects, but rather at her husband who loomed over her in a frozen, angry posture.

Fearful of either advancing or retreating due to the proximity of Barrera and Alcante, Father Pablo remained where he was, listening intently. His scant knowledge of English only allowed him to recognize certain tantalizing, but ultimately unhelpful, words and phrases that flew between the couple.

At first, he was certain that the woman wanted something from her husband, but then grew just as certain of the opposite—there was something that she did not want, or perhaps, refused.

The husband, speaking in a low, angry rumble, was no less insistent that she either accept, or possibly, do something.

Her obvious denials grew sharper and louder as her actions became more animated and erratic, due in no small part Father Pablo surmised, by her uneven contest with the mosquitoes.

The voice of Barrera carried softly, but with force, to the unhappy couple, "Too loud," he warned them in their own language.

The Americans grew quiet, and if it were not for the glow of Barrera and Alcante's cigarettes, Father Pablo might have thought that he was alone once more. Several moments passed in this manner, with Father Pablo fearful that at any time he might be discovered by his fellow countrymen, though as to why this should matter he remained uncertain.

When, at last, the woman spoke once more, it was in a low, resolute voice. Clearly, Father Pablo thought, her mind was made up; there was no mistaking that tone in a woman's voice in any language.

The American man did not respond, but instead spoke in his authoritative way to Captain Barrera. This time Father Pablo was certain that he had understood—the big gringo had ordered Barrera to drive his wife to their casa. Incredibly, it appeared as if the fearsome captain, after only a moment's pause to launch his cigarette in a shower of angry sparks, was obeying!

Taking a step closer to Juan, the captain whispered loudly and fiercely enough for Father Pablo to hear—"Pay your debts, Alcante!"

Then, without further discussion, the policeman and the American woman walked away through the squelching mud toward the entrance of the hacienda.

After several minutes of silence following the couple's abrupt departure, it occurred to Father Pablo that both Alcante and the American had noiselessly vanished as well, and that he was now in sole possession of the abandoned veranda.

Just as the stars above his head remained obscured by unseen clouds, so too did the meaning of the day's events, and it was with weary, cautious steps that he made his way toward the bed promised him within Doña Josefa's great and decaying house.

*   *   *

The cab of the police truck hummed and buzzed with angry, unspoken words as Barrera accelerated down the long jungle track to the highway. Clinging to a strap above the door, Brenda tried to keep her eyes focused to the front, but could not resist a glance at her lover from time to time.

Barrera remained supremely aloof, the only evidence of his anger being his inability to get his latest cigarette lit, and a certain crackling in the atmosphere surrounding him, something like a storm just over the horizon, felt but not yet seen.

Reaching over to seize his wrist and steady his hand, she was rewarded with a visible spark that leapt from him to her with an audible pop.

With a cry she snatched her hand away, rubbing the contact point, while Barrera gave her a puzzled, apprehensive look. The smell of ozone bloomed and vanished.

"What is the matter with you?" he demanded coolly, while at last managing to light his cigarette.

"I want you to go back and get Jim, Antonio. He shouldn't do this, he shouldn't be out there alone, you know that."

Several moments of silence followed Brenda's demands, punctuated by the groans of an overtaxed suspension system and the occasional scrape of wood on metal made by low-hanging branches.

"He is not alone; my man Alcante will take care of everything. All your husband has to do is take the sample that Juan delivers to him and walk out to a driver I will have waiting. He is on his way now and I described your husband to him in detail—he could hardly miss him in any case. It is a short walk to the place chosen by Alcante.

"He has found a spot where the wall has crumbled and been breached by the jungle. It is well concealed and there are no guards there. That is where my driver will be waiting."

"But why should he stay?" Brenda persisted. "Couldn't Alcante just sneak out with it himself? I don't understand why Jim has to take the risk; I don't know why he feels he must have the robe!"

Her lover took a moment to draw on his cigarette.

"As for Alcante, your husband doesn't trust him, and can you blame him? I certainly wouldn't. But as to the relic…that has something to do with you, I think…maybe with me, as well.

"He is afraid of it because of you...he doesn't want to lose you to something he can't understand. *Me*...he can deal with, but the robe, of that he is not so sure."

Brenda's anger flickered. "Why should he care?" she asked. "He doesn't even believe in it."

Handing the cigarette to Brenda, Barrera waited for her to take a drag, then said, "But *you* do, do you not? That is enough, I think."

She blew out a stream of smoke that was snatched away into the blackness beyond the window. "I think I do," she said so quietly that Barrera had trouble catching her words above the thumps and rattle of the truck. "I *want* to believe." Her hand trembled slightly as she returned the cigarette.

Chuckling quietly, Barrera said, "Yes, don't we all? Well, excepting your husband, of course." Across the darkened cab of the truck Barrera could see the glistening of tears.

"It's not worth all this..." Brenda began, but stopped mid-sentence, waving her hand uncertainly in the air, unsure of her own meaning or what was at stake. "Go back for him, Antonio! Promise me you won't leave him there!"

"How can I?" he answered tiredly. "I need him."

Reaching across the short distance that separated them, he made to pat her thigh, but felt her leg jerk away. In this simple reflex he felt the end of their relationship.

"I've already made plans to get him out if things turn ugly, so don't worry," he said softly.

Climbing out onto the concrete of the highway, the truck's tires settled into a hiss of contentment as Barrera sped toward Progreso.

The new silence of the empty roadway surrounded them like a held breath.

CHAPTER THIRTEEN

Jim's great head rocked forward, his chin resting uncomfortably on his chest, his booted feet sunken in the mire of the yard that lay at the edge of the veranda. His buttocks ached from the hard edge of his perch. To keep from tumbling into the muck he clasped his knees and tried to remain conscious. This was proving ever more difficult as the night wore on—the events of the day having drained him both physically and emotionally.

His fight with Brenda swirled through his semi-waking dreams like an old piece of film, the images tinted but lacking true color and vividness, the actors poorly directed and often with their backs to the camera. The editing appeared capricious and intentionally confusing, as if challenging the audience to take apart the obscure and troubling scenes and reconstruct them into some understandable drama. Jim's dreaming self felt unequal to this task yet was unable to turn away from the presentation.

It would occur to him from time to time to wake up, as he vaguely remembered that he was awaiting events that he had earlier set in motion. But as these uneasy thoughts made their way up from the black depths that threatened to swallow his consciousness altogether, they were soothed by the calming sounds of the dripping trees, the subdued, nocturnal chatter of hidden night birds. In the near distance, a woman's voice murmured soothingly, answered moments later by a child's small, sleepy laughter, then silence reigned once more.

His head snapped upright just in time to save himself from oblivion, and for the second time that week, he said, "I don't know you…" with a thick, clumsy tongue.

Only darkness lay before him, and even as these words left his lips his head began sinking once more to his chest, his only conscious thought being that he missed his wife, though it was he who had sent her away for her own safety.

Once she had understood the path he was set upon, she could not have been induced to stay in any case, and it had given Jim great pleasure to reduce his elegant challenger to unctuous chauffeur and bit player.

Jim understood where things stood between Barrera and Brenda, had understood since that day in the plaza. Even so, he knew that the greater threat lay in the purple robe and that even Barrera was at risk from its influence. Even in the dreaming chaos of his sleeping thoughts, Jim clearly grasped the challenge that lay before him—debunk the robe and all else would fall before it. Barrera would be swept away as would Brenda's nostalgic infatuation with her childhood faith and her unfulfilled dreams of motherhood. He only had to act, and act now.

Once the sample of the cloak lay beneath the pitiless gaze of modern technologies, and its true origin was exposed, then normalcy would resume its sway, rolling back the fog of superstition and longing that had enveloped Brenda and he like an enchantment—an enchantment that even now drew him ever deeper toward a dreamless slumber.

Juan had to shake his shoulder several times to rouse him, almost toppling him into the muddy morass that gripped his boots. Jim grunted angrily at the pressure and sharpness of Juan Alcante's long nails.

"Stand up and let's go," Juan demanded.

Overbalanced, Jim tumbled forward from his vantage point on the low wall and took several awkward steps while attempting to regain both his consciousness and balance. Somehow, like a drunken but lucky dancer, he managed this feat without falling headlong into the muck, turning angrily on his tormentor.

"How'd you like a size eleven up your scrawny ass?" he hissed.

Advancing upon the larger man as if these words had never been spoken, Juan said, "Walk—walk quickly away from here."

He placed something heavy and covered with a soft material into Jim's hands and spun him about. "Follow me," he commanded, stalking away, the darkness threatening to make him vanish altogether from Jim's sight.

Hurrying to close the gap between them, Jim felt his hands begin to shake. "Juan," he called out softly and urgently, "what is this?" though he knew well enough.

His guide did not answer and Jim hurried to reach his side, as even the dubious company of Juan Alcante appeared suddenly preferable to being alone with the reliquary.

Puffing with exertion he drew alongside Juan and seized his thin arm, saying, "I asked you a question...what's going on here?"

Still Juan did not slacken his pace and, as they trudged toward Jim's secret rendezvous, he shook off the American's grip. "It was not possible to take it apart for a sample," he hissed, "I would have wakened the entire house. As it was, I took risk enough."

Juan's words served to infect Jim with a dread that weighted his already mud-encased feet, even as the gold cross assumed a gravity far beyond what its size and mass could explain. A worm of panic woke into life deep within his entrails, its birth heralded by a narrowing of vision, a pressure within the skull.

"I didn't want this," he said to Alcante. "I didn't want you to steal the whole thing!"

"You should have said so," Juan answered, his breath also coming in gusts.

Ahead of them, Jim could just make out a lighter grayness in the dark. "What's that?" he whispered, able to hear the fear in his own voice.

"It's the wall," Juan assured him. "Right along here somewhere is the break in it. Your driver should be waiting just the other side."

Clutching the reliquary in its velvet wrappings to his chest, Jim whispered to himself, "Yes...I've got to get out of here, now...right now."

Even so, the sucking mud slowed his progress, just as his sense of pursuit was suddenly confirmed by the sound of men's voices coming from the direction of the house—Mayan voices.

He dared a backward glance and through reddened eyes burning with sweat saw lights moving within the grounds; flashlights or lanterns he couldn't tell. Like fireflies they flitted singly and in groups, vanishing and reappearing as they passed behind objects invisible to Jim in the distance and darkness.

"Juan," he called out in a hoarse whisper, "what's going on back there?"

"Don't worry about that," Juan ordered, "stay close and follow me."

Jim felt his hand seized in the wiry, slick grip of his accomplice, but did not complain, allowing himself to be led forward as Juan thrashed about in the brush looking for the break in the wall.

"Damnit," he heard Juan say in English, "Sonofabitch!"

Suddenly Jim was drawn forward into the vines and saw-edged leaves and felt his cheek scrape against some coarse surface even as his forehead struck something hard and unyielding. He ducked down too late and felt himself pass through the obstruction and out the other side, the lack of encumbering, suffocating foliage instantly evidenced in the freshening breeze of an open space—they had gained the road.

In the faint half-light that appeared to glow from the limestone wall and the sandy track of roadway, Jim could see

Juan's narrow skull swiveling left and right in search of their driver and car. The ghostly track was empty, its forsaken, desolate air made eerie by the distant cries that drifted to the two men from the other side of the wall.

"Where the hell is the driver Barrera was sending?" Jim asked.

Juan spun around to face him. "You stay here and wait. He will be along in a minute...I know this," he said, and without further words slipped back through the nearly hidden aperture in the wall, leaving the American to his fate.

"God almighty," Jim said quietly, his head swiveling back and forth, even as his thoughts raced wildly—there was no doubt the purple robe's absence had been noted and the alarm sounded. It occurred to him to just start walking...but what direction? He hadn't a clue.

Almost simultaneously, he considered hiding the reliquary— he shuddered to think of being caught with the relic in his hands. Besides the bowel-churning fear, his ears burned with a shame that no amount of contempt seemed capable of subduing.

He glanced about for a likely spot. Unlike the other side of the wall, no foliage or brush existed here that would suffice to hide the relic. He would have to cross to the other side of the track to once again gain the forest and the luxury and safety of its cover and concealment.

It was not far, only several yards, yet in the weird light the roadway appeared a great, glowing divide, the powdery sand awaiting receipt of his heavy boot prints.

The idea of attempting to disguise the prints with a frond or leafy brush seemed childish and futile, as the sand would remain virginal to either side, and Jim discarded it as soon as it occurred. Instead, he remained rooted to the very spot where he had emerged from the plantation, his back against the crumbling wall, his will to go forward sapped by his own intellect and imagination, the driver still nowhere to be seen.

Had he, or Alcante, misunderstood Barrera? Had they somehow arrived at the wrong spot? Or was it something altogether worse? Had Barrera betrayed him? It was not beyond the realm of possibility, and Jim considered that he had underestimated Barrera's affection for Brenda. Perhaps ambition had been trumped by love.

It was the murmur of their voices that alerted Jim and penetrated the dense buzz of thoughts that swarmed within his skull. Their actual presence remained occluded by the shadows at the edge of the roadway, the same shadows that cloaked him, their brief, whispered exchange carrying their incomprehensible words to him as a warning. In this moment, the whirlwind of possibilities that tormented him ceased their chatter and vanished; only one imperative remained—survival.

Without further thought, Jim edged back along the wall seeking the hidden opening that, only moments before, he had so eagerly passed through. At the periphery of his vision, shapes took form, ill-defined as unfinished clay figures, their faceless heads rising and lowering as if sniffing the damp, warm currents of air—casting like hounds.

Still clutching the damning, cloth-bound cross to his chest, Jim stumbled back into the jagged aperture, only his height saving him from falling through with a crash into the undergrowth. Bending his head, he shuffled beneath the opening and back into the grounds of the hacienda with a dozen tiny steps. He heard no cry from his would-be pursuers.

Turning to face Doña Joseph's tottering manse and retrace his steps, the thick, choking darkness he had momentarily escaped cloaked him like blindness. His only assurance that he was not, in fact, struck sightless was the torches and lanterns that moved restlessly through the compound in the distance. But, like Lot's wife, his turning back had rendered him immobile and senseless as a pillar of salt, and he stood rooted to the earth awaiting whatever might come next, trembling like a rabbit in a net.

"Why have you come back?" Juan demanded, his thin, dirty hands playing up and down Jim's body until they patted the reliquary in reassurance. "Wait for the car, you fool!"

Jim almost cried out at the sound of Juan's challenge and touch, but managed to contain himself. Even so, he felt his legs shaking as if he had climbed hundreds of stairs and could hardly trust himself to speak; the acrid, humiliating odor of urine wafted up to his nostrils.

"No car," he managed at last. "No one came."

"Damnit," Juan spat. "Go back before they catch us both."

"Men…" Jim stammered "…back there…men with guns."

Jim felt, rather than saw, Juan's sudden absence, and in the new silence he drew a shuddering breath, foul with his fear, and had to fight the urge to simply lie down in the mud and close his eyes.

As suddenly as he had vanished, Juan was back at his side, his restless hands prodding and poking in the darkness as if to assure himself it was still the American.

"Indios," Juan confirmed; then muttered a string of Spanish, as if talking to himself. After several moments, he apparently arrived at a conclusion and began to tug at the reliquary that Jim clutched to his chest.

"Give it to me," Juan demanded. "Let go of the damned thing. Are you stupid? Do you want to die?"

With these last words Jim released his senseless hold on the object as if awakening from a spell. "Yes," he breathed, "put it back, Juan. That's the thing to do…just put it back."

Feeling the weight of the world lifted from his chest with the cross's removal, Jim felt like dancing in the stinking mud and singing aloud. "Put it back," he repeated for good measure.

As if drawn by their voices, torches began to fan out in their direction. From where Jim stood, he could see that a rough line of searchers was being organized out of the random parties that had first responded to the theft of the robe. Soon, very soon, they would work their way towards the outer wall.

"Wait until I am gone for a few minutes," Juan commanded in his phlegmy, congested voice, "then follow. Go back to where I found you and go to sleep. You know nothing, *comprendé*...nothing. I'll come back for you later."

"Yes," Jim agreed. "That's what we'll do...we'll meet later."

Again, night swallowed Alcante and the robe, the absence of his fetid breath and sharp fingers signaling his passing, while Jim continued to stare after him into the unyielding darkness, his vision blurred by the bitter tears of his newfound cowardice.

* * *

The horses, slick and glistening with lather, pranced nervously round in a circle outside Father Pablo's window, the sound of their sharp, dangerous hooves making dull thuds as they struck the dusty earth of the yard. Pablo's brothers, awakened by their father, were already dressing in the dark of their shared room and griping to one another in muted voices, not so much in deference to their coddled little brother as in unconscious acknowledgement of the strangeness of the hour. Ignoring Pablo, as he was not expected to join them, they hurried to their impatient father to begin the task of soothing the horses and returning them to their stables.

As the last of his older siblings filed out of the room, Pablo discarded his pretense of sleep and edged across the still warm bed to peer out the window, shuffling through the individual impressions and odors that characterized each of his brothers. In their sudden absence, he found this pleasant and reassuring. At first, he could see nothing beyond but the greater darkness of the nighttime world—impenetrable and suffocating.

Suddenly the blackness was swept aside in mute violence, leaving the hidden world beyond Pablo's window awash in unforgiving brilliance. The bellies of clouds that were stacked miles high boiled with jagged streaks, or were illuminated from within, glowing and dimming by turns. For several moments, the frightened horses danced beneath the pitiless illumination, the world turned black and white, before the darkness was returned with a deceiving finality.

The colossal storm made not a sound throughout, its voice still many miles away and hidden. Not a drop of rain fell. Were it not for the horses and their shrill anxiety, and the slight, freshening breeze, Pablo might have thought he was still asleep and dreaming.

Within seconds, another display threw the yard into sharp relief as the increasingly frantic horses circled ever faster, the herd drawing closer in on itself. From within their ranks, unseen, the boy heard the foals whinny in confusion and terror—if they stumbled they would be trampled to death.

In the last split-second of light, a long, low shadow detached itself from a greater pool of darkness that lay at the corner of Pablo's vision, but was swallowed up as the heavens withdrew their power in anticipation of the next assault.

Pablo fell back from the open window as sweaty as the terrified animals that swirled and stomped without. He had never seen a great cat before, but had been told stories of them by his father and grandfather. Even so, he entertained no doubts as to what was out there, and the primal terror it inspired needed no additional proof; he was reduced to the same status as the foals.

The gray outline of the open window loomed before him like the maw of the monkey-eater that crept within yards of his bed.

From the front of the house rang the metallic clack of his father's shotgun being snapped shut on its load of buckshot. Pablo recalled the old man's stories about the behavior of horses, how they only sought man's help when they were being stalked by predators. That was why they had awakened the household instead of just running away, the boy realized, the foals might not be able to keep up! He tried to call out to his father and brothers, but his voice was dried up and made no sound.

Failing in his cry for help, he struggled to scoot himself across the rumpled geography of the bed, but his arms too failed him, and he fell back, fear having sapped his strength.

The next dazzling sheet of fire rushed across the sky, and in that brief eternity, Pablo beheld the flattened skull and rounded ears outlined like a nightmare in his window. Standing on its hind legs, the jaguar peered with interest at a quarry unprotected by the cruel hooves of rampant mares. Its green eyes glittered with a curiosity devoid of sympathy, weighing him in an instant as both non-threatening and eminently edible.

When the darkness slammed down once more, it left Pablo blind as a mole, his world reduced to one spot that he could no longer see. From that quarter all that remained of the great cat was the huffing of its breath, which grew louder and more rapid as it filled its nostrils with the scent of a sweating, urine-stained boy.

For his part, Pablo could feel the humid breath of the jaguar blowing across the sheets of his once-cozy bed, the meat-rich odor full of decay and death.

Unable to wait for the next streak of lightning to reveal the final act of his horror, Pablo struggled to release his voice.

From the front of the house, he could hear his father and brothers spilling out into the yard to corral the errant horses. He could almost picture them in his mind's eye: his father leading the way with his shotgun at the ready, his rough and tumble brothers, shaking off their sullen drowsiness with their typical rowdiness. All of them intent on the job at hand, with never a backward glance at the shadowed window of Pablo's room, his father scanning the jungle that lay closest to the horses for any sign of el tigre or his children.

"Papa," Pablo managed to mutter. Ominously, the huffing ceased and a pregnant stillness followed. "Papa," Pablo repeated more loudly, "Papa, Papa!"

A small grunt of exertion greeted Pablo's cries, followed by the far side of the bed sinking with the weight of an unseen burden. The cat's eyes glowed like merciless emeralds while its rancid breath flowed like death across Pablo's face. "Papa," he now screamed with abandon, "Papa...save me!"

The beam of a flashlight swept across the room illuminating the upper corners, even as his father bounded across the yard, his horses forgotten. Drawing rapidly nearer, the beam of his torch grew stronger yet, revealing the jaguar in the very act of seeking Pablo's jugular, its black lips drawn back to reveal yellowed fangs as long as a man's fingers.

With terrible clarity, the boy realized that his father would never reach him in time, as he was seized by the throat and his cries silenced. Even the explosions of his father's gun failed to deter the great cat's placid determination as it shook the boy from side to side, never relaxing its implacable grip, his breath sealed off by the powerful jaws.

"Uhn, uhnnn..." he grunted in unison with the jaguar's efforts "...uhn, uhnnn."

In the midst of his death throes, the flashlight's beam seared his face, piercing his tightly closed eyelids. His father, too late, had arrived.

"Father Pablo," his papa demanded in his stern way, "Wake up!"

"Yes," he agreed, his voice soggy with emotion, "it's time to get up…the horses are loose."

"I don't know about horses," Juan Alcante replied, "but I think it's time for you to get going." The flashlight beam he had directed at Father Pablo's face slid away as the priest forced open his eyes.

Father Pablo stroked his throat as the vision of the great cat dissipated from his memory like smoke. "Go?" he mumbled, sitting up from his pallet in the empty second floor room. "Go where?"

Alcante's lean face bobbed in and out of the shadows created by the flashlight and he crouched forward in his urgency. "Didn't you hear the gunfire? You must sleep like the dead," he observed in his caustic way.

Father Pablo winced, hastening to rise as the image of the nightmare cat returned with Juan Alcante's unpleasant breath.

"Gunfire?" he repeated, recalling the booms of his father's old shotgun. "What's happened?"

Alcante rose on legs that appeared spindly even beneath the denim of his jeans, gripping Father Pablo's wrist and hauling him with some effort to his feet.

"There's been some trouble," he stammered, while making several attempts to light one of his innumerable cigarettes. Puffing it into life, he continued, "The old girl has sounded the alarm…it appears someone has taken the relic, and now the Indios are going crazy."

"Oh God," Father Pablo gasped, wiping the sleep from his eyes and staring about the room in alarm. "Has anyone been hurt?"

Juan played the light around the corners of the dusty room until it fell on Father Pablo's bag.

"Not yet," he answered, "the shooting was just to wake everybody up so they could corral the hangers-on. They're not letting them leave until everyone has been searched. There are probably fifty armed Centurions out there now, kicking apart shelters and campsites, and they mean business; I can tell you.

"Is that yours?" he pointed at the bag and Father Pablo nodded in assent. "Well grab it and let's go; I've got a ride waiting outside the gates for you."

Father Pablo snatched up the valise even as he tried to slip his feet into his untied shoes. "How did it happen?" he bleated in his confusion at the strange turn of events.

"Who knows?" Juan answered, more cotton-mouthed than was usual even for him. "The old bird got up in the middle of the night apparently—you know how she worries about thieves—and discovered it gone. Who would have thought it?"

He began tugging Father Pablo toward the door by his sleeve.

"Why would anyone steal the relic?" the priest whined as the fear of what lay outside replaced the terror of his dream. A succession of popping sounds echoed through the window from what sounded like far away. "Is that gunfire?" he asked breathlessly. "Are they shooting people now?"

Gripping the priest's elbow, Juan tugged him forcibly out of the room. "How would I know? I doubt it…at least, not yet. But that's why you have to get out of here. Who knows what will happen. This is no place for you, Father."

Excited voices could be heard coming up the stairwell from the first floor and Juan pulled Father Pablo away from them and towards the back of the house.

"Where are we going?" he asked desperately.

"We'll use the old servants' stairs," Juan reassured him. "You don't want to go that way." He nodded toward the landing and the faint light that radiated from the first floor.

"But I must take my leave of Doña Josefa," Father Pablo pleaded, even as Juan threw open what appeared to be a closet door revealing a set of narrow steps that disappeared into claustrophobic darkness. "And Veronica…" he added. "It wouldn't be polite…"

Juan cut him off in a fierce whisper as they began their stumbling descent, "It was Veronica's idea to get you to safety in the first place, so please stop being so difficult! Besides, you don't want to deal with the old lady and Hernando right now, or Manny…especially Manny. You saw how they all were yesterday."

In the close confines of the stairwell, Father Pablo could barely see his escort, though the bloom of his persistent body odor left no doubt but that he was near.

"Veronica is a good girl," Father Pablo said, more to reassure himself than for any other reason, as it was difficult for him to set aside his mistrust of the rat-faced Juan.

It seemed so strange that Alcante would choose to aid him, but it made perfect sense that Veronica would intercede on his behalf—even someone as self-serving as Juan would have to bow before her undeniable goodness.

He felt himself relax somewhat at this reasoning. A breath of humid air blew across his face, and he realized that Juan had found the door to the outside and stood waiting for him on the threshold.

"Hurry," he urged the sweating priest. "You have your bag, yes? Good, let's go."

Juan clung to his arm now as they rounded the casa and began the mucky trek to the front gates. "If we're stopped by any of the Indios, let me do the talking, I know most of them by first name."

The same roiling heavens of his dreams now commanded Father Pablo's waking sky, and every few seconds the churned, devastated grounds were revealed in heartless brilliance. Each brief flash displayed unfinished vignettes of men loping along in armed packs while scores of frightened men, women, and children either fled their coming like flightless birds or huddled in fearful, bovine obedience.

The landscape was strewn with the scattered remains of makeshift lean-tos and the meager, homey possessions of their former inhabitants, and here and there smoldered the abandoned campfires of the pilgrims-turned-suspects, evidence of a spiraling, dangerous game of cops and robbers.

"Mother of God," Father Pablo gasped as he took in the full scope of the flickering drama. Turning to Juan, he found that he had hurried ahead.

"Juan," Father Pablo called after him, "Are you sure they won't hurt these people? Perhaps I should stay after all, I might be needed here."

Alcante rushed back to his side, hissing, "Shush, you fool! There's no need to demand their attention. Things are crazy enough right now as it is." Seizing Father Pablo's arm once more, he began to drag him on.

After a few moments he spoke again in a more kindly, gentle manner, "There's no need to worry, Father, I assure you. They're not going to hurt anyone; they just want the relic back."

Then he added with a nervous chuckle, "Though I wouldn't vouch for the safety of whoever they catch that has it."

They stumbled on through light and darkness.

As they neared the wall, Father Pablo heard the sound of heavy, rapid footsteps splashing through the mud, coming directly at them.

"Someone's coming," he whispered to Alcante, his heart rising into his throat at this fearful approach masked in darkness. "Is it an Indio, do you think?" His own steps were slowed by the filthy mud, making flight impossible.

Juan did not answer and Father Pablo felt the hair on his neck and arms begin to rise at the thunderous approach of this phantom juggernaut. "Who's there?" he cried, anxiety overcoming his common sense.

The heavens scorched the soggy earth with a blinding flash and Father Pablo beheld the apparition that bore down on him— a huge man made unnaturally white by the brilliance, smeared with mud, his mouth agape in silent terror, his arms extended like a blind man.

Father Pablo instinctively brought his satchel up to his chest in the final seconds before the giant crashed into him, driving them both to the sodden ground. The scream that had arisen in his throat was driven out in a useless rush of air.

Even as he fought for breath and struggled to extricate himself from his assailant's embrace, he became conscious of the steady stream of pleas being repeated over and over again in childish terror, "Help me...help me, Father!"

Father Pablo recognized the American, even as he kicked and squirmed to escape his grasp.

"Get off me," he squealed, managing to roll over and crawl like a frightened infant from beneath his great bulk. "Let me go! Please!"

Juan entered the fray as well, cursing in a low steady stream as he pulled and yanked at the American. "What the devil are you doing here? I told you to go back to the casa," Father Pablo heard him say.

Scrabbling to his feet, Father Pablo witnessed Juan slap the man's face as he hauled him up from the mud he groveled in. "Get up!" he commanded. "Get up, and be quiet, for Christ's sake!"

The big man, still on his knees, peered up at Juan like a chastened and frightened child. "Juan, Juan," he repeated in a small, terrified voice, "thank God it's you!" He spoke in English, but Father Pablo understood the simple, heartfelt words.

Raising his arms, the big man seized Juan. "Get me out," he pleaded in a hoarse whisper. "They're after me! They think I have the relic, that I've hidden it! I just managed to get away!" He threw a wild-eyed glance back in the direction from which he had come.

Though Father Pablo had been unable to understand all of the American's speech, his glance and bedraggled condition conveyed his meaning well enough, and with a start of comprehension, the priest grasped the heightened peril they were all now in.

"What is he saying?" he demanded of Alcante. "Did he take the relic?"

Juan, ignoring the priest, hauled the American to his feet. "You should have stayed put," he hissed in broken English. "I could have explained everything to them...now...not so easy. You shouldn't have run from them."

"I think they might kill me," Jim cried in apparent astonishment.

Pushing the bigger man aside, Juan peered into the darkness from which he had issued.

Though Father Pablo had been unable to follow their desperate exchange, he comprehended enough to guess that the big man was in terrible trouble. A chill wracked his damp body as he, too, stared back at the devastated campgrounds fitfully illuminated in the scattered fires that still burned in the heavy, humid air.

"Juan," Father Pablo began, "what are we..." He was halted by Juan's raised hand.

Father Pablo slowed his breathing in order to better hear what Juan was hearing. In the ensuing silence the murmur of voices in the near distance reached his ears. Then, as if in imitation of the fugitive trio, they too fell silent.

Somewhere, not fifty yards away, the American's pursuers waited for the word, the cry, the snapped twig that might pinpoint their prey in the suffocating darkness.

Suddenly, Juan's thin, sweating face appeared close to Father Pablo's own, their noses almost touching, his rancid breath filling the priest's offended nostrils. His expression was contorted in concentration, as if he were grappling with some momentous decision, even as his dilated eyes betrayed the fear that had spread like contagion with the arrival of the foreigner.

"Go on to the gate," he commanded in a shaky whisper. "If there's a car and driver there, he'll take you into town...tell him I said so. If not, just start walking in that direction...Barrera, or one of his men, will find you on the road soon enough."

Before Father Pablo could question him, he added, "And don't worry about the guards out there, you're a priest, so I don't think they'll give you a hard time. If they do, tell them I sent you out."

Thrusting the priest's mud-spattered case into his hands, he said, "Don't forget your bag." The clasp had been broken in Father Pablo's collision with the American, and Juan cautioned, "Be careful you don't spill everything. Now get out of here quickly and *quietly*." He shoved the priest in the direction of the road to town.

"What about him," Father Pablo whispered in return, "shouldn't he go with me?"

The big American remained rooted to the spot, clasping his elbows in a useless effort to calm the tremors that wracked his body, staring in the direction from which the voices had come. He was insensible with terror and clearly unable to save himself.

"Don't worry about him right now, Father," Juan insisted. "I will see to him. But you must get away from here…right now, damn it, or we'll all be caught!"

Beyond their sad tableau, Father Pablo thought he could perceive a thickening of the darkness within the greater gloom— a coalescence of shape that appeared to grow steadily more defined as he watched.

Turning away, he began to carefully pick his way in the direction he had been pointed, straining each moment to resist the animal urge to flee as fast and noisily as was necessary to escape.

Glancing back, he thought he could make out the American watching him go, but put it down to imagination, as it was far too dark to be able to determine. Even so, a twinge of guilt added to his torment.

With each step he took, the rain-soaked earth pulled at his unlaced shoes and he tiptoed forward like a small boy playing hide-and-go-seek. Nearing the gate, he was able to discern the two Centurions assigned to guard it; they were speaking to one another in low, desultory tones. Beyond them, a car idled, chugging quietly in the darkness.

It occurred to Father Pablo that it might be unwise to approach the Centurions unannounced, as they were undoubtedly on edge considering the night's events. Pausing to fish a handkerchief from his pants pocket, he pinched the gaping leather valise between his free arm and torso, carefully wiping the perspiration and soil from his face. Then, taking a few more steps, he cleared his throat in as natural a manner as he could evince.

The Indios spun about, bringing their rifles to bear on the little priest.

"It's just me... Father Pablo," he sang, "Nothing to be alarmed about!"

They looked entirely unconvinced.

After a few moments, they signaled him to come forward. As he hastened to comply, one of them produced a flashlight, playing its beam up and down on him. Father Pablo shielded his eyes from the scorching light as he trudged forth.

One of the men was muttering rapidly in Mayan to his companion, and in the castoff brilliance of the torch, their faces appeared all planes and angles, their expressions suggesting that they not were impressed by Father Pablo's collar.

Dread of this uncertain meeting weighted the priest's feet and he dragged them along like a fearful child.

From behind him, in the chaotic darkness of the ravaged hacienda, someone began to shout. It was not the frightened cries and challenging bellows that had punctuated the night when he had first awakened, but a single voice, loud and strong. It announced, "He is here! I have the American!"

Father Pablo recognized the clotted voice of Juan Alcante.

The Centurions at the gate looked beyond Father Pablo as they, too, heard the cry and registered its content. Their faces hardened into carvings at the news, and the little priest was forgotten. Sweeping by him as they hurried onto the grounds, they paused only long enough for one of them to say, "You should get out of here, Father." It did not sound like a suggestion.

Other voices were now answering the first, using his shouts to hone in on the American's location. The grounds of the hacienda came alive with questing voices calling in the darkness from every direction, all drawing inexorably closer to the spot where Father Pablo had left Juan and the American, James Arbor. Father Pablo's guilt at having left the hapless gringo in the care of Juan Alcante was exceeded only by his relief at seeing the way cleared for his own escape.

Even so, when the idling car tooted its horn he hesitated rushing to its dubious safety. But as the rattle and flash of automatic gunfire mixed with the triumphant cries of the hunters, he turned and fled toward the waiting driver.

CHAPTER FOURTEEN

As Father Pablo clambered into the back seat of the car, the driver, who appeared vaguely familiar, asked, "Who are you, and where is Señor Arbor?" even as he accelerated onto the sandy track.

Glancing back nervously at the sound of the gunfire, he didn't switch on his headlamps until they were several hundred yards away.

"The Centurions have him," Father Pablo mumbled.

"Oh shit," the driver replied. "What about the relic," he asked hopefully, "do you have it?"

"No," Father Pablo replied indignantly, "of course not."

"Oh shit," the driver repeated as he fumbled with a cell phone, careening from one side of the roadway to the other. "No signal," he mumbled frantically, stabbing at the tiny keys with his thumb.

They rode up one side of the track with two wheels and teetered alarmingly, causing Father Pablo's valise to spill onto the floorboard of the car.

"For God's sake," Father Pablo cried, "watch what you're doing—you'll kill us both!"

In the darkness of the back seat, he searched for the sacramentals that lay strewn in the sand and accumulated trash of the vehicle's floor.

"This is a nightmare," he whispered, groping about for the pyx containing the communion wafers and the bottles of holy oils that rolled about eluding his fingers. "Please let it end, Holy Father," he prayed, "and don't allow anyone to be hurt."

Ignoring his discomfited passenger, the driver continued to accelerate and swing wildly down the jungle trail while fumbling with his cell phone.

"Got it!" he shouted at last. "Got it, Father," he turned in his seat, smiling broadly, to share the good news with the priest.

Before Father Pablo could express his heightened alarm at the driver's antics, the man spun back around, becoming erect in his seat and focused as a soldier. "Captain," he spoke into the phone in a clipped, controlled manner that had been entirely absent in his demeanor just moments before, "they have the American."

A pause followed this announcement, as if the driver were listening intently to the officer on the other end. Father Pablo had no doubt that it was Captain Barrera.

"I waited an hour and he never showed," he answered, then lowering his voice, added, "Yes sir, Alcante is still inside too."

This was followed by a stream of incomprehensible and tinny declarations issuing from the earpiece that required no response from the undercover officer. Another pause ensued that was followed by a single question.

The driver replied in yet an even lower voice, "No, Captain," he threw a glance over his shoulder at his passenger who still pretended to busy himself with reclaiming the contents of his bag, "nothing was sent out. Juan or the American still have it, I guess."

Father Pablo's fingers trailed across something that lay almost hidden beneath the seat in front of him and knew what it was even before carefully drawing it out.

His touch revealed a cross-shaped object much larger than the crucifix he carried in his own bag, and as he lifted it up the weight of its gold settled into his sweaty palms and removed all doubt—he was in possession of the reliquary of the purple robe—*Juan Alcante had made him his mule.*

"Oh God…" he breathed, as he hastily shoved the cross back into his valise, "…I must go back!" He glanced up at the back of the driver's head, but the man was intently listening to instructions from his superior officer, paying him no heed.

"Yes sir," the driver said at last, "right away."

Snapping shut the phone he appeared to contemplate something in the near distance, his driving slowing perceptibly. At last, slipping the almost forgotten phone into a shirt pocket, he dug about in a gym bag at his side with his free hand, coming up with a small, portable radio. "Alpha Six to Alpha Two," he spoke into it.

A crackling of static ensued after this brief transmission and Father Pablo had just begun to think that the officer would not receive a reply, when a distant voice entered the car. "Go ahead," it said.

"Alpha One enroute to your location and says to begin operations immediately. Expect his arrival within thirty minutes, but do not wait to begin. Understood?"

"Understood," was the reply.

Up ahead, at a crossroads Father Pablo dimly remembered from his previous journeys, dozens of headlights began to come on.

"What's that?" he asked fearfully. "Who are they?"

Flashing his own headlamps twice, the driver quickly pulled into a spot just vacated by a truck in order to allow the rest of the convoy to gain the roadway. "Don't worry yourself about it, Father. Its police business now," he answered proudly.

The trucks, carrying dozens of uniformed officers replete with M-16s, rumbled by, going in the direction from which Father Pablo had just fled; the officers' features captured like snapshots in the crisscrossing headlights.

"Take me back," Father Pablo muttered as he gaped at the departing officers, the enormity of the situation threatening to overwhelm him. "I must go back," he repeated tonelessly.

"What?' his driver asked, slewing around in his seat once more. "Don't be silly, Father. We're well out of this mess, I can tell you. It's not going to be pretty." He started the car.

Father Pablo flung open the door. "I'm going back," he announced, stepping out of the car with his bag and stumbling in the wake of the convoy.

"Don't be an idiot, Father," the driver shouted. "Come on back!" He made no move to go after the priest.

Father Pablo hurried on, images of the clandestine meeting of Barrera, Alcante, and the American couple competing with imaginings of the carnage that might lie ahead. "Don't try to stop me," he warned without looking back.

The undercover officer watched the little priest disappear into the darkness, calling after him, "Don't tell the captain you were with me, Father...please," then accelerated back onto the roadway that led to Progreso.

Long before he reached the environs of the hacienda, the crackle of gunfire could be heard, and Father Pablo hurried his steps as quickly as the rutted track would allow, stumbling to his knees several times over unseen obstacles in his haste.

The roar of a truck engine swelled in volume behind him as a pair of headlight beams swung across the jungle at the last bend in the road. Father Pablo managed to slip into the trees just as the vehicle illuminated the stretch he had been walking on. Crouching down, he blended into the shadows in his black clothing, fearing it might be the undercover officer returning to forcibly seize him.

Speeding heedlessly past his position, the truck hurried toward the fray and Father Pablo thought he recognized the captain's driver at the wheel.

Breathless and sweating profusely, Father Pablo retook the road, alternately jogging, walking, and stumbling the remaining mile to Doña Josefa's hacienda. His valise seemed to be filled with lead bars and more than once he had to resist the temptation to fling it, along with its accursed burden, into the dripping jungle.

"Mother of God," he prayed, "please help me...tell me what I should do." A voice booming through a loudspeaker interrupted his pleas, and though he was unable to make out the words, he recognized the voice of Captain Barrera and ran on towards its source.

* * *

The front gate of Doña Josefa's estate was unguarded, but for the sprawled, lifeless body of an Indio who lay face-down atop his useless rifle in a black pool of blood. His companion was nowhere to be seen.

Halting to regain his breath, Father Pablo observed that the police had drawn several of their vehicles up against the walls, and were standing on them to fire their weapons over the ramparts. So intent were they on their quarry within that none noticed the little priest who had arrived almost in their midst.

Barrera's voice boomed out, so close this time that it caused Father Pablo to jump. He located its source at one of the vehicles parked very near the gate. Even as he stared hard through the cloaking darkness to discern the commanding officer, the clouds that had all evening threatened more rain marched silently south revealing a full moon and bathing the scene in a cold brilliance.

The captain brought the bullhorn to his lips and spoke once more, "Attention! Attention within the compound! Release the kidnapped American, James Arbor, and no further harm need come to you. If you do not comply immediately, the police will have no choice but to begin operations to rescue this man. Send him out to me, unharmed, at once, and let's have no more of this bloodshed!"

Though the shooting had ceased for his broadcast, Barrera's demands were greeted with silence. Father Pablo observed the tall captain glance at the luminous hands of his wristwatch as he leaned almost nonchalantly against the open door of the truck he was using as shelter.

Just as the captain appeared to have made up his mind about something and was reaching into the truck, a voice called out from within the devastated wilderness of the hacienda. "We don't have any American," the Centurion answered pleasantly. "There're no Americans here, so go away…this is private property."

Father Pablo was certain the speaker was Manny.

"I'll be damned," the captain spluttered, "Can you believe these arrogant bastards?"

Walking rapidly and erectly to the wall, he spoke quietly to a young officer who stood on a truck roof, peering over, "See if you can find that son of a bitch and make life hot for him."

The young man, armed with a long rifle with a scope on it, smiled down at the captain then swung the rifle in the direction from which the voice had issued, placing his eye to the lens.

Barrera brought the bullhorn to his lips once more, "Are you the leader of this group?" he asked of the waiting silence.

"Christ Jesus is our leader," Manny assured him. "We recognize no other."

"Good," Father Pablo heard the young officer on the wall whisper out of the corner of his mouth, "I'll have him in a moment if he keeps talking." The barrel of the rifle shifted almost imperceptibly.

Barrera keyed the speaker just in time for something dark to flit across the edge of his vision. Father Pablo strode for the gate as fast as his shaking legs would allow and into the line of sight of the captain.

"Father Pablo," the policeman exclaimed into the bullhorn, inadvertently announcing the little priest's arrival before remembering to release the key. "Come back here," he continued, even as Father Pablo entered the no-man's land beyond the abandoned gate. "Damn you, come back here! What are you doing?"

The retreating clouds revealed the landscape that had remained largely hidden from Father Pablo less than an hour before—the devastation bathed in the reflected light of a similarly desolate planet that soared above the battlefield. Here and there clusters of the desperate pilgrims caught in the midst of the earlier gunfire lay prone and shivering on the muddy earth, fathers and mothers draped over their children to form desperate barriers of flesh from the storm of bullets.

The bullhorn squealed and crackled before throwing Captain Barrera's voice across the field once more. "Father Pablo, return at once! You have placed yourself in danger and are interfering in a police matter. Return immediately!" he demanded.

Father Pablo hurried on toward Doña Josefa's mansion that glowed whitely ahead, like a great sepulcher presiding over an erupting graveyard. "I'm here on Church business!" he answered the policeman, the flesh of his back crawling with the memory of the rifles on the wall.

Even as he hurled back these defiant words, he scurried past the corpses of men and women that appeared to have been flung from a great height and now lay unnaturally heavy, and nearly buried, in the stinking muck.

"Hail Mary, full of grace," he chanted as he raced past them, as much to strengthen his own resolve as for those souls now detached from their riddled bodies, "the Lord is with you! Blessed are thou amongst women, blessed is the fruit of thy womb, Jesus."

"Father Pablo, is that you?" Manny called out from somewhere off to his right.

His prayer interrupted, his steps faltered and slowed. He was but fifty yards from the safety of the great casa.

A thick shadow rose up from a pile of debris in the near distance, an arm detaching itself from the greater bulk and waving at the priest. Father Pablo recognized the large, shaggy head of the stoically cheerful Manny. "Be quiet," Father Pablo whispered loudly.

"What?" Manny asked casually. He didn't wait for further clarification, but continued in a conversational tone that carried chillingly well across the hushed distance, "That policeman is right, Father. You should get out of here, it's too dangerous."

The memory of the eager young man on the wall with his scoped rifle turned Father Pablo's bowels to water. "Manny," he hissed, "be quiet, and get down!"

"Maybe," the Indio continued, "that captain will let you take these people out of…"

His thought was interrupted by the bullet entering his brain pan. Falling loosely to the earth the report from the rifle that had killed him followed seconds later like a punctuation mark.

Father Pablo's scream rang shrill and girlish across the debated land, and before its echoes had faded the Centurions launched a fusillade of bullets from the makeshift bunkers they had thrown together from the remnants of the pilgrims' shelters. The police replied eagerly and the air began to hum with the passage of tiny projectiles.

Some pilgrims, unnerved by the renewed roar of battle, shuttled this way and that, like flushed quail across the contested field, driven back or cut down by whichever side they chose to approach.

Father Pablo started running for the shelter of the casa, the interrupted prayer returning to his lips as if the episode with Manny had never occurred, "Holy Mary, Mother of God, pray for us sinners now and at the hour of our death."

Skirting the veranda, he ran along the side of the house until he reached the kitchen door at the rear. It was not locked and he fell through onto the cool tile of the floor.

When he looked up, it was into the round, terrified eyes of Veronica, Hernando, and the treacherous Juan Alcante. They sat on the kitchen floor with their backs against the wall like a row of owls in the darkness.

"Where is the American?" Father Pablo gasped, groping his way toward Juan while dragging his leather case. "What have you done with him, Juan?"

"Me?" the healed heroin addict replied. "I've done nothing with him! You know that, Father—you saw me helping him!"

"The American...?" Veronica asked, her cleansed face white with terror and confusion "...what about the American?"

"They want him," Father Pablo answered. "That's why the police have come. Now where is he, Juan? Tell me before anyone else is killed!"

Hernando watched this exchange with a bemused, cynical expression. Father Pablo could smell the tequila on him.

"I don't understand," Veronica insisted. "What do they want with the American? Besides, he's already gone...Juan told me so." Turning to her lover, she asked, "You helped him to get away from here, yes?"

"Yes, yes," he answered impatiently, "and the good priest knows it as well."

He faced Father Pablo, "Why the devil did you come back here? I risked my neck getting you away, you know." His eyes drifted across the valise, then cut away to the wall as a bullet thumped into the limestone hide of the house. They all jumped.

"Judas..." Father Pablo hissed at him "...Liar!"

"Pants on fire," Hernando chimed in good-naturedly. "I've tried to tell you about him," he said to his sister.

"Shut up, Hernando," Veronica fired back, turning once more to Juan. "What is this, Juan? What has happened? Tell me the truth now," she commanded.

"I *have* told you the truth," Juan spat. "After saving this ungrateful priest's neck, I got the American out, as well. Is that so hard to believe?"

"I think so," Hernando observed.

"Hernando, please be quiet...you're drunk," Veronica pleaded.

"Yes, I am, a little," her brother replied, "but as it's the end of the world, and we're all about to die, I'm not too concerned about it. *This*," he nodded at Juan and Father Pablo, "is much more interesting."

"Did he not get you off the hacienda and away from the Indios, Father Pablo?" Veronica demanded.

"Why yes, he did…" the priest replied hotly, the memory of Manny's body cooling in the mud fanning the flames of his anger as much as the girl's incomprehensible faith in her despicable lover, "…oh yes, indeed!

"Here," he cried, "let me show you *why*," he threw open the battered case, retrieving the reliquary with a flourish. "This is why! He hid this in my valise and then used me like a drug runner's mule to smuggle it out after stealing it for the American and Barrera!"

"So that's where that went," Hernando remarked lightly.

Crossing herself at the appearance of the relic, Veronica swayed slightly as if she might faint.

"That's a lie," Juan shouted. "I never touched it!"

"Judas," Father Pablo screamed at him again. "You gave up the American to save your own neck!"

"Oh and how would you know? By then you had already scampered off like a frightened rabbit!"

Juan's words hung in the air of the room like a banner of guilt.

Veronica fell against her brother, seizing his arm for support, and moaning.

"No," Juan cried, "that came out wrong! It's this priest and all the shooting! I got him out of here, Veronica; I swear it!"

In spite of his detestation of the man, Father Pablo was moved by Juan's desperate need to be believed by Veronica. In this, at least, he appeared all too human.

Bullets began to strike the house with regularity as the fighting outside drew closer.

Pushing herself away from her brother, Veronica said, "Yes…*swear it.*"

Taking the gold reliquary from Father Pablo's grasp, she crossed herself with it; then kissed the smudged glass beneath which lay the tiny shred of fabric that was all that remained of Christ's cloak.

Rising to her knees, she held it out to Juan. "Go on," she said quietly, "place your lips where mine have been, and swear it."

In spite of the bullets peppering the house, Juan rose and took a step back from the proffered cross, his face gone white, beads of sweat appearing on his upper lip. "You hurt me," he said hoarsely to Veronica. "In front of your brother and this priest, you hurt me."

Tears began to leak from Veronica's eyes, yet the cross did not waver in her upheld grasp. She said nothing.

"How you could think this…how you could think such a thing of me…" Juan muttered indignantly, even as his eyes remained fixed on the reliquary held aloft in the hands of his lover.

He took a hesitant step towards it.

"For me," Veronica pleaded, "for *us*—swear it."

Juan took another step, the soles of his shoes making a dry scraping sound as he dragged them across the tiles. "To think you have so little faith in me…" his voice trailed off.

Father Pablo and Hernando remained rooted to their spots, barely breathing and unable to take their eyes from the scene unfolding before them.

"I love you," Veronica whispered. "Please."

Juan cut his eyes to her even as he crouched over the relic and said, "You think I won't…you think I can't?"

Seizing the cross in both hands, almost wrenching it from Veronica's hold, he planted a wet, angry kiss against the smeared glass that protected the robe.

Father Pablo and Veronica gasped, as Hernando observed aloud, "That does it! No doubt about it, he's innocent!"

Juan released the reliquary as violently as he had seized it and stepped back, lifting his arms to shoulder level and proclaiming, "I swear it!"

Even as Juan struck this pose in unconscious imitation of the last hours of the cloak's wearer, Father Pablo perceived his narrow, sallow face, already white, assume the grey, stricken aspect of a man in the grip of a heart attack. Yet, he did not groan and fall to the floor in instant retribution for his sacrilege, but favored each of the three other occupants of the room with a hate-filled glare.

"You are one to speak of innocence," he spat at Hernando, "you who have sat in judgment of the poor people who have spent their last peso to come here—ignorant peasants with nothing but desperation, dragging their dirty children halfway across México to fall to their knees before…this," he pointed at the reliquary that shook with the palsy of Veronica's hands, "while you sat swilling Doña Josefa's tequila to drown your disgust at their superstitious, selfish needs; their grubby, desperate clawing for a second chance—a reprieve from their life sentences!

"Oh, how you were disappointed and dirtied by their unrelenting and self-serving needs!"

Father Pablo gaped in astonishment, at the sullen Juan's unexpected, and vehement, eloquence.

"What a cruel shock for you," he continued, almost dancing with spite, "to discover that your high-minded faith had been compromised, that you were not a high priest of the well-spring of Christ's mercy, but the ticket-taker at a medicine woman's sideshow, witness to a never-ending parade of freaks—*Pobrecito!*"

During this tirade, Hernando had blanched as white as his accuser but remained silent, his eyes on the floor.

Juan swung around to Father Pablo. "And you, little priest," he laughed, "I would be remiss if I did not address your character, as well. Let's see, what can we say about this paragon, this tower of Christian strength and leadership? That he is a good priest?

"No, I don't think that would be entirely truthful, and we are, after all, telling the truth here. In fact, the little father can hardly find his way around the liturgy, as I can attest to from the few moments I woke up in the back of the church. Really, Father, embarrassing, don't you think?

"How about restraint... strength of character... sobriety...?" Juan paused dramatically as if to give these some thought, then answered himself, "No...no...and...no, I'm afraid," counting the negative votes on his fingers.

"From what I've seen and heard, the correct answers would be," again he counted his fingers, "self-indulgence, cowardice, and a good dose of drunkenness from time to time. Or does that fall under self-indulgence also?"

He surveyed the room's occupants for insight, but only Veronica met his gaze. "Even so," he continued thoughtfully, "you did risk something by bringing the reliquary back here, so all sins are forgiven and you can now sit in judgment of me in your newfound righteousness—very good, then."

He turned to Veronica, dismissing Father Pablo with a shrug, "Enough with the clergy."

Kneeling before her, he seized her wrists, gently forcing her to lower the cross she held between them.

"Veronica," he murmured, the malice leaching from his voice, "my own Veronica. The girl I loved even when her face was splashed with scarlet and had the texture of coarse sandpaper. The very girl for whom I earned numerous beatings from the schoolyard bullies who made fun of that face."

He ran the back of his grubby hand lovingly along Veronica's smoothed cheek. "I was happy to suffer at their hands for you," he breathed. "Even though I was poor and afraid, you always looked at me like I was something greater. I knew I wasn't, but that look of yours made me a conquistador. You always believed I would be something more and I loved you for that."

Rising to his feet, he released her cupped chin, and Veronica slumped back against the wall, clutching the relic to her bosom.

"It might be enough to have your forgiveness," he said, "but I have waited too late to be a good man."

Veronica contemplated him in dawning horror, as he turned once more to the priest.

"Your American will not return," he stated simply. "It was just as you said. If I had tried to protect him, they would have known I was involved in the theft of the relic and they would have killed me, too. They never trusted me, really," he finished sadly.

Walking to the to the stairs that led to the second floor, he paused, and added, "Perhaps there is something to this relic after all—I don't normally bother much with the truth," then went quietly from the room.

Captain Barrera's voice roared into the close confines of the kitchen, awakening them all from their reverie, "You there in the house! Attention! The police have secured the grounds of the hacienda, and await my command to storm the casa!"

Clearly it was true, Father Pablo thought, Captain Barrera and his bullhorn sounded as if they were within yards of the house itself. He glanced over at Veronica and her brother, the former weeping openly now, the latter frozen in fear—each isolated within their own terrors and sorrows.

"Release the American unharmed," the policeman continued, "and no harm need come to another person. Do you understand?"

The firing outside had ceased altogether and Father Pablo scrabbled across the floor on his hands and knees until he was beneath a window. With one hand he reached up and pulled it open.

"Someone must answer me," the captain demanded.

"Captain Barrera, it's me, Father Pablo Corellas! I'm inside the house," he called out frantically.

"Yes, yes," the police commander replied impatiently, "I'm glad you are unharmed, Little Father." He paused, then said, "Tell your friends in there to send out the gringo, and no tricks— my patience is running a little thin, and let's be quick about it!"

"I will, if he's in here," the priest hollered back, "but with all the shooting I haven't been able to get up from the floor."

It was a lie, but he needed to buy a little time in order to organize a safe surrender; he must meet with Doña Josefa.

"Give me a half hour, or so, to speak with everyone here," he asked Barrera.

"A half hour?" the captain parroted. "How long does it take to find a man that big? Grandma was slow, Father, but she was old!"

Father Pablo could hear the laughter of the other policemen erupt from the darkness outside.

"Thirty minutes," Father Pablo repeated.

A long moment passed.

"Thirty minutes," Barrera agreed, "but no tricks Little Father—the clock is ticking. The Indios will be back with reinforcements before you know it, and I don't think you and your friends will want to be here when they do…I know I don't."

Hoisting himself up from the floor, Father Pablo scurried across the kitchen, pausing only long enough to retrieve the reliquary from Veronica. She surrendered it without a murmur and he stuffed it roughly into his valise, hurrying through the same doorway through which Juan had disappeared.

Still breathless from the night's events, he stumbled up the dark stairway and onto the landing, pausing only long enough to recall which of the closed doors concealed Doña Josefa's room.

Passing the door of the room next to the one he had occupied, he could hear sounds from within—a dry, cautious scraping, as if someone were carefully shifting furniture about.

He could only imagine that it was Juan Alcante packing his belongings prior to fleeing in shameful ignominy. He hurried on.

A faint light shone from beneath Doña Josefa's door and Father Pablo paused only long enough to take a deep breath before knocking.

"Who's there? Who is it?" the old woman cried out in a tremulous voice.

"It's Father Pablo! May I come in?"

Turning the handle, he shoved gently at the swollen wood of the door, peering cautiously round the edge into the dim, flickering room.

The source of the light was a votive candle placed in a chipped saucer at the feet of a wooden Madonna, her skin the dusky hue of Our Lady of Guadalupe, the sky blue paint of her cloak flaking and faded.

The statue stood on a bedside table overlooking a child's bed, the moon beneath her feet and a crown of twelve stars round her head, her arms stretched out protectively over its lifelong occupant, Doña Josefa.

The old woman, her tall, elaborate coiffure released from its combs in a cascade of crimped, grey hair, stared as the priest squeezed his way into her sanctuary, her wizened monkey's face a mask of apprehension and alarm.

"What do you want?" she cried. "Why are you coming into a lady's bedroom?"

Producing a silver letter-opener, she pointed it at Father Pablo.

Raising his own hands, palms out, the priest said, "It's all right, Doña Josefa, it's Father Pablo. I mean you no harm." He took a few cautious steps in her direction.

In the wavering, yellow light of the candle, a host of sad, dusty dolls from another era peered out at him from every corner. Near the window, a child-sized tea table was laid with miniscule cups and saucers, its spindly, matching chairs turned out as if awaiting the return of long-dead children.

Like one of her dolls, Doña Josefa lay amidst a welter of pillows, their stuffing leaking out from disintegrating seams. With her free hand she clutched one protectively to her bosom.

Her eyes widened at the approach of the priest even as she lowered the makeshift dagger to her side.

"All is lost, Father," she whispered, "I have failed Our Lady. What are we to do?"

Father Pablo lowered himself to sit on the edge of the bed as the old woman stared up at him helplessly.

"I'm not sure," he answered. "Nothing is very clear, right now. But I must ask you something."

Doña Josefa nodded her assent.

"Have you told me the truth about the purple robe of Christ...all the truth?"

She continued to stare.

"People have died...are dying, Doña Josefa; I need to be sure now."

Appearing to think this over very carefully, she said at last, "Is that why everything has gone wrong...because I embellished my story a little?"

Father Pablo reached a hand out to steady himself against the nightstand. "Embellished?" he repeated faintly. "Embellished how?"

Doña Josefa seemed to choose her next words cautiously, "The lineage part."

"Your father never told you that you were descended from one of the soldiers that crucified our Lord...that part?" Father Pablo asked. "That this relic of the holy cloak had been handed down for generations?"

"Yes," she answered primly, "he was very drunk when he discovered the reliquary in the old chapel ruins and was perplexed as to where it had come from." She paused for a moment before adding, "He had never laid eyes on it before."

Father Pablo felt the musty room begin to spin.

Smiling suddenly, she continued, "As soon as he placed it in my hands though, *I* knew what it was! It was exactly as Our Lady had told me it would be!" She winked conspiratorially at her companion before continuing.

"That time on the veranda wasn't the first time I was blessed with a visit from the Virgin Mother, but I hadn't seen her in so long that I had almost forgotten what she looked like. I guess I should have told you that," she finished coyly.

"As to how we came into possession of it, well, I made that part up so that people wouldn't have such a hard time believing. It does make sense when you think about it though; I suspect it is very likely true."

Turning his eyes to the Madonna, Father Pablo groaned softly, "What have we done…what have *I* done?"

The serene features of the Virgin gazed back at him in apparent incomprehension, the same statue that had watched protectively over the lonely, stunted little girl that had lain in this bed all her long life, a statue that was terrible in its resemblance to the Apparition Doña Josefa had described on the veranda.

Yet, how *did* one explain the miracles, he asked himself— the healings he had witnessed with his own eyes? Could it be that the pilgrims' simple, desperate faith was answered by a loving God through an object without inherent value or worth? Or did the reliquary indeed contain a tiny piece of ancient fabric that had once caressed the very flesh of Christ Jesus Himself, in spite of its now-suspect provenance?

Had the Virgin Mother appeared to the frightened old crone that even now cowered beneath the stiff, dirty sheets of her childhood bed, or was everything Doña Josefa claimed to be dismissed on her own admission of selective truth-telling? There was no denying the miracles, yet what, *exactly*, was he to believe?

From somewhere down the hallway there was a crash, as if a heavy piece of furniture had fallen over. This was followed by several moments of silence, interrupted by the sound of feet rapidly ascending the stairs.

Seconds later Veronica's screams could be heard from Juan's room.

"Is it the police?" Doña Josefa asked, pulling the pillow more tightly to her chest.

"I don't think so," Father Pablo answered, leaping to his feet and rushing for the hallway. "Stay put—I will come back for you!"

The door to Juan's room was standing open now, its occupant suspended from a rope woven of the same sisal fibers once grown on the plantation. He had tied one end to a disused chandelier hook in the ceiling, securing the other round his thin neck prior to launching himself from a wooden crate that now lay on its side beneath his dancing feet. A ring of blood running from beneath the deadly collar attested to the coarseness of the fibers.

Veronica clasped his skinny, spastic legs in a futile attempt to lift his fragile bulk and relieve the killing pressure on his windpipe, even as her Juan clawed frantically at the noose, his eyes gone black with congested blood.

Father Pablo stood frozen in the doorway, stunned at the near-silent tableau punctuated only by the grunts and gurgles of the struggling lovers.

Echoing up from the kitchen, the clear, unamplified voice of Captain Barrera proclaimed, "Time's up, Little Father!"

CHAPTER FIFTEEN

Captain Barrera's detention of the occupants of the hacienda had been brief and conducted with the stilted courtesy Father Pablo had come to expect of the police commander.

When he had discovered the priest and Veronica struggling to relieve the pressure from round his informant's neck, he had acted with cool dispatch, swiftly slicing the rope with a razor-sharp stiletto that he had, like a magician, produced from nowhere, while barking orders at the policemen that had accompanied him.

Within moments, it had seemed to Father Pablo, the unconscious and barely breathing Juan had been hustled to a waiting vehicle and whisked away on a wail of sirens. Veronica, having been allowed to ride along with him by the ever-gallant captain, stroked his limp hand, murmuring a lover's desperate litany into his blood-filled ear.

The rest, Doña Josefa, Hernando, and he, had only been questioned after a thorough search of the premises had failed to produce the American. In spite of his officers' impatient stamping about and anxious glances round the window casements into the greater darkness beyond, the senior policeman had interviewed his prisoners in an almost leisurely manner.

Allowing Doña Josefa to remain in her little bed as he spoke to her, the captain had Father Pablo stand by her side like an anxious chaperone.

It had only been when the priest repeated Juan's declaration that "your American will not return" that Barrera, at last, appeared to wilt, suddenly ashen with fatigue.

After a few moments of silence, he had mumbled something that Father Pablo understood to be, "Well, that's it then...it's all over," while clumsily lighting a cigarette and rising unsteadily to his feet. "We'd best be off," he announced.

In the event, only Father Pablo had accepted the captain's offer of safe conduct back to Progreso, Hernando choosing to remain with the old woman. "It wouldn't be right to leave her all alone..." he had said, tiredly climbing the stairs, "...especially now."

Neither he nor Father Pablo had spoken of the whereabouts of the reliquary of the purple robe, leaving its future as an unanswered question between them.

* * *

The tapping on his door was rapid and insistent and no matter which way he rolled and shifted within his tousled bed he could not escape it. Even so, his sleeping mind dodged in and out of changing, tumultuous scenes in an effort to flee the summons, as if he were running breathlessly from one strange room into another interrupting and briefly participating in inexplicable, and sometimes frightening, tableaus.

"Father Pablo," his housekeeper called out after him, "it is almost time for supper and you have a visitor!" He rolled over yet again, the blankets binding him like a straitjacket. "It's the policeman," she hissed through the door, "Barrera! Do you hear me?"

He swung his feet over the edge of the bed, compelled by the power of the personality behind the conjured name, "Yes," he managed to croak, swaying uncertainly and feeling as if he would fall down if he attempted to stand too quickly, "yes, I hear you. I'll be right down."

Glancing at his bedside clock, Father Pablo noted with a start that he had been asleep for nearly twelve hours—ever since he had stumbled through the rectory doors in the dark hours before dawn. The happenings at Doña Josefa's hacienda seemed all of a part of his recent incomprehensible dreams—impossible events involving people he could not possibly know. Yet, the weight in his chest anchored him to those impossible events and unknowable people, as surely as his knowledge of what lay hidden in the battered valise that crouched in the corner of his gloomy, twilit room.

"I'm coming," he reiterated to Señora Garza's fading footsteps while rising.

Just as he had feared, he swayed alarmingly and nearly fell, staggering over to the sink like a drunken man.

Splashing cold water on his stubbled face, he ran his damp hands through his hair in a futile attempt to smooth down the spiky, twisted strands. This effort failed to convey any dignity to the disheveled appearance he confronted in the mirror, and he pushed away with a groan of disgust.

As he had fallen asleep in his clothes of the night before, he had only to slip his feet back into his caked shoes and was prepared as he would be for the captain's interview.

Barrera awaited the priest in the same cozy room in which he had met Veronica a lifetime before, and his appearance, like Father Pablo's, had not been improved by the previous night's experience. Slouching uncharacteristically in the armchair, he made no effort to rise as the young priest entered the room, but waved a limp hand in his direction while gazing distractedly out the darkening window.

It was at once obvious to Father Pablo that the policeman had not been to bed, as his always immaculate uniform was wrinkled and creased, and large wet-looking patches stained the shirt beneath his armpits. His boots, crossed carelessly at the ankles, were still encrusted with the dried mud of the hacienda's churned grounds, and his hat lay carelessly tossed onto the floor, as if he might not have need of it in the future.

When, at last, he turned his face to the priest, it was drawn and ashen, his handsome features slack with exhaustion and something else that Father Pablo could not, as yet, identify, his dark, intelligent eyes glazed and bloodshot.

"I need to make confession, Father," he said quietly, turning once more to the window. "Perhaps I should have made an appointment."

Father Pablo looked on in astonishment; he had been prepared to be interviewed at some length about the events leading up to last night's debacle, perhaps even to be taken to the police station and interrogated, but a request for confession, from arguably the most dangerous man in Progreso, had never entered his thoughts.

He remained speechless for several moments, a craven sense of relief flooding his veins, then managed to say, "Of course not, Captain, of course not. Would you be more comfortable in the confessional?"

He made a sweeping gesture in the direction of the church and began to take steps to the door when Barrera stopped him.

"No, no," he muttered impatiently. "I don't need all the trappings—right here is just fine." Leaning over, he patted the seat of the chair opposite where he was sitting. "Come sit down."

His natural tone of command leaked through in spite of the air of defeat he exuded. It was this that Father Pablo now recognized in his haggard features.

"Oh yes," Father Pablo agreed, hurrying to take his seat, "this will do just fine. Many people prefer the more personal touch these days." He hated the unctuous manner he seemed incapable of avoiding when in the policeman's presence.

"Shall we begin?" Captain Barrera asked. "I'm really very tired."

Father Pablo hastily invoked the Trinity as Barrera followed along, his gestures impatient and perfunctory.

"Bless me, Father, for I have sinned," he opened; then continued the formula, "I haven't been to confession since last Easter, or thereabouts, sometime during Lent, I think."

He stopped speaking and rested his chin in his palm.

"Go on," Father Pablo encouraged.

Starting from his sudden reverie, Barrera continued, "I had a few shots of tequila before coming here, does that disqualify me?"

His expression appeared to indicate that the question was merely academic and that he wasn't particularly concerned with the outcome.

"Well," Father Pablo ventured uncertainly, "you really shouldn't have, but let's not concern ourselves with that now. You don't appear drunk," he added hopefully.

"No," Barrera agreed, "I'm not drunk. It was impossible to get drunk this day. That's when I knew I needed to make confession."

"You wish to be reconciled with the Church," Father Pablo encouraged.

"I wish to be reconciled with God," the policeman corrected him. "I don't always see the two as working together."

"No," the priest murmured, "but we do try. It is sometimes very hard to hear the voice of God in the midst of this noisy life—even amongst the clergy."

Barrera almost smiled. "You surprise me, Father, there is a bit of poetry in you—the poetry of the martyr, I'm afraid."

"I don't know what you mean, Captain," Father Pablo replied nervously. "Now, do you wish to confess your sins, or no?"

Fishing a cigarette from his tunic, Barrera held it up inquiringly, even as he lit it before gaining permission. He blew out a stream of smoke, then while casually searching about for an ashtray said, "My wife has left me and taken the girls."

He found the receptacle and leaned back once more in his chair. "It seems she heard all about my arrangement with the Americans—it's all over town apparently and, well...she is ashamed of me.

"Extraordinary, isn't it?" he continued softly, staring up at the ceiling now. "That poor woman has put up with my affairs all these years and never wavered in her love for me, then when I try to do something that might really have put us up in the world, she's shamed."

Looking to his confessor for commiseration, he found him staring uncomfortably at his hands. "Women," the captain breathed. "I guess they're just as much a mystery to you?"

"Yes," Father Pablo answered quickly, feeling his neck flush. "She *knew* about your other women?"

Barrera laughed softly, "Oh yes. It's like I told you that day in the café, everyone knows everyone's business in a place like this.

"She's ashamed of me now, though," he continued, "and oddly, now that I know that…I am ashamed of me, too."

Stubbing the cigarette out abruptly, Barrera turned away from Father Pablo. "When I saw that look on her face, it was as if I no longer knew who I was, or even who I had been.

"I'm glad she left," he continued huskily, "I couldn't bear her looking at me anymore, and the girls, though they know nothing, made me weep. I didn't even try to stop my wife from taking them."

Father Pablo contemplated the policeman's hunched back, saying nothing for a long while.

Pulling a handkerchief from his pocket, Barrera brought it around to his hidden face, and Father Pablo waited for him to finish before speaking again. "This is a result," he said quietly, "but what are your sins?"

Swinging back around in his seat, Barrera cast a long bloodshot glance at Father Pablo. "Very good, Little Father…worthy of myself…I would never let a criminal get away with such a lame confession, either."

He resumed with more gusto, "I am guilty of the most serious of all the sins—my crime is pride—the great, overweening pride that justifies all things and brooks no opposition."

Rising suddenly from his chair, he began to pace the room as he continued, "The pride that made me believe in myself, and my abilities, and placed me head and shoulders above every other man in this sad, little town, that allowed me to rise to the rank of captain over dozens who were my seniors, that gained me the prettiest bride in all the Yucatán. This was my sin! *Me*—I was my sin!"

Barrera flung himself into his chair, appearing to shrink before Father Pablo's eyes.

More softly now, he went on, "And now, Father, now that I need me to be me more than ever in my life, now that people lay dead in the mud of that hacienda, now that the commandánte is conducting official inquiries into my actions, now that my family has abandoned me, *I* no longer exist—there is nothing left of Antonio Francisco Barrera, yet I will be held responsible for his crimes—his sins."

"Your sins," Father Pablo corrected him. "*Your* sins—do you sincerely regret them?"

"Hah, that's a good one," the captain turned his still-leaking eyes on the priest. "Maybe the real question is would I regret what I've done, what I've become, had I succeeded. If things had turned out as I planned, would I be crying in front of a priest at this moment?"

Father Pablo said nothing, as he had no answer to this, and Barrera laughed, "I wrestled with God and He cast me down— His robe was my undoing, that is all we are left with…so in answer to your question, yes, I regret my sins mightily, and not least the lives of those poor people who are now dead because of me. I will never lose enough wives and daughters to atone for just one of them…and I don't even know who they were."

"And do you resolve to sin no more?" Father Pablo asked after an interval.

Barrera laughed more weakly this time, "I've been stripped to the bone, Father, I don't think there's enough of me left to sin again…I only wish I had never begun."

There was a rap on the door and Señora Garza stuck her head into the room without waiting for an answer. "Supper's on the table," she announced, glancing disdainfully at the disheveled police officer. "Shall I set a second place?"

"No," Father Pablo replied more forcefully than was his wont. "Bring my valise from my room, Señora."

Unaccustomed to commands from her young priest, she quickly shut the door again and hurried away.

Father Pablo turned once more to Barrera.

"Am I forgiven, Father?" the captain asked tiredly.

"Of course you are, so long as your confession was sincere."

The policeman looked at Father Pablo. "You know it was," he said.

"Then you are absolved, Antonio," Father Pablo answered, following with a prayer of absolution. When he was done, he murmured, "Give thanks to the Lord for He is good."

"His mercy endures forever," Barrera completed the ritual.

"Then all that is left are prayers and penance."

Señora Garza entered without knocking in order to demonstrate her annoyance at being ordered about, and Father Pablo took the valise from her. She scurried out without waiting for his thanks as he opened the leather satchel and placed it in Barrera's lap. The policeman glanced down at its contents.

"Mother of God," he whispered in exclamation, "it's the reliquary—the purple robe—you've had it all the while!"

Looking up at Father Pablo with a wan smile, he added, "Just my luck these days—I finally have what I've been after now that it's become worthless to me."

"Worthless?" Father Pablo asked, sitting up a little straighter, "Don't be a fool, Antonio, and for God's sake, stop feeling sorry for yourself, it doesn't suit you at all."

Wincing at the priest's words and tone, Barrera said nothing in reply.

Father Pablo seized the crucifix containing the robe and thrust it at the policeman. "Take this," he commanded, "and give it to the American woman. Her husband died for it, so it is only right that it should go to her—I trust in God that she will know what to do with it—I certainly don't."

Reluctantly, Barrera took the cross from the priest in both his hands, regarding it at arm's length as he would a snake capable of striking him. "Perhaps you missed your calling, Father, you would have made a good policeman—you certainly have a sense of justice—rough justice in my case—I would rather return it to the Indios naked and alone than face Brenda Arbor this night."

"Yet this is what I require of you—this is your penance."

"Penance," Barrera repeated with a quiet laugh. "Isn't that what life is anyway?"

CHAPTER SIXTEEN

The crowd that awaited Father Pablo in the plaza lacked the festive, holiday spirit that had characterized the earlier pilgrims. They milled about aimlessly, their voices subdued and querulous; forming an angry murmur that rose and fell like the ocean waves that rushed the nearby shore. Though food and trinket vendors worked the scene as they had in days past, no banners were to be seen gaily waving over the faithful in anticipation of their pious journey, no waiting buses chugged and wheezed on the silenced streets. The stalled pilgrims lay in the morning shadow of the church as restless as an army in arrears of its pay—vicarious victims of the battle at the hacienda.

As Captain Barrera had predicted, the Centurions had indeed returned with reinforcements from the surrounding Indio pueblitos and followed the retreating police to the very outskirts of Progreso. They now controlled the only highway and the few secondary roads that led into the city, thereby effectively laying siege to its inhabitants and visitors alike—the pilgrims could neither complete their journey nor return to their homes in other parts of the country. It was of no comfort to them that the governor was, at that moment, mobilizing troops to break the cordon, as they had no wish to be caught in the middle of the Battle for Progreso.

Father Pablo's appearance at the church doors had the effect of increasing the volume of the people's voices to that of a sullen mumble, and as the last of the morning's communicants nervously shook his hand and made their way down the steps to join the mob or hastily skirt it, he glanced furtively in their direction and made to return to the sanctuary of his church.

After all, he reasoned, there was nothing he could do to alleviate their plight and he must put a call to the archbishop to bring him up to date on the events surrounding the holy garment—it wouldn't do for the senior prelate to learn of them only from the news broadcasts. As to the current whereabouts of the robe, Father Pablo found himself guiltily uncertain of what he would relate to his superior.

Doña Marisa surprised him at the door, appearing to materialize out of the cool darkness of the church like an apparition, the black of her widow's dress and veil taking shape from the greater blackness within as she glided soundlessly toward him. Forcing her head downwards in painful genuflection, the dowager's hump perched like an incubus on her back, and Father Pablo felt the hair on his neck and arms rising at her unexpected, stealthy approach, heralded only by the tapping of her walking stick. The altar boy sidled away like a frightened horse as she halted in front of the priest.

"Good morning, Doña Marisa," Father Pablo managed to stammer.

Doña Marisa continued to look past him at the impatient assemblage in the plaza, lines radiating from pursed lips. "You've done it now," she assured him, still staring down the mob, "you and all your hocus-pocus!   Just look at this superstitious rabble, would you!"

Maneuvering herself to face him, she continued, "What now, Little Father? We're overflowing with idiots and surrounded by hostile, armed Indios—any new tricks up your sleeve?"

Father Pablo stared back speechless, his tongue gone dry even as a cold, damp hand gently massaged his heart.

The old woman looked at him oddly. "What's the matter with you?" she asked as beads of sweat gathered along his hairline.

Her eyes were the grey of the bleak tundra that he had seen in schoolbook photos as a child—a strange, cold place where no one could possibly live and be happy.

"I…I *have* made mistakes," he mumbled.

Continuing to study him closely, Doña Marisa snorted, "Mistakes? That's what you have to say? Now that's a fine confession, a mea culpa worthy of a priest such as you!"

She swiveled back around to face the plaza once more. "Well, that's that then, I'll just be on my way; hopefully I'll make it through this gang without being robbed or murdered." She set off down the steps, her cane rapping a warning of her approach.

Father Pablo hesitated in the doorway, his own responsibility for all that had happened weighing heavily upon him, thoughts of the penitent Captain Barrera foremost among them. He had hoped to celebrate the Mass of a new day and a new beginning with the poor man, but the policeman had failed to show.

Shrugging, he gestured for his altar server to go ahead of him. In his haste to close the great doors behind him, the boy did not even look back.

Having effectively blocked his own retreat, Father Pablo turned back to the crowd, trying a smile that came across as sickly and insincere. "Good morning," he said too loudly.

A handful of people returned his greeting in a faint, scattered chorus. The silence that returned boomed in Father Pablo's ears. Just cresting the spire of the church, the sun threw its warming rays over the farthest edge of the plaza in a brilliant bar.

"God has given us a beautiful day," Father Pablo exclaimed, raising arms still draped in his cassock to the whitewashed sky, but the people did not appear to share his sentiments.

He could see that Doña Marisa's progress had been blocked by a knot of young people who were talking quietly amongst themselves and lounging full-length on sleeping bags thrown carelessly onto the flagstones. Even from where he stood, Father Pablo could see that the widow was admonishing them with righteous fury. Several times she struck the stones with the tip of her cane as if, like Moses with his staff, she would part this sea of the unwashed.

A middle-aged man who appeared to have not shaved for days pushed his way up to Father Pablo, saying, "The police will not let us go out of the city, Father; they are preventing us from returning to our homes."

He waited as if he had asked a question.

"Yes, I know," the priest replied distractedly, as he witnessed the argument between the widow and the youths grow more heated. "I believe they are right in this; it isn't safe to travel out there just now."

He began to descend the steps in order to extricate the old woman from the altercation.

Several men in the dress of campesinos moved in front of him as he stepped onto the plaza stones.

"There is a rumor that the *Church* has possession of the holy relic—is that true, Father? Is it here?" the smallest of three asked peremptorily, while pointing his stubbled chin at the church to emphasize his question.

"Here?" Father Pablo repeated guiltily, his alarm heightened by their aggressive actions. None of them had even bothered to doff their straw hats. "No, of course not," he answered, attempting to push through them, but they would not part to let him pass. A few yards away he heard a young woman's voice join the argument with Doña Marisa.

"Let me through," he demanded, but the farmers' dark faces remained blank and unconvinced.

"The Centurions don't have it;" the spokesman for the campesinos continued, "otherwise, why would they blockade the city?"

Others in the crowd began to draw closer in order to better hear Father Pablo's inquisitors.

"I can assure you that the Church is *not* in possession of the robe," Father Pablo snapped nervously. "Now I must insist you let me pass!"

"You filthy rabble," Father Pablo heard distinctly above the increasingly curious hum of the crowd. Several heads swung in the direction he had last seen Doña Marisa.

A young woman's voice answered, "You old bitch!"

"Well, if you don't have it, and the Indios don't have it, who does that leave, Father?" The small, flinty man persisted. "Is it the police? Do the police have it?"

An alarmed murmur ran through the crowd at this last conjecture and several people began to shout angrily, "The police have it! They have stolen Our Savior's cloak!"

"No, no, that is not what I said," Father Pablo cried, raising both hands in the air, even as he blushed unconvincingly.

Over the heads of his interrogators he saw the walking stick of Doña Marisa rise into the air and remain poised above the heads of her enemies.

"Really, I must go," he shouted and began to push his way through the sullenly yielding mob.

Even as he focused on Doña Marisa's cane to guide him to her rescue, he witnessed another hand shoot upwards and wrest it from her grasp.

"You stupid hag," someone cried. "Who do you think you're speaking to? I'm not some peasant to be whipped like a dog!"

Father Pablo broke through in time to see a squat, tough-looking woman slash Doña Marisa's legs several times with her own stick. With each stroke a thin veil of dust rose into the clear morning air from the older woman's black dress.

"We've seen the way you look down your long nose at us," Doña Marisa's punisher hissed, dancing and flailing around the old woman.

The faces of the witnesses wore amused expressions and some were even laughing and joining in with catcalls.

"Stop," Father Pablo demanded, "stop that this instant!"

The young woman with the cane froze in the act of raising it once more and the watchers grew instantly silent.

Flinging himself into the circle, Father Pablo seized the stick from the woman's chubby fist. "Shame..." he cried, wielding the cane as if he might strike the woman and her supporters as well, "...shame!"

Though they remained respectfully silent, the crowd did not fall back, but continued their bovine scrutiny as if indifference rendered them innocent. The offending woman melted into their midst as if she had never existed.

Spluttering to a halt, unable to think what to say beyond his single declaration, Father Pablo rushed to Doña Marisa's side. Large, heavy tears dropped from her downturned face to splash, unheeded, in the dust of the plaza, yet she made no sound.

Halting before her, Father Pablo was arrested by her startling, silent grief; an aspect of her character that, until that moment, he had no inkling could exist within her forbidding personality. Without a word between them, she retrieved the contested walking stick from his grasp, resuming her interrupted journey to the far side of the square and the street beyond.

Father Pablo followed wordlessly at a respectful distance, as shamed as if he had been amongst the jeering onlookers to her chastisement. The restive pilgrims made way for her this time and Father Pablo followed her trail of tears through the narrow chasm of humanity.

Without slackening her usual, inexplicably rapid gait, she trundled into the roadway as if it were not possible for the car that was boring down upon her to exist. The driver, having found the normally congested streets of Progreso strangely deserted, was going faster than was usual even for him, and had no time to apply his brakes before the two figures crossed into the roadway before him.

Looking neither right nor left, Doña Marisa scuttled in front of the oncoming vehicle and gave out only a slight, surprised squeal as she was suddenly struck from behind.

The force of the blow propelled her against a car parked on the far side of the narrow street, sending her walking stick dancing along the sidewalk as if escaping her contentious company. Dimly registering a dull thud and the sound of shattered glass, she suddenly found herself sprawled across the trunk of a parked car, her tiny feet pedaling furiously in the air.

Behind her, the mob that had so recently enjoyed her humiliation cried out as one, then groaned in unison before a great, expectant hush fell over the plaza. The scream of a car driven at great speed and in the wrong gear receded into the distance.

All at once, hands were pulling at her, while a cacophony of voices anxiously inquired as to her wellbeing, even as others gave conflicting opinions on her condition.

She lay with her cheek against the still cool metal surface of the trunk assessing her condition for herself, and after several moments of this, concluded that, other than some soreness to the right side of her face, she was unharmed.

With a huff, and the assistance of some bystanders, she managed to regain her footing, and as she did so a sprinkle of glass rained down onto her shoulders, dislodged from her hair by her movements. She felt slightly woozy and it was only after someone had returned her troublesome stick that she was able to steady herself and take in the scene.

A crowd had gathered around someone that lay in the street, and it occurred to her that it might be the body of one of her recent tormentors. With this not altogether ungratifying thought, she resumed her interrupted journey to the police headquarters to demand the removal of the unruly occupiers of the plaza; then hesitated.

Someone had pushed her, she suddenly remembered. At first, she had assumed it to be one of her attackers, but now, as the sickening thud of the impact returned with greater clarity, it occurred to her that something altogether different may have happened. She found herself moving somewhat painfully toward the object that lay at the heart of the knot of onlookers.

Stepping forward to gently grasp her elbows, two women led her over, while many of those gathered about the victim turned to watch her approach with expressions of great concern. Doña Marisa found herself hurrying to join them in spite of a growing soreness in her back and joints.

Parting respectfully to allow her entry into their circle, she noted, even in her haze of confusion, the sudden change in demeanor of the rabble she had so recently castigated.

Father Pablo lay at her feet looking up at the morning sky, his expression not unlike that of a man resting contentedly in his hammock on a warm summer day, only the wine-colored pool of blood that had seeped from his skull betraying his circumstances.

Doña Marisa squatted down to brush the flies, which had already begun to gather, away from his placid, immature face— but for his morning stubble, she thought, he resembled nothing more than an altar boy caught masquerading as a priest.

Several women were praying their Rosaries, the click of the beads audible in the great hush.

"How did he get here?" Doña Marisa asked one.

Looking up in apparent surprise, her hands arrested in the act of moving from one decade to the next, the woman answered, "He was following *you*—he saved your life."

"I was unaware of it," Doña Marisa replied. "I was very upset and thought I was being pursued by…well, never mind."

A siren sounded from the nearby hospital signaling the dispatch of an ambulance and Doña Marisa touched Father Pablo's cheek with the back of her hand.

"He is still breathing. Do you think he is in much pain?"

The praying woman shook her head in answer, continuing with her meditations.

Turning back to the stricken priest, Doña Marisa found that his eyes were open and that he was looking at her. It occurred to her that she should thank him for his sacrifice as she might not get another chance, but he forestalled her by raising his right arm and pointing upward.

A number of people craned their necks to follow, but saw nothing more than the wispy cirrus clouds that swept across the morning sky.

"Blue…" Father Pablo muttered as happily as a toddler with his first word, "…Our Lady is clothed in the blue of heaven," then quite deliberately placed his hand on the Dowager's Hump that rested between Doña Marisa's shoulder blades.

With a small cry, she twisted her torso painfully away from the injured priest's shocking familiarity, and his arm fell back to his side once more. Closing his eyes, he began to snore as gently as an infant.

The tears that sprang to the older woman's eyes were less for the injuries and sacrifice of a young man she hardly knew and greatly disapproved of than it was for the loneliness his touch revealed—she could not remember anyone, other than a doctor in the practice of his cold profession, having chosen to touch the great deformity that rode her back and spread its deadening tendrils into her very heart and soul. Even her late, beloved husband had avoided contact with it, averting his eyes when chancing upon her in a state of undress.

The arrival of the police broke the spell that had descended upon the crowded plaza, and the pilgrims scurried out of the way of the phalanx that pushed its way to the injured curate.

Following closely behind were the ambulance attendants hauling their gurney with careless haste through the recently opened channel.

Captain Barrera closed up the procession, striding behind, his normally intimidating demeanor somewhat mitigated by his lack of headgear. Halting at the prone figure of his confessor, he looked down at him. It was not possible from his expression to know what he was thinking.

Rising shakily to her feet with the aid of her newfound attendants, Doña Marisa slapped at the dust on her knees. With some effort she was able to peer upwards at the tall policeman and was shocked at the change in the man; besides being unaccountably hatless, his normally smooth face was darkened with several days growth and his uniform was dirty and unkempt, even his tunic was unbuttoned almost to the waist, and he fidgeted with a kind of nervous energy foreign to her experience of him.

"You have arrived too late," she pronounced.

Barrera studied Father Pablo for a moment with a practiced eye and said, "I believe you are wrong there, Señora, God has other plans for our little brother."

Placing a plastic mask over Father Pablo's mouth and nose, one of the medical technicians began to administer oxygen to him through a tube attached to a green metal bottle. Meanwhile, uniformed officers roamed through the crowd, writing pads in hand, collecting eyewitness information on the accident.

Kneeling, Captain Barrera patted the chest of Father Pablo in an affectionate manner, whispering, "All will be well...I know that now. I know you do, too."

Opening one bloodshot eye, Father Pablo studied the policeman blearily for a moment before lapsing into unconsciousness once more.

Barrera rose in a cloud of flies that had been skating on the congealing blood beneath Father Pablo's head.

"You there," he pointed at a man with his morning's newspaper, "keep these damn flies off his face until we can get him aboard the ambulance."

The startled man sprang to the task as if it were his life's work.

Captain Barrera gestured to the ambulance crew to remove the patient and, with some effort, considering that he was a small, if plump, man, they lifted him onto the gurney and wheeled him away to the waiting ambulance.

Doña Marisa and the captain watched him go, but neither made any attempt to accompany him.

"You will get the devil that did this?" she asked of him.

"No," he answered without hesitation, staring off in the direction of the church doors and a knot of rustic-looking men that appeared to be creating a ruckus, "that will be left to someone else. I'm afraid my days in authority are numbered.

"Now, if you are certain you do not wish any medical attention, I must excuse myself, as there is at least one service I can provide Father Pablo this day."

With a nod at the gathering mob being exhorted from the church steps, he left her to march alone across the plaza.

Doña Marisa watched Barrera stalk away with a dizzying feeling of uncertainty—it seemed the captain's announcement and the brazen touch of the young priest had thrown her world into chaos. Nothing appeared as it should now and her staid, ordered life seemed artificial and terrifyingly fragile. For no reason that she could account for she thought of calling Captain Barrera's name across the plaza and having him return to her, but common sense prevailed and she kept her peace.

Reluctantly, she turned away, resuming her interrupted journey home, and wondering if she too might have suffered a head injury.

Behind her, the small, angular farmer that had so rudely accosted Father Pablo addressed the growing press of citizens and visitors drawn by his inflammatory speech.

Making his way through the crowd, Barrera began picking up snatches of the fierce little man's tirade—phrases like "corrupt priests" and "crooked cops" were being thrown to the mob like food to the hungry.

They must be starving, Barrera thought with contempt, if their rapt attention is anything to go by. He noted uneasily the exhorter's coterie of companions that formed a semicircle behind him like a security detail.

As Barrera mounted the short flight of steps leading to the portico of the church, the fiery orator marked his coming with only a glance from the corner of his inflamed eyes. He recognized the legendary policeman by description, even in his current disreputable state, and felt a small thrill of terror run down his spine. At the same time, he noted that Barrera had advanced alone into the midst of the throng—the few officers that had responded with him leaving with the ambulance.

Barrera's boldness infuriated him while filling him with fear, and he let his words fly like arrows.

"You heard my questions to the dishonest priest," he sang out to his audience, "and saw how he fled before the truth! The Church has become a web of deceit that cowers before the truth of the purple robe—they have stolen that which they cannot control or explain and hidden it within this building!"

He threw an arm up to point accusingly at the church itself.

Barrera walked casually past him to the church doors. Leaning against them, he folded his arms across his chest while crossing his booted ankles. For added effect he yawned hugely, only belatedly covering his mouth with a few lazy pats to his lips.

The restive crowd grew suddenly silent with this affront to their orator; a few tittered; then went suddenly quiet.

Stumbling in his homily, the eloquent farmer glanced back at the policeman with genuine hatred.

"The priest has been judged before our very eyes!" he resumed. "Did you not see it yourselves? He was struck down by the Hand of God!"

Many had seen and were vocal in their agreement.

"The Blooded Mantle must be returned—we cannot allow the Church and its corrupt agents," and here he favored Barrera with an arch glance, "to withhold the very cloth that touched our Savior's body!

"Many of us have traveled hundreds of miles to be here, some have spent their life savings in order to bring their loved ones to the foot of the cross!"

The majority loudly and vehemently concurred with this, even as others were drawn from all corners of the plaza by the swelling ruckus.

"Within!" the hard little man exhorted the crowd. "Just within these walls they have hidden it from its rightful owner and from us—the faithful! Will you allow it?" he thundered.

Hundreds cried in return that they would not, could not, allow such an injustice.

"Then join me now," their newfound leader demanded. "Let us go within the walls of our own church and search for that which rightly belongs to the people!"

He reached out, palm upwards, as if to assist the crowd to its feet and up the steps.

They rose in response like a flooding tide to surge upwards, even as their commander and his fellow campesinos turned about to lead their fledgling army through the portals of the enemy.

Barrera had not removed himself however, and his continued presence had the unexpected effect of reducing the mob to puzzled silence and their surge to a subdued lapping at the uppermost steps. He still maintained his casual stance, and in fact, disconcertingly, was not even looking at the advancing mob, but appeared to be studying something off in the distance, his stubbled chin resting in his palm. Silence spread out from him like oil on water.

The wiry campesino regarded the policeman coldly, his very presence a challenge to his newfound authority, and an insult to his manhood. For once, he had trouble finding words.

His people waited.

"Stand aside and I will allow no harm to come to you," he lied unconvincingly and loudly.

"Me?" Barrera asked as if waking from a reverie, turning at last to face the mob and its leader.

"*You* can do no harm to me in any case," the policeman assured his would-be protector pleasantly. "But, as to you sacking the church...I cannot allow it."

As if the subject were now closed, he turned his face away once more.

Even so, the angry little farmer and his followers noted Barrera's hand drift down to within inches of his holster. "You cannot kill us all, you pig," he spat.

"This is so," Barrera agreed. "But I will certainly make a point of killing *you*."

Those closest strained to hear this exchange over the rising angry voices of the press behind them. It was becoming increasingly difficult to not be shoved forward, and those in the front ranks struggled to maintain a safe distance.

"This is the butcher of the Centurions," the little man screamed at his followers while leveling an accusing finger at

Barrera. "Will we bow before his authority...will we answer to this *antichrist*?"

A wave of fury swept through the crowd at this announcement and the tide of angry humanity began to rise once more.

Stepping forward, Barrera raised a hand to silence the mob, saying loudly enough for most to hear, "This man is right enough about me!"

The people went silent once more, this time in amazement at such honesty from a government official.

"I am responsible for the deaths at Doña Josefa's hacienda!"

Barrera paused to allow this news to travel across the plaza and silence the mob with curiosity before resuming, "No one, but me, is responsible. And I confess before you now, brothers and sisters in Christ, not only asking for your forgiveness, but so that you will believe what else I have to say and no other lives will be senselessly lost.

"The Purple Garment of Jesus is not within this church, I assure you, so there is no sense in following these bad men..." he pointed at the knot of similarly-clad men and their leader, "...into sacrilege and crime—don't do it, I ask of you...please."

"Oh ho," Barrera's opponent chortled theatrically, turning back to his stolen audience, "he admits to stealing the reliquary and now wants us to believe it's not inside there!"

He danced with spiteful glee at his deductions. "Murderer *and* thief...and we are to believe him...even as we are besieged by his victims! Satan is the father of all lies," he exclaimed triumphantly, pointing back at Barrera.

The crowd was returned to his control and angry that they were so nearly duped. They came on.

Barrera took several of his long steps, unholstering his .45 and striking his antagonist a practiced, unhurried blow behind the right ear. The little man collapsed like a house of cards and lay there as small and deflated as a dog's carcass.

"This is a bad man," Barrera reminded the crowd, "perhaps as bad as me if given the chance."

The rabble-rouser's cabal of protectors looked on in impotent fury, ever mindful of the pistol in Barrera's capable hand, maintaining their distance even as their hands went secretly to hidden knives.

Again the mob was halted when confronted with this graphic reminder of authority, even as a furious roar arose from the multitude.

"Walk away from this," Barrera pleaded with them. "I have no wish for anyone to die or be hurt, but I cannot, even now, allow this in my own city. Though this may be my last day, I am still captain here, still responsible, and I *cannot* allow this to happen."

At the rear of the plaza he saw his fellow officers arriving in twos and threes as word reached them of the trouble on the plaza. They milled about uncertainly awaiting leadership and more reinforcements. To Barrera, it was like watching the mysterious antics of men on a distant shore, and he smiled slightly.

The stone that struck his forehead was thrown with great force, and the senior officer sank to his knees with a sigh, his recent smile replaced by a look of puzzlement. Barrera teetered for a moment before toppling over onto the flagstones, his gun skittering away to be instantly snatched up by eager hands. The mob rushed toward him like a tsunami.

Belatedly, he reached for the pistol only to find it gone. In any event, he found himself much too tired to care, and was rewarded for his efforts by having his fingers cruelly stomped on.

Quickly surrounding him, using their bodies to shield their actions, the campesinos pierced him repeatedly with their blades. When they were satisfied they had avenged the insult and injury to their voluble brother, the one who had seized the pistol discharged it twice into Barrera's skull.

The surging, now-leaderless mob shied away from the explosions to mill uncertainly before the great doors of the church, while in the near distance, as if in answer, the pneumatic thump of a heavy machine gun could be heard pounding away at the roadblocks just beyond the city limits.

Within moments, the grind and roar of heavy trucks and armored vehicles heralded the approach of the liberating federal forces, and as they entered Progreso, the mob regained its senses and slunk away without doing further harm. The body of

Barrera, bearing mute testimony to their momentary madness, lay where it had fallen, his disgraced uniform stained with his own blood.

CHAPTER SEVENTEEN

The archbishop sat at Father Pablo's bedside, studying his haggard features for several minutes before closing his eyes. The dim lighting the nurses maintained in the room had the effect of making him tired and sleepy, no matter what hour he chose to visit. It seemed the poor boy was to be preserved in eternal twilight. His doctors had assured the archbishop that this was often the case with severe head injuries—extreme sensitivity to light, sound, or touch being normal byproducts of head trauma. Given time, these discomforts should fade away.

As his young priest was still sleeping (something which he did for twelve to fourteen hours a day—this, too, being a natural outgrowth of trauma, he was told), the Yucatán's senior prelate shifted in the uncomfortable chair to fish his rosary from his pocket and begin his daily devotions.

Whispering the Apostles' Creed in the silent room, his eyes strayed once more to Father Pablo. The change in him was shocking—the childish, chubby cheeks had vanished, leaving behind the seamed, hollow jaw line of an ascetic, while his black, tumultuous hair had threads of grey woven throughout, giving him the appearance of a much older man.

The baby fat that he had carried into manhood had melted away as well, his months of recuperation having apparently required the absorption of all that was extraneous about him.

And strangely, even the tiresome adolescent complexion that had troubled him into adulthood had faded, leaving behind a clear, if somewhat scarred, skin tone.

The overall alteration to his person being so great that upon her arrival a week after his accident, Father Pablo's own mother had gone in search of him in other beds convinced that she had been given the wrong room number. When she was shown a childhood scar on his backside as proof, she had thrown up her hands and fainted dead away.

Working his way through the Joyful Mysteries, the archbishop thought also of the silence of Father Pablo. In the two months since the accident he had spoken only those few words on the plaza.

Baffling, really, the archbishop thought, to simply point upwards and say, "Blue," followed by a few muttered words about Our Lady, and this be your final utterance for the foreseeable future. Perhaps he had been speaking of the sky; by all accounts it had been a brilliant day.

The whole affair was troubling and even the neurosurgeons were clueless—Father Pablo's silence was not organic they assured him—he maintained the power of speech, but for reasons unknown, and unknowable, he did *not* speak.

On the few occasions that the archbishop pressed him for details of his condition, Father Pablo simply wrote in his weak, shaky hand, "I cannot," and then fell back onto his pillows.

Sometimes, the archbishop had uncharitable suspicions that his young pastor was hiding behind his silence like a child in a roomful of adults.

And now, months after having had him moved to the archdiocesan medical facility in Mérida, little had changed but Father Pablo's outward appearance. Though the archbishop visited often, sometimes several times a week (no easy feat considering his schedule), Father Pablo continued to lie in semi-darkness, seldom conscious and never speaking.

The pain and mystery of it all spurred the archbishop's troubled conscience like a cruel rider. In the matter of the purple robe, he reckoned that he had been unforgivably foolish in leaving so much up to the young priest, the proof of it being the wreckage that lay before him on the narrow hospital bed and, worse yet, at Doña Josefa's hacienda. In short, he felt stained with the guilt that his bungling of the whole matter had laid at his door—so many dead, so many hurt.

In the two months since Father Pablo's accident the archbishop was still struggling to put into perspective the extraordinary events that had occurred in Progreso. Though he was greatly relieved that the relic of the purple cloak (if, in fact, that was what it truly was) had been returned to Doña Josefa's hacienda, settling the unrest brought about by its theft, he still had no understanding of the details—who had taken it, who had returned it?

The person who might best answer these questions lay before him, and would not, or could not speak, and evaded in-depth communications of any kind through near-perpetual somnolence—real or feigned, who knew?   It was all so maddening.

The priest he had chosen to rush into the gap left behind by Father Pablo had found his feet rapidly, restoring order within the parish within a matter of a few weeks.   This came as no surprise to the archbishop, as the man was a retired priest with a lifetime of service and a certain gravitas of which young Father Pablo had been completely devoid.

Additionally, the fervor surrounding the holy garment had quieted somewhat with its return, and the pilgrimages had slackened.   The gold rush quality that had characterized the earlier venerations had apparently succumbed to a more sedate and decorous homage.   It seemed to the archbishop that Father Pablo's removal had presaged a return to some degree of normality in that region, and he felt the need to put some perspective on these troubling events for his own peace of mind.

But, as he attempted to contemplate the Presentation in the Temple, he nodded off still mumbling his prayers, even as his thick, freckled fingers fidgeted senselessly; then grew still.

When he awoke, he glanced guiltily at his watch and made to rise, fearing he had missed the confirmation rites at Our Lady of the Angels school.   Instead he found that he had only dozed a scant five minutes.

"I'm sorry, I'd hoped not to awaken you, as you seemed to be resting so peacefully," a woman's husky voice whispered across Father Pablo's bed.

Archbishop Valdés started at the words, peering hard into the barred shadows made by the sun through the wooden shutters.

"Was I?" he asked. "It didn't seem so. I'm not sleeping well these days and find that I doze off if left alone for even a minute."

Nodding in sympathy, the woman replied, "Oh yes, I know exactly what you mean, Your Excellency, I used to be troubled with the same problem—I don't believe I slept more than four hours a day after the death of my husband."

Suddenly remembering his manners, the old priest slid off his chair holding his hand out, saying, "Forgive me, dear lady, you have the better of me, I'm afraid."

"Señora Marisa Elena Sáenz, Your Excellency," she murmured in return, standing before bending ever so slowly over his ring, and rising with the same protracted stiffness after kissing it.

"Señora…ah, yes…Doña Marisa! Father Pablo has spoken so often of you," he exclaimed, even as he dredged his memory for any tidbits of useful information, but all he could recall was that she was a widow, with a capital W, and a dreadful scold. He had met many such women during his own days as a parish priest.

Though he understood himself to be a very small man, he was nonetheless surprised to find Doña Marisa to be taller than he—he had been under the impression from Father Pablo that she was much smaller. Perhaps he misremembered.

In any event, the remarkable eyes were just as the young man had described them—gray as a sea storm. Even so, the archbishop observed, they contained warmth, a hint of merriment, which winked like the sun behind a passing cloud. Perhaps she would not be as burdensome as he had been led to believe, he thought with some relief.

"I have been hoping to meet Your Excellency these past months, but it seems we have always managed to miss each other in our visits to Father Pablo."

"What good luck then," he said as they reseated themselves. After a pause that threatened to grow too long, he asked, "What news of Progreso?"

"I suspect you know the most of it already, Your Excellency. Things have certainly quieted down, though our visitors continue to arrive in a steady stream, much to the delight of the hotel owners and shopkeepers."

"I'm glad to hear it," the archbishop replied, returning his rosary beads to his pocket. He nodded at the shuttered windows. "Perhaps, now that the sun is on the other side of the building, we might open the shutters a bit."

Hopping to his feet, he trotted over to the windows to make the adjustments.

"I like to be able to see who it is I'm speaking to...I'm certain you feel the same," he added pleasantly. "Besides, it shouldn't hurt for our dear boy to get a little sunlight and fresh air, I would think."

"No," she agreed, "I should think not. I don't like him looking so pale. Very soon, I hope to be allowed to return him to Progreso and his beloved sea."

"Yes," the old prelate murmured, regarding the woman across from him in the improved light. "This is much better— fresh air—we can breathe." He thumped his barrel chest with a fist.

That was another thing, he thought. Surely, Father Pablo had informed him that this woman always went about in black, and yet, here she was in a sky-blue dress that went wonderfully well with the gray of her eyes. It was extraordinary how wrong that young man seem to have gotten everything.

Suddenly a thought occurred to him—perhaps this woman could fill in the details of the events in Progreso.

"Tell me, Doña Marisa, whatever became of the American woman? You know who I mean—the poor woman whose husband was killed by the Indios."

James Arbor's murder had been in all the papers and threatened to create a stir with the American Embassy. In the end, however, the authorities agreed that he was caught in the crossfire of the fight at the hacienda and inadvertently cut down. Several witnesses were produced to corroborate this version of events and the American investigators were able to retire with dignity, if not satisfaction. But as to his tragic widow, little had been written.

"Señora Arbor," Doña Marisa said quietly. "There has been no word here of her bravery...her generosity? I am astounded."

The archbishop leaned forward in his chair, rounding his eyes. "Nothing that I have heard of, I assure you," he said. "Please do continue."

Doña Marisa leaned forward as well.

"Somehow...the exact details are not known, she came into possession of the reliquary of the purple robe. It is rumored, and these are only rumors mind you," the archbishop nodded in eager understanding, anxious to hear the story, "that the late Captain Antonio Barrera made a gift of it to her just before his heroic death. How it had come into his possession can only be conjectured."

"Yes...well, he showed great valor in defense of the church by all accounts," the archbishop observed reverently, politely avoiding any issue of Barrera's culpability in the whole affair.

"He did indeed," Doña Marisa agreed. "When I watched him walk away from me that day on the plaza, I wanted to call out to him...to call him back. I wish I had now...I don't know why I didn't."

"How could you know what would happen?" the archbishop asked.

Doña Marisa appeared to study the fingers that twisted nervously in her lap for a moment; then said, "I think I knew."

She went silent and the old priest studied her face.

"But this woman," he exclaimed at last. "Will you not tell me her story? I am dying to know, Doña Marisa."

She looked up at him once more and smiled broadly. "Please forgive me, Your Excellency. Of course you must know her story. Her name is *Breenda,*" she pronounced carefully and incorrectly for his edification.

"*Breenda,*" he repeated obediently; then added to help her along, "She mysteriously came into possession of the reliquary..."

"That is exactly right," she resumed, instantly warming to her story. "It appears that shortly after the..." she appeared to be choosing her words with care, "the...*events* in the plaza, she took up the golden crucifix of the Holy Garment in her own hands, and walked out from her casa in her bare feet holding it aloft. It was quite a striking image by all accounts.

"No one knows, but her of course, whether she had received the news of Barrera's death by then...but she most certainly knew of her husband's.

"In any event, she strode without fear to the main crossroads that had been held by the Indios just minutes before, raising the reliquary into the sunlight and crying, 'Children of Christ...follow me!' in her excellent Spanish.

"Hundreds had already followed her from within the town, and the soldiers were so amazed at the sight of her and her precious burden that they didn't know what to do. So they let her be while their superiors made frantic calls to Mérida for guidance.

"So there she stood, like a dusty Joan of Arc atop a dismantled barricade, never once lowering the crucifix and calling out every few minutes for followers. Within an hour, a thousand, or more, heeded her call as word of her extraordinary summons swept through Progreso.

"Then, so I am told, as I was not there Your Excellency, as the church bells struck noon, she turned and marched with the throng of believers she had gathered over the twelve miles of rough roads to Doña Josefa's hacienda.

"Many in the crowd emulated her fervor by removing their own shoes, tying the laces together and looping them over their necks. After only a few miles of this rough trek, it is said the followers of the purple robe of Christ could be traced by the trail of blood they left in the dust of the road."

"But what about the Centurions...the Indios, Doña Marisa?" the archbishop interrupted.

"Yes...the Centurions," she replied, raising her thick, arched eyebrows and withholding her answer for just an extra moment. "They did them no harm, but watched their progress from the surrounding jungle, finally meeting them at another crossroads several miles on and out of sight of the army. Without molesting anyone, they provided an armed escort back to the plantation where everything had started.

"Beyond that, all that I know is that the reliquary resides there still, and that the American woman was allowed to take her husband's remains away from there and return him to his own country to be buried."

The archbishop sat in silence for several moments digesting all he had been told. At last, looking up at Doña Marisa from beneath his unruly eyebrows, he said coyly, "You appear to have very good sources…very close to the action, it would seem."

Smiling coyly back, the widow replied, "He," she nodded at the still sleeping Father Pablo, "has had me acting as his secretary. Naturally, I wish to be helpful to him in any way that I can, so have corresponded with Señora Arbor at his direction. In any event, I don't believe I have violated any trust by sharing these confidences with the Archbishop of Yucatán."

The prelate cast a suspicious glance at Father Pablo, half expecting to find him watching from beneath his eyelashes. "Really…I had no idea. Is there no one who will not amaze me in this matter?"

"There is one bright spot in all this for Señora Arbor, that I am sure she would want me to share," Doña Marisa added tantalizingly.

"Yes, yes," the archbishop answered.

"Even as she lost her husband, she has been blessed with child at forty-five years of age and after a lifetime of barrenness."

This announcement hung in the air between them as the archbishop considered the possibilities, then said simply, "She has been greatly blessed indeed."

"Like Saint Elizabeth," Doña Marisa agreed.

"But you also mentioned her generosity," he prompted.

"Ah yes," she exclaimed. "How could I forget? She has posted an enormous sum of money to an account for the widow of Captain Barrera and her daughters, anonymously, of course. They will never need for anything, I think."

"Extraordinary," the archbishop breathed, entranced by the idea of a man's mistress caring for his wife and children. It seemed the purple robe had turned the world upside down.

Rousing himself suddenly, while glancing anxiously at his watch, he asked, "And the young woman with the marked face, the disfigurement...what was her name? Ah, yes, Veronica...what has become of her? I believe Father Pablo is very smitten with her," he added confidingly.

"Oh don't be shocked, Doña Marisa," he continued, "it's not at all unusual; he is still a young man even with the collar. I, myself, have held secret crushes that took a lot of praying to be released from. In the end, it was all rather harmless and inevitable."

"She, her brother, and her young man all reside with Doña Josefa still," Doña Marisa answered, not in the least shocked.

The prelate leaned forward confidentially and asked, "Her young man…? Isn't he the one who hung himself?"

Conflicting details of the siege of the hacienda had swept through every parish in the days following the fight and there had been talk of little else wherever the archbishop had gone. The characters surrounding the Cloak had assumed the mythic proportions of soap opera stars and were endlessly discussed in the markets, squares, and cantinas.

"*He lives?*" This was a tidbit unknown to him and others, he felt certain, as the common talk was that the young man had quite deservedly died for his betrayal of the relic.

"Oh yes," his visitor replied matter-of-factly, "I have seen him several times at the mercado and in the plaza when they come into town for supplies. Though *lives* may be too kind a description—he sits in the sun and drools while Veronica holds his hand and dabs at his mouth; no one knows how much he understands of what is said to him, as he cannot speak and shows little reaction to anything. She will not leave his side, though," she continued, referring to Veronica, "and appears content enough just to care for him. Remarkable, isn't it Your Excellency, what love does to us?"

"Yes, yes," he agreed absently as he contemplated the image of the tragic young couple. "I'm sorry I haven't met her."

He shook his head after a few moments as if awakening from a dream, then sat up straight once more.

"So, you spend time out at the hacienda?" he inquired. "Is that what you wished to speak to me about, Doña Marisa? There remain so many unanswered questions about the relic..."

"No, Your Excellency," she interrupted him, "I have never ventured out to Doña Josefa's plantation, my news is hearsay, I'm afraid—I am too set in my ways, too rigid, for such an unorthodox, communal environment. Father Pablo understood that about me...."

She smiled warmly at his sleeping form, even as her eyes grew unfocused, her expression that of a young girl remembering her first kiss.

She continued as if speaking to herself, "...but he didn't want me thinking that I was all alone; his touch that day on the plaza told me that. The robe, you see," her eyes suddenly quickened and sought the archbishop's own, "had been spread out for me long ago—for all of us," she added happily. "Father Pablo simply lifted its hem for me to slide beneath, as snug as when I shared a bed with my sisters as a child."

She clapped her hands together in delight at the thought; then grew serious once more.

"It's not that the purple Robe itself is unimportant, Your Excellency, for I too shall someday walk on my knees to venerate it, but in my case it is joy, not need, that prompts my pilgrimage—Father Pablo showed me that I had been woven into its fabric two thousand years before my birth."

She stopped suddenly, as if perhaps she had said too much. "But the Garment is not why I had hoped to speak to you. I wish permission to act on Father Pablo's behalf."

"Father Pablo..." the archbishop repeated dazedly "...on his behalf? I don't follow you, dear lady."

"Since we are currently without a permanent pastor in Progreso, I came to ask for your permission to raise money to complete the chapel—a chapel to Our Lady of Guadalupe—I believe that would please him very much."

"Yes," he murmured, "poor boy...he saved you from that car, didn't he? I can easily understand your desire to make him happy, to honor him."

He poured himself a glass of water from Father Pablo's jug and looked inquiringly at Doña Marisa, but she shook her head.

"I certainly give my blessing on your efforts and, if you wish, I would be most honored to come to Progreso and speak on the subject at a Sunday Mass. However, as to fund-raising throughout the archdiocese, that may be another matter, I'm afraid."

He took a sip before continuing.

"As you know, Doña Marisa, the Yucatán is a poor state, warm-hearted and generous, yes, but poor for all that, and it's hard enough to keep some of the parishes going as it is. And though you and I know and love Father Pablo, many people in the archdiocese are only just hearing of him.

"You understand, I hope?   Please don't think of me as stingy, it's just that I have to think of the good of all."

Doña Marisa smiled at him, reaching across the bed that separated them and patting his hand with an easy familiarity.

"Of course not, Your Excellency. I understand very well; perhaps, in time, all that will change."

She rose with a sudden energy, and the archbishop followed suit.

"In the meantime, I will begin."

The archbishop sketched the Sign of the Cross in the air between them, and she kissed his ring once more.

"Thank you," she said simply, then spun about and hurried for the door, as eager as a schoolgirl it seemed to the old priest.

"I will send a letter to your current pastor endorsing the effort," he promised to Doña Marisa's retreating back.

Wandering over to the window that looked out on the busy street below, he was in time to see her emerge from the building. As he watched Dona Marisa slip into the stream of mankind that flowed along the broad sidewalk, he envied her litheness of movement, her gaiety of step—so at odds with the long years her iron-gray hair suggested.

Suddenly Father Pablo's words of weeks before, his description of the widow's crippling deformity, returned to him, and he smiled.

"Poor boy," he said aloud to the silent room as he watched her drift away, her dress a restful speck of sky in a riot of earth-bound color, "did she so frighten you that you had to invent a hump for her back?"

THE END

19418494R00202

Made in the USA
Middletown, DE
19 April 2015